A Nickel and A Trinket
By Max Watson

Max Watson Books LLC

Max Watson Books LLC
PO Box 821641
Dallas, TX 75382
www.MaxWatsonBooks.com

This is a work of fiction. Names, characters, places, and events are products of the author's imagination or are used fictitiously. Any resemblance to actual events or persons, living or dead, is entirely coincidental.

First edition June 2021

Max Watson Books LLC and colophon are trademarks of Max Watson Books LLC

To book an event, contact the publisher, request an interview with the author and more contact Max Watson Books LLC at PO Box 821641 Dallas, TX 75382 or visit our website at www.MaxWatsonBooks.com.

Cover design by Sarah Kil Creative Studio
ISBN Print: 978-1-955527-00-2
ISBN eBook: 978-1-7340197-9-7

Also by Max Watson

Bubble Bath Romance
Charli's Sexy Valentine
Scarlet's Naughty Christmas
Arlina's Hot Barista

Standalone
Chains of Nurture
The Drunken Promise
A Nickel and A Trinket

A Nickel and A Trinket

"Backup security at the altar."

The tall man's walkie crackles from its mount on his shoulder. A smirk twists his full lips. Sharp white teeth flash as he chuckles into the small black device. "Another one already? This town is full of groupies."

"What do you expect, he's a real-life prophet after all." The walkie man's voice laughs back.

This makes her frown. *He isn't some mere prophet, heathens. He's the messiah, can't you see that?* Her pointed-toe pumps squeak as her leg bounces with excitement. Today's the day. She's been tracking this tour for months, biding her time and saving her dough for this moment. Well, *the* moment. Whenever it happens. Hopefully in three hours.

She's been in line since one this morning and still ended up with a spot far from the entrance. They're lined up through the mega church's massive parking lot. She can hardly see the building from here. It's already seven, the sun stretching above the horizon and spreading fingers of heat through her wool pantsuit. She has to be at work by noon. A doctor's appointment, she'd told them. She's never taken time off, not for an appointment nor a sick day, and certainly not for any kind of vacation.

Her palms itch with the anticipation. *What will it be like?* She wonders if she'll feel like weeping at his feet. Or maybe singing uncontrollably. Her savings took a huge hit for the right to see him on the first day. But it will be worth it to see him first, while he's still fresh. Maybe he'll remember her. Maybe her name will be sugar on his tongue. She's seen his billboards. Watched every video and replayed every ad. He's perfect. Who would expect anything different from the messiah?

Everyone here is in line for the magic. Not her. She's here to hold his hand, to feel his grace. That will be enough to purify her impure thoughts, her dark desires. Even now they plague her. The line inches forward at the raise of the security guard's bulging outstretched arm, and she feels it. The tingle beneath her skirt. Her eyes roam over his toned legs flexing under the tight dark denim. A few stray curls of dark hair poke out from the bottom of his light blue t-shirt. Her eyes follow the trail lower.

"Move forward, madam." His baritone reverberates through her. She takes a trembling step and nearly collapses. The man's accent. It does something extra to her. She wonders what words he would use to woo her, to lure her into his bed. That heathen. All men are heathens. Disgusting simple creatures motivated by breasts and perfume.

She called her bank's corporate office twice this week. She always asks for the same employee. She wanted to hear his accent, much the same as this security guard's. From somewhere possibly thousands of miles away, this employee answering her calls would always tell her the same thing. *You can sign in to your online account and view the charges at any time, madam.*

What was that, I'm sorry, did you it was a fraudulent charge?

No, madam, you need to...

Madam. How she loved when he called her that. How she loved the thick sound of it. She imagined that man from the corporate office, sprawled before a raging fireplace, thin sheets draped over his bronzed skin. His fingers twirling lazily in a bearskin rug as he repeated the instructions to her. How had such vile images entered her mind? It didn't matter. None of it will matter. Not after today.

She stamps her foot with anger. Hatred for her curse. These disgusting men. With their sultry voices and tempting flesh. Sins of the flesh. That's her curse.

Before she returns to that cold office filled with more filthy men, her curse will be purified. Purified from these men. These men who rule the world and pump into society all those ideals that she should lie with them, bear their children, and bring forth more of them to rule over her and her body.

The line has moved farther ahead. She's beside the building now. Safely away from that guard. The one near her now is a broad burly woman. Unsightly. Her sin is of pride. How dare this woman stand so proud with her muscular form while she works for such purity? Filth. Filth all around her.

Roars from inside pull her attention. The pungent smell of bodies huddled around the altar waft from the propped open glass doors. She's so close.

How gracious of this church to host the messiah on his tour. She should think about trying them out. She's tired of her old church anyway. She loved that old curmudgeon Baptist preacher, Rob. But he retired and left his daughter in charge. A woman leading the church. How uncouth.

By the time she makes it up to the altar, three patrons behind, she suddenly finds herself terrified. What if he looks upon her with scorn? What if he can see her sin and finds her too tainted to purify? She can't look at him. Not until she stands before him. His voice is soft, subtle. Not the commanding force she imagined. But that's okay. It means he's kind. Maybe he will forgive her sins after all.

"3:14 a.m.," he says.

"Oh, thank you. Thank you!" The man who had stood before her cries to the messiah before running from the room with his hands in the air. He was a short, smelly thing souring her mood these last several hours. He was guilty of gluttony. Perhaps now he will take better care of himself, what with his sin purified.

"Keep it moving!" An older gentleman seated off to the side hollers from the altar. He must be important. Someone trusted by the messiah. She keeps her gaze lowered.

"What's your name?" His sweet voice surrounds her. Already she feels lighter, brighter.

"Amanda Thompson." She curtseys before raising her eyes to him. A gasp escapes her. He's but a child! A young man with medium brown skin and a mop of unruly brownish-red curls. Golden eyes pierce her. Tears prick her eyes. The messiah is beautiful!

"Don't look away, Amanda, let me see you." His hand tips her quivering jaw up, gently urging her eyes to meet the gold shine of his.

A guard behind the messiah clears his throat, uncrosses his arms, and points to a sign that reads "Time of Death: a nickel and a trinket". Oh! She'd forgotten the trinket part! Amanda pats around for something to give him and her hands fall on her white gold cross necklace. She rips the chain from her neck and hands it to the beautiful young man.

He shakes his head, pulls off a tiny silver ring that the lobster clasp attaches to and hands the rest of the necklace back to her. That inexpensive and easily replaced little loop is all he wants from her? Tears pool in her eyes as she is humbled in the messiah's presence.

"12:43 p.m."

She blinks, confused. "What?"

"Your time of death is 12:43 p.m." His smile is tight, weary.

"Next!" The man in shadows calls, and she's ushered aside by the throbbing crowd behind her. Their voices roar, drowning out the messiah—no, the gifted young man—who'd uttered those few words to her.

Another guard appears, his or her body obscure. Amanda cannot see as the guard guides her back outside. Everything is blurred around her. *12:43 p.m. Your time of death is...*

What time is it now? 12:43...that's forty-five minutes from now. Her feet move as she stares at her wristwatch. Has she only minutes to live? Did he purify her of her sins as his eyes probed her?

Her sin...what was it again? Forty-four minutes. What can she do with so little time?

"Keep moving!" That handsome security guard with the bulging arms draws the attention of a circle of teenagers holding up the slowly moving line.

What could it hurt? She's been so pure, lived as the warrior God intended her to be, fighting for his cause, casting out evil from her life. That's why she'd come after all, to purify the last remaining darkness prayer wasn't able to cure.

Her pumps are clacking, smacking against the pavement as she runs. She sees ghost images of clocks all around her, tick-tick-ticking away the minutes she has left. She'll never have to go back to that hellish office of gropers and catcallers ever again! She can call that corporate office man with the sexy accent one last time! And best of all...

"Whoa, what's she gonna—"

The security guard whirls toward the direction of the pointing teenager just as Amanda launches herself at the guard. Her lips crush over his, her tongue forcing between his teeth. She expected some kind of masculine spiciness to invade her senses, how foolish she has been. Still is. There isn't time left to worry about things like that anymore. Who cares if he tastes like the honey mustard of Little Joe's Brats food stand on the next block over? Not her. And he might just be enjoying her kiss, if his lack of forcing her away is any clue.

A cluster of frantic yells farther up the line has him pulling his attention from her mouth. "Hey, hey! You're going the wrong way!"

She stands there, lips and other places tingling, watching as the guard jogs toward the vehicle causing the uproar. The car idles a few feet from the line of patrons, the driver already sliding from his seat, a massive smile plastered on his face.

Where once she would have looked at him with his expensive suit and high-end sports car with disdain and judgement, now she finds herself merely curious. She watches as the driver realizes he's trapped himself with no hope of getting out any time soon. Yet he smiles.

She can't hear the sexy guard as he reprimands the driver and points at the bright chalk-drawn arrows directing traffic toward the exit. The driver shrugs, still smiling.

"Who wants my car?" His yell carries over the roar of the queued crowd, a hush falling around her. *Tick-tick-tick.*

The driver flings his key fob into the crowd like a bride's bouquet and skips off in the opposite direction. The old woman who catches his key calls after him.

"Wait! What about the title?"

But he's halfway across the parking lot. Suddenly, Amanda wants to know where he's going. She takes off after him, the ticking in her head fading beneath the clack of her heels. So what if she has forty, thirty, or twenty minutes left? There's not enough time to care about time!

"Take me with you!" she screams at the expensive-suited man's back. And as she runs, her head falls back as laughter spills from her. She hasn't laughed like this since she was a child. No, she's almost certain laughter like this has never bubbled so out of control from her lips.

Why had she wasted so much time judging, judging, always judging and never living? She should call that corporate office man and ask him out. It doesn't matter if he's her neighbor or halfway across the globe, she wants to put a face to that voice. She could be dead in minutes! She could die in less than twenty-four hours. Or maybe a week. Who can say? But she does know the time it'll happen and by God, she's not gonna waste any more of it.

The only thing she cares about right this minute is seeing what Expensive Suit Man feels like doing for her next—maybe last—fifteen minutes.

I was five the first time it happened. Being five, I didn't know what it was, what it meant, and certainly not what to do about it. I kept to myself, kept my head down, and was frequently lectured for the amount of my time prescribed to my own little world. I don't even remember what it was that was so enticing and fascinating back then that kept me unintentionally isolated. Perhaps I knew without knowing what would happen the day I started looking up.

It was a German shepherd. A classmate had her dad bring the dog to school for show and tell. As I stared into his giant glossy brown eyes, I heard *12:02 a.m.* in my head. I couldn't read the analog clock on the wall then, so I thought nothing of it. It was after spring break the girl missed a few classes and came back dejected and broken. Her dog had run away late at night and was hit by a car. It wasn't until reflecting on this experience with Gramps that we concluded this was when my ability, or in his words, "obsession", first manifested.

In his eyes, my mind had altered that memory after facing death at such a young age. He believes this time never popped into my head at all but was an idea I came up with as a young child. Young kids blame themselves for everything, after all. I must have connected with something, that dog, for the first time in my life, and then faced with the harsh reality of death so young, I must have come up with my own blame game. To him, I was telling myself when he was going to die and therefore blamed myself for not preventing it. The idea of preventing death had never even once occurred to me. The knowledge of other people's deaths was simple fact and nothing more.

Needless to say, I had seen enough to know this was no obsession or blame game manifestation from childhood. After that, I stopped talking about it with Gramps, and now I hide that I share my hobby with strangers. It wasn't like I was hoping he'd help me find some miracle cure from this power, anyway. I only wanted to learn how to cope with the profound ability I had been granted. Imagine if you could give someone such powerful information that it would entirely reshape their lives in equally drastic positive and negative ways. Could you bear such a burden? And all of it in exchange for a mere nickel and a trinket.

The first time I realized what was happening was a few years after the dead dog incident. What's a child's typical experience with death early on beyond a pet, but their own grandparents? While he wasn't my actual grandfather, he was a close friend of Gramps and he loved when I called him Pop Pop. Pop Pop's presence always granted 4:16 p.m. to form in my mind. It just so happened that this particular 4:16 p.m. occurred on a fishing endeavor where little ten-year-old me watched as his face screwed into a wrinkled pinch, his hand clutched his chest, and he fell forward, nearly tipping his fishing boat on his descent. Gramps worked the puny engine and maneuvered us to the docks, where EMTs would work on Pop Pop until calling "TOD 1616".

I will admit that I did briefly become obsessed with death at this point. And military time. I didn't realize 1616 meant 4:16 p.m. until emptily staring at Pop Pop's grainy picture in the paper and glazing over the words that appeared beside it.

This was when I made my first mistake. His name was Will. He was one of those bratty classmates who was always class clown, never intentionally bullied but frequently took his hijinks too far and had a constant rotation of mindless followers. I, being the young boy with the label of "awkward" as my sole identifier, wanted desperately to become a follower. But to do so, one must demonstrate his greatest talent.

Keith had tried to show off his ability to walk on his hands, promptly fell and sprained his neck, and was denied access to the group. The latest recruit, Tommy, had won his spot by beating all the other boys in class with his spitting distance.

Will never believed my ability was real. But if dollar signs truly manifested in the eyes when an idea forms in a little boy's mind, his eyes would have been tainted green throughout the rest of elementary school. The nickel per person was his idea. He kept the money, of course. To get something out of it, and to hide the method in which I obtain the time of death, I created the lie that I must be handed a trinket. It was out of some strange fear that someone else could learn my ability if they knew it was only eye contact. I was but a stupid kid, after all. Luckily, so was Will, who didn't question how I could read the time for the German shepherd that had no ability to give me a trinket of any kind.

My first transaction was for Annalise, who paid the price and traded a brand-new doll outfit. Will snickered when I accepted the trade but happily pocketed her nickel. I regret that I had not yet started documenting every person I read at this point but am happy to learn Annalise still lives in some small town halfway across the country. I stalk on social media many of my more familiar patrons, always updating the log I keep and marking off those who've passed, always at my predicted time.

"5:08 a.m.," I tell an old man as he hands me a nickel and an army man. Today's spoils have a common theme—older toys. In my collection I now have my sixty-seventh army man, my thirteenth Mr. Potato Head, my sixth twisted Slinky, and numerous other toys given to me in exchange for a time and a ticket for freedom.

TOD. One nickel and one trinket. Is what my sign reads. I sit on the street corner, a different one every couple days, for a few hours in the evenings. And anytime I'm bored.

"Are you Tod?" a boy of not more than twelve asks, his hand clutched behind his back.

My name is Stefan but because of my sign or because of starting this endeavor as a little kid, my nickname became Tod. Not very creative, if you ask me, but you wouldn't. There's only one question anybody ever asks me.

"So, when am I gonna die?" His nickel is sticky and was likely pulled from a cup holder and his trinket is a pink sparkly hairbrush, likely swiped from his little sister's room.

"7:01 a.m.," I tell him after he gives me his name, Harrison Habib. I should be more sympathetic, and in the beginning, I handed out this information like I was giving out a cancer diagnosis. People are strange, but you know that mystery power, since you've been witness from the beginning.

The boy skips away with fists pumping in the air. I can just imagine the conversation he'll have when he gets home.

"I can't go to school anymore, Mom, Tod says I'm gonna die at 7:01 a.m.! If you make me get up to go to school, you're gonna kill me!"

Or some nonsense like that. I'm sure both Mom and little sister missing her favorite brush will be looking for me tomorrow. Time to pick another street corner. Perhaps I'll spend a few weeks in the next town over, it's not too far on my bike.

"What're you doing? You're in the wrong neighborhood, boy." I look across the street for the source of the feminine voice. A dark figure leans against the squat old liquor store, tossing a coin into the air. I jut a thumb to my sign and turn back to staring ahead, waiting for another person looking to be saved from their boring life.

"TOD? What's that mean?" I jump as the figure materializes next to me. It's a tall white woman with a tan that looks like it came from a can. Her hair is a fake gold tinsel wig and she wears the biggest hoop earrings I've ever seen. Gold glitter paints her eyes and lips. Her lips are huge. She flashes a smile when she catches my stare, and I see her whole mouth is huge and eye-catching. I blush and drop my gaze.

"Well?" She cocks a hip and rests a fist against it. Her curvy body is encased in denim and fishnet. Fishnet tank top, fishnet tights, fishnet gloves. I gulp.

"Time of death. T.O.D." I sound out the acronym.

"For a nickel and...a trinket? Like a glass statue old ladies have on their shelf?"

I nod. "Or a bouncy ball. A button. Can be anything. Payment is a nickel and I can tell when someone will die if they give me something of theirs, no matter how worthless," I lie. The trinket part is still a continuation of the lie from elementary school. But I liked getting something out of it, something I could hold that meant even a little bit to somebody once. Even if they pick that something off the ground to give to me, they were thinking of me for that little second while they did it and somehow, that makes even a plastic fork special.

"Sure don't look like anybody got anything worth giving," the woman says as she stoops low to rummage in my box of today's spoils. She drops a little pink coin purse at my feet as she picks up a filthy Raggedy Ann doll with both hands. "Her hair as bright as yours."

"Here, I'll show you how it works." I grab her coin purse and pop it open in search of a nickel.

"Hey, fucker! Give me that! You wanna die?!" she screeches and rips the pouch from my grasp. But not before I saw what was inside. A thick roll of cash and a stack of square foil wrappers.

"I'm sorry, I wasn't trying to steal. Just looking for a nickel," I mumble and turn to pack up. I think I am in the wrong neighborhood after all. It was new territory and full of bums, so I thought it would be the perfect place to find someone wanting a second chance at life. Guess I was wrong.

"We're fine," she calls over my shoulder. I look back but she turns my face abruptly back to face her. "Never mind that. I didn't mean to yell at you. Can't be too careful around here. My bad for laying it at your feet like that, I was asking for it. What's your name, sweet pie?"

"Stefan," I say against her hand cupping my jaw. Sweat beads in my armpits. She's a whole lot of woman—tall, curvy in all the right ways, demanding in her grasp, captivating in her beauty.

"Name's Mona. This place ain't safe, you hear? You look my age, still just a boy. Get on outta here before somebody snatch you up and do to you what they did to me. Pretty boys like you are no safer than a girl. Go on now." She releases her firm grip on my jaw, picks up my box, and shoves it against my chest. I stumble back.

"I'll read you for free. No trinket, neither." I stumble as she push-es me down the sidewalk toward the brighter, safer main strip. I'm not ready to be away from this striking woman.

"Naw." She shakes her head, making her earrings flop against her long, thin neck. "Knowing when don't change a thing. Knowing how neither. It's how you live that matters. Death don't tell you how you lived." She blows me a kiss, smearing glitter on her fingers, and I stand across the street watching her watching me.

Behind me, the smell from the few local shops and restaurants builds to a mix of garlic, coffee, and smoked meat. Children laugh and people jabber with smiles in their voices. Behind Mona, the streetlight bulb is busted. The street sign is bent, the stop sign torn out. Shadows loom and brown paper bags with bottles inside litter the gutters. A car creeps to a stop beside her.

The box slips from my grasp, spilling broken toys in every direc-tion. I drop to gather the collection and glance back up to Mona. But she's nowhere to be found.

Her shimmering mouth moving over her large, bright teeth fill my mind as I wander to the park a block down where I'd locked up my bike. I contemplate finding another corner in my usual spots and get a few more readings in.

But fifteen readings, I suppose that's enough for today. I haven't found a new hiding place for all my trinket goodies yet anyway, so I might as well spend the next hour doing that instead. Autumn blows heavy in the air, swirling leaves tremble and scurry in my wake as I soar on my bike past the lively main strip and into the rest of the neighborhood. On either side of me are old boarded businesses and even older boarded-up houses.

A pale and faded yellow school bus creaks by, little kids screaming in all directions away from it. For the briefest moment, a pang of envy pumps in my chest at the kids getting off the bus, grabbing their mommies' hands, and trudging up their little stoops into pink and yellow houses that probably smell like fresh-baked cookies and perfume.

I pedal harder, letting autumn chill away the heavy feeling. The houses get farther apart, less lit up and more boarded up, and even strays steer clear without any garbage nearby to poke a nose through. Down an overgrown alley, up a steep hill of gravel, and through the dark patch of dead trees is where Grandpa's house sits.

A short little cottage with nothing but dead trees and empty pavement for neighbors, Grandpa's house is my second favorite place to be. No noisy kids losing a ball in the backyard, no dirty dogs barking at the wind, no pestering salesmen banging on the door asking if my mom is home. It's just me and Grandpa in our private little cul-de-sac at the edge of the neighborhood.

His old truck isn't in the driveway, which means he's either still at the railyard or it's at the shop again. I tuck my bike along the rose bushes and the hydrangea that he makes me divide and plant all over the yard every year. With my sign tucked under one arm and my box under the other, I sneak around the house, peering around the edge for any signs of intruders or spies.

Land mines hidden beneath the surface could go off at any moment if I don't tiptoe extra carefully on the way to the shed in the far back corner of the gardens. Pansies and zinnia scent the air along with the sweet ooze of honey.

"Hi, Queenie," I whisper to the buzzing box of Grandpa's bees as I dive into the shadow of the shed. My spoils spill into the patchy grass that doesn't grow no matter how much shade grass seed he has me sprinkle here. I gather the goods and duck into the shed, peeking out of the small windowpane for any stalking onlookers.

Another reason I love not having close neighbors—no one can see me playing around like a little kid. With a sigh, I add my goodies to the stash hidden under the last shelf at the back of the shed, squirreling away my hoard with the spiders and dust bunnies.

It's quiet in the house, the creaking of the back door sending golden fall light into the dusty dark of the kitchen. The chill of outside lingers inside, the thermostat likely won't be waking up for a few more months when the snow starts to stick. My heavy pocket full of nickels jangles and my muddy shoes squish on the white tiled floor. My anxious breath rattles in my lungs as I grip my pocket to still the noise and kick off my shoes as quietly as I can.

The newly varnished wood floor of the living room catches the light filtering in through the white lacy curtains, and I peer in the dim light for a looming shadow dozing in the rocking chair. Finding it empty, I make a mad dash for my bedroom up the stairs. The thick fluffy quilt Gramps made me is cold but welcoming as I dive underneath and await any lurking monsters that might pop out of hiding. When a swirl of wind knocks branches against my window and no other sound echoes through the dark cold house, I leap from bed, yank out the wooden chest buried deep beneath it in the depth of the darkest shadows. With a quick gyration, I shake all of the coins from my pocket into its overflowing cavity filled with more nickels than I know what to do with. A glint on the back of my hand catches my eye. A piece of Mona's gold glitter sticks to my hand. I rub the tiny square between my fingers, watching the tiny piece flash brightly as it catches the light.

The smack of the screen door sends a jolt through me. I shove the chest back into the black pit under my bed, a few stray coins scattering just as my door trembles with a heavy pounding.

"You in there, sonny?"

"Yeah, Gramps." My door opens slowly. Grandpa stands hunched against the frame, a bulky burden in his clutches. His blue-black skin—just like Mama's—shines with sweat and his white clumpy hair stands on end around his head. The package in his hand has brown paper plastered to something dark. Blood seeps through and stains the paper. His suspenders hold up baggy dark jeans and rise to his shoulders, clad in crisp white and black plaid flannel. Black socked feet wiggle, catching my lowered gaze.

"Uncle David and Barry are comin' for supper. I scored us some deer. Hurry on now and get to your chores. I need all the help I can get with cookin'."

"Yes, sir. What you need?" I climb up from the floor and dust off imaginary filth from my thighs for something to do. A nickel clatters from a fold in my jeans and rolls under the bed.

"Set the table, wash yourself up, uh...I need you to clean the guest bathroom, empty them drains with that snake like I showed you. Then go out to the garden and dig me up some potatoes, carrots, onions. Snap off some lettuce. While you at it, see if any my tomatoes redden yet."

Knowing his list always works backwards, I collect the garden veggies first. The smell of dry soil and freshly broken vines fills my nostrils. I bury my hands in the dirt a little deeper and claw until I find the perfect sized carrot. As I pile my spoils into my shirt, turned up into a makeshift basket, I peek over at the house and see Grandpa through the window bouncing around the kitchen, steam billowing around him. His white clumpy hair dances in the rising clouds and I can almost smell his sage herb broth from here. Dumping the veggies into the sink and smacking the loose dirt from my shirt, I pause and bask in the warmth filling the house.

"Go on, git! They'll be here any minute!" Grandpa shoos me from the kitchen with a swat of a kitchen towel to the behind. "Get that bathroom sparklin', you hear?"

The plastic pointy thing he calls a snake scrapes and catches on something deep in the tub drain. They're only coming for supper, what do I need to empty these drains for anyway? Grandpa and I share a bathroom upstairs. This tub hasn't been used in who knows how long. The monster extracted from the drains doesn't have the usual stink of the wet mush I pull up from our bathroom. It's dry and long, gold shining amid the black flaky goo. I pull out a strand. The thick long hair is blond except for a small part at the end that's black like mine. *Mama.*

I've seen the pictures. Her dyed and straightened blond hair. Sometimes red or light brown. Never natural black. Would she have smelled like hair dye? What perfume did she wear? Mama's hair rinses off easily in the sink, and I slip it into my pocket just as the front screen door smacks and two great big voices fill the air.

"Boy oh boy, do it smell tasty in here."

"Hello! Thank you for having us!"

"Uncle David! Barry!" They capture me in a bear hug that takes my breath away. They smell like wood smoke and the same after-shave.

"I said seven, it ain't done yet!" Grandpa comes clambering in from the kitchen, flour streaked on his dark wrinkled cheek.

"I know, we got out early is all." Barry shrugs, his big shoulders rising and falling in his flannel of green and yellow. All the men of the railyard dress pretty much the same. Dark jeans, suspenders, flannel in the cold months, white tanks when it's hot or the trains are heading for a south run. Uncle David holds up a dark brown bottle like a peace offering. Grandpa flashes his white dentures and waves us into the kitchen, where he gives marching orders and puts us all to work.

After dinner, Barry volunteers to help Grandpa clean up the kitchen, leaving me and Uncle David to rock on the porch and watch the lightning bugs challenge the twinkle of the night sky. The chain of the porch swing rattles loose on my side, Uncle David's weight making me fight against the tilt of the seat sliding me into his thick arm.

"Did you ever know my mama?" A barking howl erupts in the distance. I strain to listen, hoping for a coyote but my shoulders sag when I hear it's just a far-off backyard dog when its owner screams at it to hush. Grandpa's friends have all wanted me to treat them like family—Pop Pop when I was a kid and now Uncle David and Barry. I've always thought of them like uncles even though we're not related.

"I met her once or twice. Only in passing though. She was always heading someplace, running somewhere. Your grandpa said she never could sit still." He swats at a mosquito and sips the brown liquid from the bottle he'd brought. His breath smells of sage and liquor.

"Was she pretty?"

"Sure, I suppose so. You know I don't really see that way, but I think she was like a painting. Everything in all the right places. What I can say for sure, you take after her. You got her kind eyes."

My breath puffs in the cool night air. A frosty sheen settles out on the dark grass within the porch light's glow. I swallow.

Uncle David sips from his bottle. I take the bottle from him and sip some too. "Don't tell your grandpa, he'll have my hide. Course, by the time we was your age, we all'd split one of these and drank it full between us. Did that 'bout every weekend." His belly jumps at his bellowing laugh.

The liquor burns my throat but tastes like nothing. Silence surrounds us, except for the buzzing of mosquitos as they dance around our ears. We swat, sip, and swing, saying nothing else. I hiccup. The booze warms my skin from the chill of the night air. I hear a clank from inside the house moments before the screen door flies open and Barry stumbles out.

"Don't blame me when David and I get filthy rich, you had your chance, old man!"

"Old man! Boy, I may be old, but I'm still spry 'nough to whoop you." Grandpa comes out, one hand on his hip and wagging a bony finger at Barry as he dances away from the door and bounds down the front steps backwards.

Uncle David chuckles beside me, the porch swing chains shaking with his big body. "I told you he wouldn't go for it, baby."

"Think about all them crazy cat ladies, Jeb! They love themselves a buncha cats. All we gotta do is make some cardboard little kitty houses, slap some pretty flowers and gold glitter on 'em. We'll be rollin' in it!" Barry gestures wildly with his hands and his bushy black eyebrows waggle with excitement. The dim porchlight glistens against his dark black skin. I look down at the skin on my arm and wonder if I glisten like that.

"You'n your ideas. Always ideas. Ain't you tired from working the railyard all day? Ain't you got anything else to waste my free time with? I wanna retire. You think I wanna cater to some old lady's cats?" Grandpa harrumphs into the patio sofa on the other side of the porch, arms folded, foot already tapping. Uncle David and I look at each other and grin.

Later that night, I slip the golden strands of Mama's hair into my treasure box where I keep the real important goodies. Mama's picture. An old comb. One of her scarfs. And big things people give me when I read them. A sparkly necklace with probably pricy jewels. A hundred dollar bill. But most of all is my notebook. The names and times of everyone I read this year. The rest of all I read before are written in the stack on the top shelf in my closet. I add the names and times from today to the book and slide the treasure box back into its hiding place beneath the loose floor plank. Hopefully, Gramps won't want to redo these floors too or I'll have to find a new spot, and I'm running out of hiding places.

I find it hard to sleep. Maybe I'm afraid I'll dream about death again. It's almost every night. But mostly I'm afraid to tell Grandpa that I got fired again. A big, loud woman came barreling in the gas station looking for soda and to pay for gas but she was so loud and bright, I got scared and hid in the back till she left. Her gas will come out of my check, leaving nothing for me. It's the fifth job I've lost since I started trying to work this year. Grandpa's gonna be angry.

I wish I could read people for work and not have to save up money for college for a career in I don't know what. I got good grades and graduated a little early, what with Grandpa's homeschooling me and skipping summers. But I wasn't in any kind of hurry for anything other than not doing homework or going to that community gym place I hated so much. Maybe I'll apologize and ask for the job at the grocery store back. That one wasn't so bad if I got to stock shelves and not ring people up, at least.

Too soon, the screech of crickets lulls me to sleep. And too soon, I'm dreaming again.

Harrison Habib drags his feet as he readies himself for school. His heart pounds as he watches the clock. His mean mother refused to believe him about his time of death and she forces him to go to school every day.

To beat death, he now takes the early bus so that by the time his predicted death time comes, he's already safe inside the school building. It has been six months of jumping at the screaming minute hand as it approaches the time that will haunt him the rest of his life. Weekends are so easy, all he has to do is stay in bed until it's safe to play.

But Monday comes around again and his battle against his clock continues. He breathes in relief as he settles into the cafeteria stool. His breakfast of a PB&J bar settles like cement in his stomach as he watches the clock on the wall. He reminds himself that he's in the school, safe and sound.

One minute to go. That's when he hears something loud. Bangs. Bang-bang-pop! Everything around him freezes as the sound grows closer. His ears start ringing. The cafeteria door kicks open.

7:01 a.m.

Chapter Two – Desdamona

"Can I help you with something?" The old white woman looks me up and down with her eyes, her nose never leaving the air. The urge to cover myself is a sensation I've grown accustomed to over the years.

I bow my head with a sweet smile. "I'm looking for a present. For my friend."

"Uh-huh. We don't have anything I think your *friend* would be interested in. Try the back of the video store down the road."

My head cocks to the side. The back of the video store? Where the eighteen and up section is hidden? Oh...that witch! "Actually," I rise to my full height and hide a snarl, "I'm looking for *Crime and Punishment*. It's by Fyodor Dostoyevsky, maybe you've heard of him?"

The old woman smirks a knowing smile and my cheeks heat. "Of course I've heard of him." She rolls her eyes, turns on her heel, and points down an aisle. I stare at the spines of various copies of the book I've tried finishing for five years now. Shit. My pride had to get in the way. I'm running out of time and this is far from any streets I'm familiar with. This was stupid. She'd have been happy with a damn chocolate bar.

· · · ·

THE BROWN BAG CRINKLES under my shirt as I rush back home. Trey catches my eye as I cross the street. He hovers over Sandy. He licks his lips and my stomach turns. He traces a hand down her neck and along her collarbone. She shivers and shrinks away from him.

"Sandy! I was looking everywhere for you. Come on, girl, we got a thing to do."

"But I gotta make—" Sandy looks torn between following me and enduring Trey's constant pestering until a trick comes to save her. Easy choice.

"Come on." I pull her from our spot beside the liquor store, ignoring Trey's content stare. As if all he's got to do is wait and she'll become his. Sandy limps beside me. With a glance back at her I can tell. I screwed up. I shouldn't have risked going to town to the bookstore. This stupid little gift wasn't worth her working by herself. Dammit.

My house smells like old fryer oil, hair spray, and perfume. "Mama, what you got cooking?" I call into the dark, but she's nowhere to be found. Two plates coated in grease and bones sit on the counter by the sink. Mama's purse is gone. I turn to Sandy. "How much you need?"

"I can't take your money all the time, Mona. I appreciate the help but you can't turn for both of us." Sandy's eyes have lost their luster. Her words fall like feathers to the linoleum floor.

"How much?" I stand firm, one hand on my hip, one clutching my surprise tight to my stomach.

Her dull green eyes flick up to me and every time our eyes connect, the strange words fill my mind. *By car.* She drops her gaze back down to our feet. "Why you holding your stomach like that? Don't tell me you're—" Her head whips up with fear plastered on her makeup-smeared features.

"Naw, naw. Ain't like that. I'll tell you, but first you gotta tell me how much. I owe you for disappearing for a while."

"A hundred." Her upper lip quivers. She looks away.

"Mm-hmm. Here." I take out two hundred from my coin purse and push it into her hand. Mama won't be happy that I'm short my day, but I can make it up to her. I'll just have to work the dangerous hours and be careful who I come out of the shadows for is all.

"Mona! I can't, or you'll—"

"Hush, now. Come on, I said we had somethin' to do."

With the bath water hot and steamy, I pull Sandy's green lacy bra from her bony shoulders. She devours the peanut butter sandwich I made for her and lets me slide off her heels, then her stockings. She turns away from me as she slides her thong from her hips, but not before I see it. She's bleeding.

"Sandy, are you—"

"It's nothing." She hops into the tub too quickly, splashing water on the pink towel laid out on the floor.

"Don't lie to me. What happened while I was gone?"

"It was three of 'em. But...they only paid for one." Her voice breaks. But where I expected her to fall apart, she lifts her chin and squares her shoulders. I can almost see the words in her mind, *I can do this. I can hold on a little longer.*

"I miss my mom. How come she sold me and didn't keep me like your mom? If I had to do this anyway...wouldn't it make more if she kept me?"

I slide in behind her and make work of unraveling her long matted hair tied into a pinned French twist at the back of her head. The scab from Deshawn's outburst last week flakes on my fingers. Sandy sucks in a breath.

I don't know her mama but if she comes from a place anything like this, selling Sandy outright was worth more to her addiction once than waiting and earning a little at a time. Sandy's been Deshawn's for several years now. She started the next day, showing up to stand beside me in my spot. She was only eleven then, a few years younger than me. But where I'd been at this as long as I can remember, she was so innocent to this way of life back then. She wasn't meant for a life like this.

"Here." I turn over my present to her after our bath. We sit on my bed, both of us wrapped in ratty matching pink towels. Sandy's pale skin is flushed almost as pink.

She tears apart the brown paper and stares at the cover of *Bridge to Terabithia*. "It's my favorite movie! I didn't know it was a book. Thank you, Mona!" Her smile splits, flashing white teeth with a little black gap in the front. Fat tears pool in her eyes. There it is.

Sandy is the only reason I've kept on like this instead of running away the moment I came of age. I've looked after her and saved up for her from the first day I met her.

"Go on and cry now. Hold on for me a little bit longer, Sandy. I'm saving up for you. I'll buy you one day, just you wait."

A blue jay squawks an ungodly tune outside my window, jarring me awake from the endless dreams of death. I lie here irritated for a moment, collecting my thoughts. The bird lands on the windowsill beyond the pane and screeches louder. I leap from bed and bang on the glass. Blue jays are the worst. But even that rude awakening is quickly forgotten as I recall the day's agenda.

"That you bangin' around? Get a move on!" Gramps hollers from downstairs. Stomping fades and gets louder and fades again. I image him throwing everything he can think of into various bags. Food, clothes, extra life jackets, blankets.

The sun beats heavy, reflected off the water, and sears onto our cheeks. My line hasn't budged all morning while Gramps can hardly stay seated with all the attention he's getting. Uncle David and Barry are still trying to bait their hooks.

"Where's that sunblock? I'm burning up over here," Barry complains, digging through Grandpa's numerous duffle bags.

"Well, shit." Gramps strains with another fish. "Musta forgot that. Knew I was missin' something. Get that net!"

I net the heavy largemouth bass and add it to his nearly full cooler. My mouth waters thinking about the fish fry we'll get to have later.

"Here, take my hat, Stefany." Barry plops the gaudy sunhat on my head. "You'll be burned to a crisp once the sun's through with ya."

I toss the hat off my head with a snicker. "You know I hate that name. I ain't afraid of the sun."

"Suit yourself." Barry shrugs and sticks his women's gardening hat back on his head. I stifle a giggle and reel up my dead line, going over to steal some of Grandpa's action. No sooner am I settled, I hear Uncle David hoot and turn to see his pole bent near in half. He reels in a big pink and shiny trout right where my line had been.

"You bes' shut up, yer scarin' off my fish!" Gramps swats Uncle David with the net.

I like to fish. Bait the hook, chase the hot spot. But I hate killing them if they're still swimming around. I hate stripping off their scales, fileting them even as their dead bodies still flop. Most of all, I can't stand the stink. *Sweetheart*'s cabin fills with the reeking stench as the three old men prep some of the fish for the grill. My stomach growls but not in a good way. I bury my head into the blankets and hope the gentle sway of my hammock will rock me into a dreamless nap until dinner.

I love Grandpa's houseboat. I love being out on the water, taking her to new places along the coast of beautiful Lake Michigan and exploring outside of our hometown of Michigan City, Indiana. The lovely people who dock all around us take care of her when we can't get out in time before a storm.

Barry says Gramps and the grandmother I never got to meet used to live on *Sweetheart*, traveling something he called the "Great Loop". With school over, my dumb job ended, maybe Gramps and I can pick up where they left off. The main deck is big enough for potted plants so we could take our garden with us. We could sell the house and use the money for other expenses. We'd have to buy stuff sometimes but with our own garden, we could make the money last a long time.

The more I start to think about it, the faster my heart pounds in excitement. Our little fishing trips give me only a little taste of sailing but it always leaves me yearning for more. I want to see the ocean without any land in sight. Gramps wouldn't have to work so hard anymore; hell, I'm sure he should've retired ages ago.

A swell rocks the boat and jars me half out of the hammock. The charcoal and lighter fluid stink of the deck grill fills the cabin with smoke so thick that a coughing fit has me fleeing for fresh air.

"Quit with that cancer fluid! Ain't nobody teach you how to light a grill before?" Gramps' voice cuts through the smoke. The wind blows the thick cloud along the shore, beachgoers and people tying off after sailing cough, waving hands in front of their faces, and scowling at us.

"Yeah, yeah, it's lit now, ain't it?" Barry challenges back.

Uncle David coughs. "How was your nap?" He swipes a meaty paw over his face, wiping the tears in his eyes.

"Hard to sleep with all the stink and noise." I grumble, grab a stalk of corn prepped for the grill and rip back the husk. The sweet flesh pops between my teeth, spilling the waxy raw liquid on my tongue.

The first batch of grilled fish is half raw, half burned, and all grill-fluid flavored. Begrudgingly, Grandpa hands over a few of his prized fish for a second attempt, reducing the numbers for the promised fish fry tomorrow night.

I chomp the rest of my raw corn and stare out at the lapping waves. I remember a story about a siren that was beautiful and her singing would draw sailors to their deaths on hidden rocks beneath the waves. It's not a pretty lady singing to me but the ocean herself, whispering words of freedom and exploration.

"Stefany..."

"Boy!"

I wonder what New York looks like. Could we chug *Sweetheart* right up to the liberty lady's skirt? What about going all the way up to Canada and the north pole? Down to Florida. So many places we could go!

"Ow!" Grandpa swats the back of my head, forcing me to turn from the water and back to the table. "What was that for?"

"Uh-oh, I know that look. What's her name?" Barry leans forward, fish chunks in his beard, and winks at me. Grandpa's face turns red. I immediately think he knows about Mona.

"Or his name." Uncle David offers a half-smile.

The Atlantic Ocean is her name. "Hey, Gramps, why don't we sell the house and live on *Sweetheart*? Let's sail the world!" The conspiratorial smiles around me fall. Barry suddenly gets a second wind and jumps up to grab fourth helpings. Uncle David makes himself busy clearing the rest of our plates.

"Well, how 'bout it? We could see all the old folks vacationing in Florida! Or see the big city! I bet we'd even find unclaimed islands out there." I jump up and peer over the edge of the boat, squinting in the distance for land masses calling my name. I know Lake Michigan connects to the ocean somehow, but where?

"Hush, help clean up," Grandpa says quietly.

"Wouldn't it be fun? There's so much we could see. You wouldn't have to work anymore or take care of the house. We could—"

"Stefan. Grab a trash bag." Gramps cuts me off. Annoyed, I flick open the plastic, fighting the wind that tries to steal it from me. Barry pretends to be interested in a cluster of seagulls floating nearby looking for scraps. Uncle David offers me a sympathetic look.

"We could take the garden with us, put all the plants in big planters." I hold open the trash bag and he scoops our dinner trash off the table. "There's enough space if we move this table over—"

"I said hush!" Grandpa yells, standing tall and staring down at me.

"Come on, you hate your job! You're always so tired all the time and complain that your back hurts and you're too old to be working still. You don't have to work so hard if you sell the house."

"Boy, you best shut up now. We're not living on no houseboat and that's that." He never raises his voice. Not in real anger. I've never seen the look he has in his eyes right now.

"What are you so afraid of? What is it with you old people and wanting to work until you die? Don't you wanna see as much of the world as you can?"

"Not another word about it, you hear?" Grandpa punctuates each word with a fierce poke in my chest and I stumble back, tripping over my feet and falling to the deck. The trash spills from the bag into my lap, smearing ketchup and barbecue sauce onto my favorite white shirt. I stare up at him, heart pounding, an unfamiliar terror bubbling within me.

"Hey, hey now. That's enough. Let's leave it be." Uncle David comes to my side, scooping the trash back into the bag and dabbing napkins at the stains. Tears spill.

"What the hell is wrong with you, old man!?" I scream at him, pushing Uncle David back. Grandpa ignores me, pouring water onto the coals in the grill, putting out the embers with a menacing *hiss*.

"Screw you!" I leap from the boat, narrowly landing on the deck, and run for the parking area.

My tears have crusted to my cheeks by the time they join me. Their round silhouettes block out the sun and I turn away, arms folded over my chest.

"Hey, come on out of there. Let's get you home," Barry tries, coming up alongside his truck bed where I sit.

"No. I'm not getting in the car with him!" Uncle David tries next but I refuse until they eventually drive me home in the bed of their truck, taking it slow on the back roads.

I can't sleep that night, angrily tossing and turning, trying to figure out what could've set the bitter old man off so bad. So what if I want to sail around in the boat? What's the harm in that? I'm almost eighteen, maybe I'll just ask for the boat and part ways. Then he won't have to see me ever again since he clearly can't stand me. He wouldn't have shoved me like that if he cared. Maybe he never cared about me. Maybe he's just been stuck with me since my dad wants nothing to do with me. Fine. A few more months and then I can be out of his clumpy white hair. Bitter old man.

I doze off just before dawn, only to be woken by that god-awful blue jay again. No blue jays would bother me out on the open sea. The sooner I'm out of here the better.

A faint tapping sounds from my door as I slip on yesterday's jeans. I spot a ketchup stain over the pocket and scowl, throwing off the pants and storming to my closet to look for a different pair.

"What?" I yell.

"Just seeing if you're up. Time for chores. I made breakfast." Grandpa's voice is soft on the other side of the thin brown door.

"Whatever."

• • • •

THE SUN BEATS ON MY back, high noon rearing its head with triple-digit heat on its coattails. I swipe the dirty garden glove across my forehead and glare at the house. Old man taking the easy chores in the nice air conditioning, making me do all the heavy lifting. I add the day's pile of weeds to the compost pile and turn the debris.

Thirst compels me back into the house, but I keep my back turned as Grandpa slathers oil into the butcher block countertops. His cast iron skillet collection lines one side of the kitchen, all glistening with their own coat of oil and ready to be put into the oven. He knows I love seasoning the skillets and oiling the countertops. They're my favorite chores. Jerk.

"You leave the marigolds around the tomatoes?" Gramps asks, his voice quiet. I glance at him, ready to give him a piece of my mind. When I was younger and left to weeding on my own one day, I yanked up all his companion marigolds planted around the tomato plants, mistaking them for dandelions. It was a running joke between us, but I'm in no mood for that crap today. But his sheepish look halts the hateful spit on my tongue.

"Yup." I stomp out of the kitchen, aiming to get the rest of my Sunday chores out of the way and get out to reading people or something, anything to get me out of this house until the old man goes to bed. I know the train is off to the West Coast somewhere tomorrow, meaning he won't be back for a while and I can get some peace.

"Wait…" Gramps calls to me, chasing on my heels. I whirl around to face him. Where he'd towered over me yesterday, now he suddenly looks small. His back is hunched more than ever before, lines on his face look depthless. A weariness in his shifty gaze ages him. The unshakable grandfather who's been my only family as long as I can remember, the old man who appeared ageless and immortal, now looks ancient. Why had I never noticed? How old is he anyway?

"Look, I-I'm sorry about…y'know."

"What?" I cross my arms over my chest.

"Yesterday…what I said." His hands wring around the oily rag, smearing the oil on the backs of his hands, squeezing and twisting the gray cloth. A dollop of the concoction plops on the floor.

"You mean when you shoved me." I step up to him, glaring down, anger and a new hatred forming within me.

"Now look here, I didn't—" His eyes snap up to meet mine but he immediately drops his head. "Yeah, I'm sorry. I love you, sonny." He pins me with a look full of his words, spilling the affection we don't speak of, the words we've never shared.

I stumble back a step, startled by this strange side of him. "O-okay. Thanks."

We awkwardly stare each other down. The tension eases from my shoulders.

"How 'bout you help me fry up the bluegill?" He offers a small smile.

"Sure." I beam. "But you gotta tell me why you won't sail around the world with me."

His face falls. Just as quickly as love and warmth had filled his eyes, it disappears, a flood of anger resurfacing. His nostrils flair.

"Not happening. I said drop it. Now, I'm sorry I pushed you and all that. But the topic ain't open for discussion."

What the hell? "Then I don't want your crappy fried fish. I'm leaving."

"Now just wait a damn—" But I cut off his stomping retort by slamming the front door. It swings open, the knob ripping from my hand, but I don't look back. "Stefan!"

• • • •

"CAN I STAY HERE TONIGHT?" I pant, sweat on my brow from pedaling hard away from that vile old man.

Barry stares at me, eyes wide, looking over my shoulder for the fire that chased me here. He stands in the doorway of their cottage, a towel barely wraps around his waist, his hair dripping in time with my whooshing breaths.

"Who is it, baby?" Uncle David calls from inside. He walks up behind Barry, takes one look at me and pushes Barry aside to bury me in his fluffy chest. I begin to cry right then, my tears refusing to let up until a cup of cocoa is pressed into my hand and Barry has long since gotten dressed.

"Tell Uncle what happened. Lay your troubles on me, sweet baby," he coos, rubbing my back as I sip the hot liquid. A half-melted marshmallow sticks to my lip. I lap at it and relay the argument to them.

"Well, shit." Barry grumbles and leaves the room. I stare down at my empty mug.

Uncle David leans toward me, bumping his shoulder into mine. "Don't worry about him." But I know he's going to go call Grandpa.

"I don't get it. He says he wants to retire all the time but turns around and yells at me when I come up with the perfect idea. He could retire, sell the house, and we could spend our days sailing the open waves. Sounds like a dream to me. If he's too old to sail, alls he's gotta do is say so. No reason to get violent. Like damn." I hide my shaken demeanor behind feigned anger. Uncle David isn't fooled.

"Why don't you stay the night and cool off, eh? When we all get back, you two need yourselves a heart-to-heart. It's not 'cause he's old, he's afraid. Afraid to lose you. He's got good reason to." The empty mug is pulled from my grasp and I'm left alone to my thoughts.

Barry comes trudging in, Uncle David behind him looking worried. "What?" I say, indignant and still shaken over the whole thing.

"Sit yo ass down, boy, you 'bout to learn real quick," Barry belts out, even though I've been seated since I got here. He falls into the recliner across from me and crosses his arms over his broad chest.

Their cottage is smaller than my house, only one bedroom and hardly any yard. It's brown everywhere. Wood siding outside, wood paneling inside. Brown furniture, brown paint. It's ugly as sin. But it always smells of wood smoke from the fireplace and dried meat from their dehydrator making pounds of homemade beef jerky every time I come over. The smell is faint today, but I imagine meat's in the freezer just waiting for their return after this coming trip.

"It's not our place, baby. Let Jeb tell him." Uncle David stands unsure in the small brown living room looking between Barry and me.

Barry waves his words away as if they were bugs pestering him. "Your granddaddy pushed you around 'cause he's scared. Ain't you ever wondered how come he has that big flashy boat but such a tiny house?"

"It's not that tiny, it's bigger than ours—"

Barry waves Uncle David's words away again. I think about the boat compared to the others at the docks. I guess it is pretty big and flashy. Most other houseboats are little flat things that never go anywhere. The other regular boats are smaller, too. Sails propelling them for small treks not far from shore. The closest I've ever seen in size or shape to Grandpa's boat is the big multiple-story yachts that pass by, their decks crowded with bikinis and laughter.

"Your granddaddy was a big shot in his day. Selling properties all up and down Lake Michigan's coast. Naw, he wasn't one of them park bench sellers with a fake smile, he was a wheelin' and dealin' machine, pairing the worst lot to the highest and happiest bidder. He was good at what he was doing, let me tell you. But he wasn't chasing paper for a McMansion of his own, nope. He was fixin' to buy that flashy houseboat for your grandmama. Susie had her heart set on cruisin' the coast and never settling nowhere. They made a run for the Great Loop one day.

"This goes without saying, boy, but you don't know this, understand? I'm tellin' you what Jeb ain't ready to tell you. But the fact you know is a secret, you hear me? Good. It's like I'm sure you expect I'm gonna tell you by now. A storm came, that *Sweetheart* of your granddaddy's was good for rough waters but they wasn't sailors and soon, like he tells it, they was over their heads. Tryna not capsize and what have you. But it was no use. Wave after wave crashed the deck and your grandmama went right over. Never to be—"

"That's enough, baby." Uncle David's gruff voice is soothing, halting Barry's tale. He sits on the sofa beside me, his hand returning to rub my back. I stare at the brown carpet. So Gramps was afraid I'd get washed out in a storm? I never asked what happened to my grandma, just always thought it was old age or something. Barry sits on the other side of me when I start to cry again. He swats at my back awkwardly.

I sleep in until the sun heats up the cottage so much, I'm sweating. They left before dawn for the railyard. I lock up and put the spare under the flowerpot with nothing but dirt in it that sits in the middle of the tiny front deck. I take my time pedaling back home now that I know it's gonna be empty and I'll have the place to myself for almost two weeks.

There's fried fish in the fridge when I get home. The kitchen is all clean, the chores all done. I feel sour and mixed up and decide not to think anymore. After a few days collecting nickels and names in town, I wandered to the back streets in search of Mona. I caught a glimpse of her getting into another car, pink glitter heavy on her eyes but if she saw me, she didn't seem to recognize me. I stay home the next few days moping, thinking.

There aren't any old family photos up on the walls. Nothing mounted up but fish plaques, deer heads, and one school photo of Mama with her blue-black skin, big white smile, and flattened blond hair. With no attic to the house, I go straight to Grandpa's closet and dig around for something useful there. I don't even have to look. The shoebox sits right in front on a low shelf as if he looks through it all the time. It's filled with family photos, some still in frames. A woman who looks like an older version of Mama laughs beside a weird young version of Grandpa. There they are outside this house, back when all the surrounding trees were still alive but not a single blade of grass seemed to be. They kiss on the deck of *Sweetheart*, tall thin champagne glasses in their hands. They pose for a family portrait holding a tiny baby wrapped up tight.

Chapter Four – Desdamona

"Are you still reading that?" Mama offers her lopsided smile from my doorway.

"Yeah. But I don't remember the beginning. Guess I'll have to start over." I'd finally reached the halfway point, but I last tried reading it over a year ago based on the snippet of newspaper I'd used as a bookmark.

"Why bother? Read this instead." Mama hands me an old worn copy of *The Call of the Wild*. "It used to be your favorite."

"Yeah, yeah. I read it already. I wanna read something new but this is all I got."

"Well, work the main strip Saturday and you can buy books with the extra you roll in, how 'bout that?" Mama smiles so sweetly, as if she offered me to do the dishes and she'd let me buy myself a gift with my allowance.

I force a smile back at her. "Maybe I will."

"Mama Lucy!" A young male voice echoes through the house, followed by the slam of the front door. Our smiles fall.

"What is it, what happen?" Mama calls out, almost sounding exasperated as she takes her time sauntering to the main room. I bounce behind her, impatient yet terrified. I can guess what happened. But I'm not ready to see it.

"Deshawn, he..." Deshawn's little brother, Jeremy, looks at his shoes. Mama bends to the figure piled on the floor. With a breath to steel myself, I tiptoe into the room and look at the heap.

Bloodied rags wrap around the head, blankets cover the body. No. No, please, no.

"Mona," the whimper sounds from the doorway.

"Sandy! I was so worried, I thought..." I run to her, wrapping her tight in my arms. Damn that Deshawn.

"What happen?" Mama pulls a rag from the head. A sorrowful moan erupts from the body and we all jump.

"It's Martin. He got jumped and they cleaned him out. Deshawn just…he was so angry." Jeremy grabs Martin's head and holds it in his lap. He's been Jeremy's best friend as long as anybody can remember.

"I was so scared," Sandy whispers against my neck as her hand massages her jaw. A deep red and purple bruise has begun to spread across her left cheek. I can almost see the outline to the gaudy ring he always wears.

"Will he be okay?" Jeremy looks at Mama like she's the neighborhood's doctor. She opens her mouth, a doubtful look in her eye, but before she can say anything the room lights up from outside. Headlights from the street flash off, on, then back off again.

"I don't know, baby. You take care of them, I take care of him." Mama nods to the door. Jeremy looks out into the darkness toward the waiting car, then glances at Sandy.

"This on you." He says under his breath as he passes us, tossing a look of pure hate at Sandy.

"She ain't get him jumped, the fuck your—" I step to grab the asshole and make him see reason, but Sandy pulls me back.

"That's enough!" Mama yells. "Leave him be. Get me some towels. And close that damn door!"

"He tried to get up on me. But he was on something. He was so angry. I told him I didn't want to and he hit me." Sandy gathers towels from under the sink while I fill a mop bucket with hot water in the tub. "That was when Martin came in just jumped. I've never seen him like that. What could make somebody so angry like that?"

"Anything. Probably everything. He should know better than to do what he deals."

Sandy's dull eyes look at me with barely any light inside. If I hadn't just held her and felt her trembling with fear, I'd think she didn't feel a thing. "You think...guy like that, you think he'll make good on it?"

"Twenty thousand?"

She nods.

"I'll make sure he makes good on it, don't you worry."

Martin doesn't look as bad after Mama fixes him up. A couple broken ribs, swollen eyes, busted head. He'll live. Jeremy doesn't stop popping in and out between dealing all through the next several nights. Sandy shares my bed when she's not out working.

That bloody heap could've been Sandy. Little thing like her wouldn't survive it. I manage to add another hundred to my stash by the time they both return to that bastard's side but the little bit I can stash isn't building fast enough. I have to figure something out quick.

Eighteen thousand six hundred to go.

"There's been an accident."

Why is it always in the middle of the night? I collect times of death for a living, I know accidents don't all happen at night. Even if the probability is higher, people are tired, surroundings get dark, mischievous works are at play. And why does the death always have to be announced with those same four words?

I had it all worked out. An apology in the form of the family photos all hung up on the walls. Dinner planned and ready. I wasn't gonna bring it up ever again. Life would just move on. Grandpa's time of death was 7:37 p.m. So of course I couldn't wrap my head around the possibility that the man on the other side of the phone was telling the truth. It was six in the morning. Grandpa wasn't dead.

I never saw him again. They brought him home after everything was already taken care of and all that was left of him was a tiny box. Why had it taken nearly twelve hours to tell me? I called them liars and ran to *Sweetheart*, planning to make good on sailing the coast with him under my arm. The waters were calm, the sky clear, the sun shining brightly. It wasn't fair. How could the sun have the audacity to rise? How could our neighbors be so cruel to sail and water ski on such a grim day?

Our dock neighbor, Mr. Howard, set sail and chased me, drawing me back to shore, to Barry and Uncle David, who waited on the dock for me. An awkward search for my father, my legal guardian after Grandpa's passing, came up empty. I never even knew the man's name. It was a forbidden word in Grandpa's house. I turned eighteen one lonely summer day on August 14, waiting for news of my new home once the lawyer of Grandpa's estate tracked down my dad.

I never found out what happened to him. Maybe he has a new family somewhere. Or maybe he's dead like everyone else and I really am all alone. The house creaks and pops at night when the wind blows now. I'm restless.

College and what I want to do with my life all seem so far away. With the inheritance from Grandpa's stash from his salesman days, I could live here for quite a while and not have to even get out of bed. It's six a.m. Five months since he died. I stumble out of bed and into the dark of the house, down into the kitchen, hoping to see his ghost. The smiles of my dead family surround me, all bright teeth and crinkling eyes.

The moon illuminates the garden beyond the kitchen window and I see myself out there, sweating in the heat, scowling in at Grandpa the last day I saw him alive. If only I said it back that day. *I love you, too.* Why are those words the hardest to say?

Sick to my stomach, I run back up the stairs, throw clothes into a bag, grab my special treasure box, and pedal as fast as I can from that house. I'll never go back there. Never, ever again. Grandpa's ghost can have it.

I didn't think about where I was heading until I was there, pedaling up and down the dark streets, bouncing over mashed-up beer cans and small plastic liquor bottles. The neon lights of the liquor store flash, a lone figure lounges in the dark beneath them.

"Mona," I squeak, my tires making that humming noise as I grip the handle brake.

She steps into the red light from the neon sign, green glitter illuminating her face like a beautiful dark fairy. Her matching green tinsel wig sparkles in the light. She puts a hand over her eyes as if to shield the sun to see me better. "Who's there?"

"Don't you remember? It's—" I start to sob, my grief cutting the words from my throat.

"Yeah, yeah, of course I do. Stefan, right?" Mona snakes a hand around my waist and guides me with my bike in tow to lean against the building. "What're you doing here? Weren't you listening when I said you aren't safe here?"

I nod frantically and between sobs I say, "Can we go somewhere? I got a place."

She gives me a skeptical look in the red glow of the neon lights buzzing above us, and I remember her coin purse.

"I can pay! Whatever it is, I can pay!" I sniffle.

"Okay, okay, baby. Let's go." Her arms surround me again and we hobble into the darkness. I feel her head twist against my shoulder bobbing and nodding to someone in the darkness behind us. I don't allow myself to think about it and instead focus on the smell of her. Candy, beer, smoke, but something else. Underneath all that there's a crisp clean smell that reminds me of when the dryer died once and we had to string up the clothes in the yard for a few weeks. I remember the snap of sheets as Gramps flicked them over the line. I ran between the rows of clean and cool sheets, breathing in that smell.

The memory brings more hot tears to my eyes. "I never said it. I'm such a coward!" I bellow to the sky. Mona shushes me and keeps me walking farther from the dark streets.

"Where to, honey?"

My sobs are the only sound as we make our way to the harbor. The breeze picks up and for the first time, I notice Mona's wearing a skirt. It's pleated and green like her eyeshadow and isn't very long. She's wearing the same fishnet getup as the first time I met her too.

"Like what you see?" Her head twists against my chest and she smirks. I sniffle and hope it covers the sound of my heart pounding in her ears. Her legs woggle unsteadily as she steps onto *Sweetheart*'s deck. "What is this place? Not like any boat I've ever seen."

"It's a houseboat. But it's not affixed or nothing," I say, but thoughts turn to our fishing trip not long ago and I collapse onto the deck. In gulping sobs, I confess my sins of the argument and the stupid idea to sail the world in the contraption that was more house than boat. She helps me into the cabin and into the hammock, all the while cooing and rubbing my back.

It takes awkward juggling but eventually we figure out how to both sit in the hammock, heads at opposite ends. The bobbing waves gently rock us. My tears have long since dried and idly I wonder how much she charges. Is it like an hourly thing or by the night? Afraid to ask, I bask in the strange girl's company.

"Don't you gotta girlfriend or something?"

"Naw, I haven't been to school since elementary. Everybody my age thought I was too weird anyway."

"How old are you?" Mona turns toward the porthole window and inhales the lake air deep into her lungs. Moonlight sets her face sparkling when we rock close to the window, then she's cast in shadow as we rock away from it. In the dark, I shamefully let my eyes linger on her small black tank top and how it strains over her chest with every breath.

"Eighteen, you?"

She's silent a moment. "Twenty-three. So you never finished school?"

"I finished, Grandpa homeschooled me the rest. I refused to ever go back."

"How come?"

I shrug and the hammock creaks. "Just don't fit in nowhere, I guess."

Mona snorts and her eyes glint in the light enough that I can see she's staring at me. "Boy as beautiful as you, I bet you stand out everywhere you go."

"Boys ain't beautiful." I smirk at the thought, but a warm tingle dances over my chest. She thinks I'm beautiful?

"I like you, Stefan." She says it point-blank like she's telling me her favorite color.

"M-me too." I swallow the dryness in my throat. Dammit, now it just sounds like I like myself. Stupid.

"I gotta get back. You feeling better now?"

I nod. We struggle to balance the hammock as she eases to the deck. I hold back laughter watching her stumble as *Sweetheart* dips and sways.

"Can I see you again?" I ask, laughter in my voice. But Mona stands so still at my question, staring at me with such an intense look that the smile dies on my face. Without a word she walks to the hammock, stills its rocking, and crushes her lips over mine. Her mouth tastes of candy, something cherry, something cinnamon. A strange noise escapes me.

I watch in a daze as she staggers out the cabin and I listen to her tall heeled boots clamber over the deck. I picture her struggling between the dock and *Sweetheart* in those tall things. And then there's silence.

Shit! I forgot to pay! I leap from the hammock to stop her but stand on the deck staring out into the empty darkness. She's gone. Lips still tingling and heart pounding and grief momentarily forgotten, I hop off the boat, toss my bike on the deck, then slip back to the cabin for the night.

Sweetheart bobs in excitement the moment I jump into the hammock. I slide onto the side where Mona was minutes ago and breathe in her lingering scent. The hammock stretches, wrapping around me and holding me close. I enter a deep dreamless sleep.

By morning, I decide to find her and pay for the night so that she doesn't get into any kind of trouble. After stopping at the ATM and withdrawing the max amount allowed, a hefty thousand, I bike to the liquor store in a rose petal cloud.

The sun is shining bright, the birds chittering a chorus. The air smells sweet. Not the sweet stink of tobacco pouches drying on the sidewalk and fermenting soda bottles smashed in the gutter or any of the other smells of this part of town, but a distinct sweetness. Like cinnamon. And cherry. And clean sheets billowing in the wind.

The spot under the neon sign is empty so I perch beneath its dark looming presence and wait. Even the pigeons at my feet look brighter, their feathers glistening with shimmering green and pink, a cluster of brown here, white there. Not one is the drab gray that usually pecks around the pavement.

I whistle to the love song stuck in my head and hobble on my bike, balancing against the brick building. She's probably working and is running a little late. Which means...I shake my head, afraid to go down into those dark thoughts. No, I bet she's getting dressed for the day.

One long limb stretches in my mind. The smell of cocoa butter as she lathers higher and higher. The shimmer of glitter as she smears it over her vibrant molten chocolate eyes. Her plump ass squeezes into a tight denim mini skirt. Yeah, I like that.

Her breasts expand with a deep breath as she slides the fishnet tank top over a flashy red bra. Her fingernails are painted a glistening red to match. Her plump lips make a smacking pop sound after she applies a layer of hot-pink cherry-flavored lip gloss. A stick of cinnamon gum slides between those thick lips.

"Hey, man, you live around here?" A deep voice startles me from my thoughts and the whistle dies from my teeth. I twist to look over my shoulder and stumble from the wall, my feet smacking the pavement on either side of the bike.

"Huh? Naw—yeah, not far." The man's silhouette blocks the sun as he towers over me. His baggy navy shirt billows around him, flapping in a sudden vicious gust of wind. He stands in the light preventing me from meeting his gaze, and I stare at his pristine white shoes instead.

"Who you here for? That's a nice bike, man. Can I see it? I won't do nothin.'" The man pushes me from the bike before I can say anything. He stoops low as if to inspect the chain and gears. My heart starts to pound. Where is she?

Afraid to look in his eyes, I stare at a piece of gum that has flattened and turned black over time as it was ground into the cement. "Mona. I'm lookin' for—I'm here to meet Mona."

"Mona? How you know Mona? What you want with her?"

"Have you seen her?" I kick at the black gummy spot and a string of the grime sticks to the toe of my shoe.

"What you want with her?" The man stands and steps closer, the bike the only thing separating us. His voice is tight yet loud. I swallow the lump that forms. My pits sting with sweat.

"To pay for last night," I squeak. Shame and fear flush my cheeks. She's probably late because she's getting yelled at for not getting the money. I should've come after her last night and not waited until now.

"Aw, yeah?" A flash of something shiny catches the light and draws my gaze to the man's broad smile. "Why didn't ya say so? I'm her pimp, you pay me. She workin' right now. I'll tell her you made good and didn't stiff her after all. How kind of you to come all this way."

His arm loops around my shoulder and he pulls me awkwardly around the bike. It clatters against the building before sliding slowly to the ground.

"Wait, I—" I reach for the bike but the man jerks me backward. I stumble over my feet. His large hands grab my shirt as my back is thrust against the side of the building in the alley. I glance out toward the street and see two men passing a brown bag back and forth, sitting on the curb at the next corner, laughing, watching.

His elbow pushes into my collarbone and against my neck while his other hand shoves into my pockets. His breath smells sickly sweet, like overripe and rotting apples.

"W-where's Mona?" I briefly catch his eyes. *12:25 a.m.* I drop my gaze to his hand, holding the money from my wallet. He said he was her pimp and I said I was here to pay. What's with this harsh treatment? I guess I deserve it for not paying last night.

"This everything?" He shoves his hand back in my pocket after taking my cash. My wallet plops to the alley dirt.

"It's a thousand. I don't know what she charges a night. I thought maybe five hundred would be enough. I wanted to pay ahead for another night. I was thinkin', I don't know, I thought maybe she could, th-that she could come by once a week. I could pay in advance every time."

His hand comes out empty and he grunts in annoyance but steps back. Spits flies from his mouth to the dirt at my feet and I stare and the pinkish slime. "Once a week, huh? Yeah, sure, I can arrange that, no problem, sir."

I smile and look up. "Thank you—"

But the words are cut off when a sharp pain hits my stomach. I double over, clutching my stomach just as a flash of something fills my eyes and everything goes dark.

"Man, he already been cleaned out." A dull thud hits the back of my head. I blink open one eye and groan at the sting.

"Shit, he's awake." The sound of scampering fades. Dust is kicked in my face and I cough, sitting up and peering around me. The two men across the street wave, then laugh.

My side screams as I hobble to stand. My wallet is ripped in two and stomped into the gravel. I shake the pebbles and dust from it, then stuff it back in my stretched pockets. My left cheek burns, the lid over my left eye swollen.

The sun sears into my one good eye. The birds screech a cacophony that has me clamping my sweaty hands over my ears. I stumble toward the street to get to my bike and get the hell out of here. A shadow lounges beneath the sign and my heart leaps.

"What you lookin' at? I already know you ain't got any money, so move on, boy," a short loud woman proclaims.

"Where's my bike?" My hope dies when I see a woman the total opposite of beautiful Mona.

"The fuck I look like, the help desk?" She steps from the spot where my bike used to be and puts her hands on her narrow hips. I step back and my foot plops into a puddle. It hasn't rained in a week. I grimace at the mysterious fluid and the woman cackles.

Where are my shoes?

· · · ·

A FEW DAYS LATER AND my eye finally opens fully. The bruise on my side turned an angry purple but at least the one on my face is only a hint of green. If Mama was around, I bet she'd pat a powder on it to hide it, like I see in movies. She'd clean it by dabbing it with a cloth and I'd wince and she'd yell at me to hold still.

The sun has been especially mad at me since that day. It always shines right on the water and straight into my eyes with such intensity, I swore I was gonna go blind. The new moon night is a relief to my sore eyes. Stars glitter on the water's surface in dancing elongated shapes stretching over the ripples and gentle waves. A soft breeze kisses my stiff cheek.

"Here I am."

I whip around to the dock and there she truly is. My angel of the evening. Mona. A smile bursts the crack on my lips but I ignore the warm trickle of blood. Her silhouette on the dock is outlined by a faint silver glow that highlights a bit of fishnet, a large hoop earring, a coin purse dangling from a thin wrist.

"Well, let's get to it." Her tall boots smack onto the deck and she lurches forward. I rush to grab her but she quickly recovers her balance, grips my wrist, then yanks me after her. The cabin door slams shut behind us. Her name gets stuck in my throat like peanut butter.

"How you want me? Like this? Here?" Her words bite. I blink and her clothes are heaped at her feet. A beam of pale light illuminates parts of her. A dark nipple on a perky breast. A clenched fist. The upper half of her face. Her molten eyes shine with tears and crinkle with a look of rage. I swallow.

"How 'bout here?" She moves in the light and it now casts over her plump ass. Blood rushes south but my heart pounds in fear.

"M-Mona." I step toward her.

"Or maybe like this." She sprawls into the darkness at my feet. *Sweetheart* tilts over a wave and I stagger, trying to avoid stepping on her.

"What—"

"I thought you were different." Hands materialize out of the darkness and shove me.

I fall against the door and Mona's naked body presses into me. My throat closes.

"Like this? You paid for it, tell me what you want." Her hips sashay and grind into me. My body quivers at her touch. A hot breath puffs over my ear.

"S-stop it," I wail and sink to the floor. The only sounds that fill the cabin are my choked sobs and her angry panting breaths.

"I'm just some whore, right? You paid, here I am. You want me once a week, fine. Let's get to it, I got other places to be."

"I'm all alone!" The wail escapes before I can stop it. I sound like the pathetic child I am. "I just wanted a friend. I thought I had to pay for your time, for you to be free for a little while."

"Oh, so you're my hero now? You tryna save me, is that it?" Her boots stomp and the beam of light flashes over bits of bare skin and cloth. I imagine her slipping into each article of clothing but shake my head to clear the sultry thoughts.

The door shakes and a smooth leg sidles up beside mine as she slides to the floor with me. My eyes adjust to the darkness enough to see the whites of her eyes as she stares at the ceiling. I sniffle and stare up with her.

"The hell is wrong with you?" she mumbles. Not sure if I'm supposed to answer but not having a response, I say nothing and shrug even though she can't see it. My tongue touches the throbbing split on my lip and the taste of iron fills my mouth.

"His name is Trey. He's mostly harmless 'less you do something stupid like wave money under his nose."

"Your pimp?"

"My—?" Her head whips in my direction, casting her face in the darkness, the only light forming a halo around her head. "He ain't nobody's pimp. He thinks he's so hard. Trey say you came by tryna pay two hundred for that one night and another two for one night a week." She sucks her teeth. "Why won't you stay away? I told you it's not safe for you there."

"It was five hundred, er, a grand. I was—"

"How much? A grand! That slimy sonofa..."

"I was looking for you. Sounded like he could help." I shrug again. *Sweetheart* bucks and her head knocks into my shoulder. A puff of sweet candy fills my nose.

"Do you live on this thing?"

"Yeah." I don't wanna talk about Gramps or his rotting house. I don't wanna think about it either.

"Must be nice to get rocked to sleep each night. Kinda makes my stomach swirl, though."

The ticking minutes fly. If Barry were in my shoes, I imagine he'd be hearing the cha-ching of money being wasted. All I wanted was more of her company. But now that she's here, I have no idea what to do or say.

I swallow back the fear building with each passing second. Will I have to get beat and robbed every time I pay for a night? Not wanting to squander the price my face and ribs and bike paid, I try reaching for her hand. Companionship is what I crave. Surely holding her hand wouldn't cross any lines, right? Fumbling between us in the dark, my fingers walk like an Addam's Family pet in search for her.

"Come on," Mona says suddenly, startling my searching hand into a sweaty fist. She grips my shoulder and yanks me to my feet. "I wanna try that net swing again."

Net swing? Oh, the hammock. She stands beside me, hand still bunched in the fabric at my shoulder, and stares at the swinging contraption. With a smile, I slide onto it with the ease of someone who sleeps in it every night. The pale light catches her wide eyes looking at me as if I had performed complex miracle surgery. The plastic leather of her boot creaks in protest as she attempts to join me. She pushes silver tinsel strands over her shoulder.

Her foot pushes heavily and the hammock dips. I call out and a startled Mona jumps back. Stifling a laugh, I steady the swaying hammock, excited to watch her next attempt. A fishnet-encased arm snakes around me and she angles her body half over me. Then she tries hopping off her other foot and swinging her weight up, but the motion is too abrupt. The room spins. The hammock swings empty above me. Mona stands with one leg raised in vain, mouth open, and eyes wider than ever.

She clamps a hand over her mouth as snorting laughter spills from her luscious lips. An ache forms at the base of my skull where it had connected with the floor. A bubble in my gut expands until it gurgles up my chest and billows out in a loud belly laugh. I roll over and pound my fist on the floor.

"Ain't you ever sat in a hammock before?" I choke between laughs.

"Shut up and help me on this thing." She snorts. I used to think snorting laughs were so obnoxious and childish but with her, it's adorable. "Stop lookin' at me like that!"

"Okay, ease your weight—easy! Slowly, sit here and—"

"You just plop on it like it's nothing but act like I'm gonna shatter it." Mona sits beside me and shifts to follow my instructions how to climb on. But she twists her back to me instead of angling her feet my direction like last time. Before I can say anything, she lies back, her body draped over half of mine, her head beneath my chin. My pulse skyrockets. I've never been this close to a woman before.

My mouth dries. Words disintegrate on my tongue. A gentle breeze turns harsh and sprays a mist of cold water through the small window I always leave open. I squeal at the cool droplets against my heated flesh and Mona chuckles. My skin burns hotter.

"You were gonna pay five hundred just to see me? Why?"

"I'm like you." Shit. I meant to say I'm lonely and almost said I like you. What the hell do I do with that? "I-I mean…I'm lonely, like you."

Is she lonely? What the hell do I even know about her? She could do this for fun and have tons of friends. Or maybe she just wants to pay for college and this is the only way she could. *I'm nothing like you.* Of course that's what she'll say. I'm a spoiled brat with a paid-for house and fancy boat, a lifetime's supply of money in Gramps's account and a talent that could pay for anything else. I mope around doing nothing and piss away his life savings while she's out doing awful things for tons of men. Maybe women too.

But she doesn't say anything. Is she mad? Would she say if she was mad or keep it to herself like some kind of professional courtesy? Say it. *I'm sorry.* Say the words, it's not that hard!

"What was your grandpa like?" Mona finally says, and I blow a breath of relief.

Her head angles against my chest and I can feel her looking at me. I pretend not to notice and focus on the stars bobbing in and out of view through the window.

"Stubborn. Hot-headed." Memories of him rise. "It feels as if I've only run away from home. Like if I just go back there, he'll be in the kitchen, waiting for me to bring veggies in from his garden and life will just go back to how it used to be."

I want to change the subject. I'm not ready to think about Gramps yet. I want to ask her the burning question: why does she do what she does? I want to ask how long she's been doing this but I'm afraid to know the answer. Maybe she lost everybody too and had no choice. If Gramps hadn't left so much behind, where would I be? What would I be doing to get by?

Sitting on a corner selling time instead of my body. Why can't Mona play an instrument or something? I've seen plenty of other talents on the sidewalk that earn strangers' money, and they're always tossing more coins to the musicians over me and my weird talent.

Thankfully, Mona changes the subject so I don't have to choke on my words. "Can you sail this thing?"

With each sway of the lapping waves, the hammock creaks and groans rhythmically. A tiredness settles into my bones and I want nothing more than to wrap my arms around Mona and drift off into a peaceful sleep.

"Not really. I tried when Gramps died. I took off to dump his ashes on the water but stalled out. Our dock neighbors had to haul me back." I wince, knowing this will lead back to what I didn't want to talk about. Gramps' ashes are probably buried under so much dust by now, sitting in that empty house. All the food I left to rot in the fridge...the fried fish he made for me when he left and never came home again...

"I don't wanna talk about Gramps, though. So, if Trey isn't your pimp, then who is? Do you have one?"

"I don't wanna talk about that kinda stuff. Let's not talk about bad. If you could go anywhere, far from here, where would you go?"

"Anywhere? Hmm...I don't know. You?"

"Dallas, Texas. South, far, far from here. A place where the sun is always there to wrap its warmth around me." Mona nuzzles against me.

The night ends far too quickly but when sleep finally claims me, the dreams of death that frequent my nights are absent once again.

• • • •

"11:59 P.M."

"Seriously? Not midnight? Are you sure?" the young boy, Nate, asks. No, he's about my age maybe.

"Of course I'm sure." I scowl at the rock he handed me, still filthy from the garden he likely pulled it from on his way over.

"Move it, there's a line here! I ain't got all day!" An old woman swats Nate with her cane until he scampers off. She smiles wide as she hobbles up to me, her gray dentures about to pop out of her thin lips. "Name's Henrietta Selma Albright. Whatcha got for me, sonny boy? Make it good!"

The old woman has clumpy white hair, leathery skin. A hunch-back and bowlegs.

"6:03 p.m." I stare at her, seeing someone else. She nods sagely, hands me a nickel and something before scooting off. I stare after her until she rounds the corner.

"Well?" the next person, a middle-aged white man asks, tapping his shiny brown loafer on the pavement.

I look down at my hand. The old woman handed me a packet of marigold seeds. Tears threaten to spill. Shaking my head, I toss the seeds into the box beside me and turn to face the man.

I ask for his name, read off his time, and accept my third dirty rock of the day. The soda-coated coin clacks in my coffee tin. Twenty-five reads today. Not terrible for two hours of sitting at this street corner.

"What the hell is this? A nickel and a trinket...what parlor tricks you workin' on?"

My head snaps up to find Barry leaning over my box, toeing it with suspicion.

"Nothing." I say, bending to pick up the box and get back to *Sweetheart*. "Just leaving."

"Hold on now, you haven't gotten to me yet!" A small girl behind Barry peers around his large frame, waving frantically for my attention. "Please?"

I nod at her and Barry steps aside. "Name?" The girl hands me a coin and a lucky rabbit foot dyed purple.

"Um, it's..." Her eyes shift to Barry and back to me. He takes a few steps back. "Leslie. Um, Leslie Ray Umble."

I nod at her, take her hands in mine, and peer deep into her wide brown eyes. She's kind of cute if not a little plain. Dirty dishwater blond hair, pale skin. She looks to be older than me, later twenties, maybe?

"4:15 a.m., Miss Leslie."

"Wanna tell me the hell this is about?" Barry asks as we watch Leslie stumble away, her gaze locked on the clouds above. I shake my head and continue packing up.

Barry stomps on the sidewalk at my heels. "You hardly come by in the last, I don't know, year maybe, and I find you offering parlor tricks on the sidewalk. The hell's goin' on?"

"Nothing's going on, like I told you. Just having fun is all." I hasten my pace, nearing the library where I'd locked up my bike. Barry huffs but keeps up.

"Who's Tod?"

"It means time of death." I explain the header on the sign tucked under my arm. I scurry across the street to my new bike and flip my bike lock code in, trying to get it free before Barry gets through traffic and joins me.

"'Time of death, a nickel and a trinket.' What's that mean?" Barry pants, hands on his knees and standing in front of me, blocking my path. I lean one foot on the pavement and one on the bike pedal.

Annoyed, I look into his eyes and say, "12:41 a.m. That's when you're gonna die. Now you owe me five cents and a worthless trinket." I pedal around him and peel around the corner before he can say anything.

Dinner is a tomato sandwich and a sliced raw potato with salt. Thoughts of Mona surface but I quickly squash them. With a sigh, I slip one nickel at a time into the plastic coin jar and watch the digital counter flash the total with each added nickel. The waters slap against *Sweetheart*, announcing a bumpy night of sleep ahead. I smile in anticipation.

Collecting the watering can, I fill the green plastic container at the dock's public drinking fountain. Grandpa's plants took to the giant containers well, I only lost one tomato, two potato, and two jalapeno plants in the transfer. Water pools at my feet by the fourth can of water but the sun quickly sets to cleaning it up from the deck.

"Well look at the little garden you got going. How nice." Uncle David stands on the dock, hand raised in soft greeting.

"Barry tells me you've been begging on the street corner? You know you can come stay with us if you need to." Uncle David does a poor job of prying as I put a plate in front of him with a tomato sandwich and chopped carrots on it.

I know he's just trying to get me to talk. The inheritance amount was no secret. They know it wouldn't have been possible to blow through it in a year and a half with nothing to spend it on. They also know I wasn't begging. Saying nothing, I turn back to the plants, massaging a fingertip into the blossoms of the cucumber vines and spreading the pollen between each yellow flower.

Around a sweet carrot, Uncle David says, "What's this time of death nonsense?"

I shrug.

"Okay, not nonsense. What does it mean?"

"It means exactly what it sounds like. For a trinket and a nickel I tell people when they'll die."

He ponders this for a moment, crunches on more carrot, then says, "This got to do with your granddaddy?"

"It's got nothing to do with him!" I yell, and the seagulls flocking on the dock waiting for leftovers flap into the air, then settle back with loud screeching protests. I whirl on Uncle David and flop onto the seat across from him. "Why did the paper say he died at 8 p.m.? He died at 7:37. Better yet, why didn't I find out until the next morning? Ya'll were there!"

His gray-blue eyes widen at my outburst. A sailboat coming into the no-wake area boasts a large family who all lower their waving hands at my grimace in their direction.

"How did—"

"Doesn't matter how, I just know."

"We-we found him that way. We didn't know how long he'd been there, pinned behind that crate like that...we didn't know."

"Why didn't you call me sooner?!" I yell, and the seagulls squawk in impatience. I throw the bread crust from his plate at them, nailing one between the eyes. A flurry of white and gray dive after the scraps.

His silver wedding band glints in the sunlight as he strokes his beard, watching me. "You said we were lying when we brought the ashes home. Just like you, we didn't want to believe it, neither. The first aid specialist on board announced it, but we didn't believe it. At the hospital we wouldn't believe it then neither. It took four different people to tell us before we could even sit down and consider it for ourselves. We—I just kept waiting for him to walk up out of that bed and tell us all to quit foolin' and get back to work." Tears pool in his eyes. I look away.

The seagulls migrate down the dock to a neighboring houseboat with orange cheese puffs flying in the air off the railing and into their greedy beaks. The waves lap viciously one after the other, making water splash up one side while we grip the table and wait it out. A large party barge chugs out far enough so we don't smell the booze and perfume but close enough to hear nothing other than the blasting pop music until it passes.

When I turn back from gazing over the water, Barry has materialized behind Uncle David, a stack of pizza boxes in his grasp. He offers them up with a sheepish grin.

"So you know when someone's gonna die, just by looking in their eyes?" Barry shovels the fifth slice of pepperoni and banana pepper pizza into his gullet. Uncle David watches me with a probing look. I toss a slice at the gulls. A grackle joins the flock and pecks its way to the front lines.

"Yup. As long as I can remember. I been reading people like you saw since I could ride a bike." I think back to my stashed trinkets all over the shed and under my bed and in my closet back at that house. My hoard of nickels waiting for a group of invading drunk teenagers. Maybe it's already gone. Maybe the whole house is too.

"So you haven't raised your rates?"

"Honey."

"What? It's business, ain't it? Inflation effects every business no matter how small."

I turn away from the birds fighting over a pepper ring. "It's for fun, not money."

"It's a talent that shouldn't go to waste." Barry wipes his hands on his blue t-shirt and rises, his cargo shorts—the same as Uncle David wears—are spotted with old food stains. "Here. A quarter and a knickknack, right? How 'bout we raise that a little?"

He hands me a twenty and a money clip.

"So your uncle wants to make your talent into a business?"

"Yeah, I turned him down. I'm not interested in taking people's money for this kinda thing. I mean, a nickel for a time seems plenty to me. He wanted me to charge like twenty bucks or something. And how am I supposed to make that a business?"

"Mr. Stefan, the mystic psychic of mischief!" My voice booms theatrically. "Come one, come all...to his little shop in a strip mall. Yeah, sounds like a great idea to me."

He doubles over in laughter and I can't help but join in.

The crickets quiet as our footsteps echo through the surrounding bushes along the walkway. The nature park is a long ride from where his boat is docked. When he said he wanted to go to the park, I thought he was talking about the park near the beach, but as I perched on the pegs on the rear tire of his bike and the short ride stretched on, I found myself easing into the trip.

I try to keep our visits short but tonight, right now, my hand brushing his, our steps in sync, it feels right to linger. For the few hours once a week we spend together, I'm not a whore in the slums working for money that goes straight to my mother. I'm not a friend desperate to free her best friend from an evil man's clutches. I'm not a girl in tight clothes and too much makeup. I'm just a girl whose heart is hammering and palms are sweating with a boy's name stuck in my throat.

At first, Stefan was a sweet taste of innocence in a dark world of survival. He was a distraction from the violent men, the groping and gruesome, foul and vicious life I lead many nights. But he was also an easy source for good money. The sour sensation in the pit of my stomach twitches at the thought of taking advantage of his kindness. At the end of every night together, he bikes me home but stops at an ATM and lets me pull the money out with his card and pin. He says he doesn't want to know, that it's not about the money. But his innocence and trusting behavior piss me off.

Over the past few weeks, I've taken five hundred each time. But last week, I snuck eight hundred. I can be sweet on him, keep him chasing on my heels, and keep milking the extra money from him. The five hundred was already more than my usual amount but even with Mama's cut, I've managed to add fifteen hundred to my stash for Sandy's freedom.

So why does this easy money feel so dirty?

The moonlight catches his fiery brown hair and in this light, he looks almost ethereal. His brown curls with hints of red, odd golden eyes, coupled with his medium skin...he's like something out of a fantasy novel. His square jaw and rounded lips, thick lashes, perfect nose...he's a chiseled fairy creature caught in a filthy black widow's web.

With our shared past, I should feel even more foul for doing this to him. I'd be lying if I believed this wasn't partly out of jealous spite. I promised Ira I'd get him to safety and here I am, all this time later about to become his worst nightmare. He could've been so much like me, forced to a hard life on the streets doing things nobody wants to be doing for a dollar they don't even care to spend.

Despite this jealousy and the guilt of what I'm doing churning in my gut, I'm still enjoying every moment with him. It's a cruel twist of fate to find someone so beautiful, so sweet and innocent, so tempting when he's so far beyond my reach.

"What's got you so quiet?" Stefan asks, his deep voice stirring things that have no business stirring.

"You." I should've already started heading back an hour ago. But the night is warm, the breeze soft, the air fragrant. He's wearing a light knit sweater and soft-looking dark jeans and a cute pair of leather sandals. If I were any other girl and my life was on any other path, I'd venture to say tonight was perfect.

But I'm wearing fishnet and cheap perfume and dollar store lipstick. My heels—dangling from my fingers with their pink chipped nail polish—are three inches too tall and four years too old. My body is sore and worn. The world lay at his feet while the only thing in my future is a gruesome end in a ditch or a sad fizzling out like a wet old cigarette.

If I were any other girl, like one someone loved enough to beg a little girl to take to safety, if I were lucky enough to be raised in love and warmth, I'd probably reach for his hand. I'd push him against a tree and have my first real kiss. He'd walk me home and never look away from me. I'd pretend to be cold and he'd give me his sweater, knowing full well I'd never return it.

"What about me?" He looks bashful. Damn, he's so cute.

"Why you wanna hang out with me? Ain't there any hot girls that live on them boats next to yours?"

"I like hanging with you. And yeah, I mean, I guess so. Nobody lives on any though, just come by sometimes. I've never talked to any of 'em and they always have jocks hanging on 'em. Not my type anyway."

"So I'm easy, that it?" I can't help the edge that leeches in. He looks sideways at me. I think of his bruised face and split lip. Nothing has been easy about being with me. A park bench comes into view, illuminated by the moonlight, perfectly centered in a shadowy wreath from the surrounding trees. My heart squeezes at the sight and I glance up at the sky searching for a wishing star.

His hand reaches out, grabbing at my wrist with such determination that a squeak bubbles from my lips. He runs with me in tow the few feet to the bench and once we reach it, he stands there, me beside him. He stares at the bench with trepidation etched in his features as if this were our marital bed and he was unsure who should lie in it first. The thought dampens the momentary elation I'd felt when his cool fingers laced with mine.

Stupid! Stupid! I'm nothing but a used up whore. I have no right to hope for gentle touches, stolen kisses, sweet whispers, or for those cool fingers to reclaim tarnished lands. But God, do I wish things were different. I wish I were different.

Stefan plops on the closest edge, our laced hands awkwardly stretched across him. He half stands as if to move down, sees our hands, then pulls me to sit beside him instead. We stare at our hands as if it were a new element we'd only just discovered and upon naming it, thought, *my God, how has this magnificent thing existed for so long without our knowing it?* My hand looked like somebody else's wrapped up in the large softness of his.

"I don't think you're easy," he says, and my sluggish mind replays everything up to this point in search of what the hell we were talking about.

I want him. I want him unlike I have ever wanted anyone or anything in my entire life. I want him in the awkward, stumbling, laughing way I was robbed of. I want to give him all my genuine firsts and all of my lasts. Dammit, I want to be somebody else. Anybody else.

His body turns stiffly over me, angling in front of me, but I can't look away from our laced fingers. I'd heard once about a place couples go to where they dip their hands in wax and make little wax statues of their hand holding. Something I once thought sounded so trite and flowery I now crave with such intensity that tears prick my eyes.

"Can-can I..." His face is close to mine, his eyes darting from our hands to my lips. Without thinking, I close the gap to kiss him, then stop short. It comes so easily to me. Like going through the motions. It shouldn't be like this. I should be shaking with nerves, sweating with anticipation. Instead I nearly leapt in and made good on his intentions for him, like I'm taught to do. Like I'm paid to do.

Staring into the shadowed gold of his eyes, I lose my nerve. I should kiss him like he wants me to, like he's paying me to. As much as I wish I were somebody else, this is who I am. A whore. A vagina for money. Or mouth. Or... I shake the thoughts from my head. A coin-operated orifice need not feel, think, doubt. Who the hell did I think I was for a moment there? But as I lean closer, it feels so damn wrong.

His hand slips from mine. No, it doesn't feel wrong. *I* feel wrong. I don't belong here, on this bench, beside this man, under these stars. My place is somewhere far from here. With smoke in the air and substances of many colors in my veins and someone else much closer than I want them to be.

"Mona." Stefan's voice sings my name and snaps my thoughts away. His large hands frame my face and his question burns in his eyes. Another girl nods my head and closes my eyes. A quiet thud goes unheard as my heels fall to the ground. And his lips find mine. A surge of emotion and feeling and fresh air fill me from the warm earth beneath my toes up to the playful breeze tickling my neck.

"Mmmph..." A moan drips from my lips and he laps at it, eating the sound as if it were honey on my tongue.

I want to ask him for his sweater to cover my shameful body. I want a stranger to walk by and see two young kids making out on a bench at a time in life before things get too complicated. I want this kiss to be the start of something real, something beautiful.

But too soon is the magic broken. And the bike ride to the ATM and closer to those darker, dirtier streets recasts the night in a filthy light.

"Hey, Mona." Stefan's voice sounds wistful. The ATM whirs as the debit card is sucked from my fingers. A glance over my shoulder finds him gazing up at the stars, a faraway look in his eyes.

"Hmm?" I wonder what his pin number is from, maybe his birthday? His grandfather's? Or maybe it's Ira's but I doubt he'd know that. The ATM flashes to the "withdraw amount" screen and my finger hovers over the eight.

"I think I'm falling in love with you."

The soft chitter of a bat flies overhead, stilling the flutter of dusty wings. The breeze bursts in a violent gust, whipping the trees in a cacophony of rustles and snaps. As soon as the wind assaults us, it settles as if it never happened.

My heart pounds in my ears in time with the beeping of the machine in front of me. A timeout countdown flashes. The excitement and elation within me burst and sour. My heart increases tempo but a new fire ignites through my body. Hatred. Rage. Nostrils flaring, I stab at the screen.

Requested amount exceeds maximum withdraw amount daily of $1000. Would you like to withdraw the maximum instead? The machine prompts. With another glance over my shoulder, I stab the green "yes" button and slip both the fat stack of cash and his card into my coin purse. With a breath to steady myself, I turn and grasp his waiting outstretched hand.

Easy innocent virgins like him are simple to distract. I coil my body against his, the center bar of his bike digging into my hip. His brown-red curls tangle in my fingers and I slam his mouth over mine. His body trembles beneath my fingers that stroke his chest, stomach, the waistband of his jeans.

A gasp has him pulling his head away from me. With his face turned in search for the source of the sound, I etch this moment into my memory. A dark scruff peeks through the soft skin of his cheek. Overhead, the sky is outlined with pink and white, the morning forcing its way through the black and purple blanket of night. He smells earthy, musky, clean.

A woman done up in a business suit with a traveler coffee mug in hand steps around us, eyeing me with scorn and distaste, before hurrying to the ATM. She thrusts her card into the slot then turns to look at us with expectant dismissal. With a fist rested on my cocked hip, I give her my best saucy smile.

"Um, let's go, Mona." Stefan's bike clanks under his foot and he waits for me to hop on the back.

I sidle up behind him slowly as if he were a pole on a stage. His body stiffens as I press my chest against him. "This is the part where you thank me for last night." I fake whisper against his ear, my eyes stuck on Miss Business Priss. Her features scrunch up as if she's caught a whiff of something long dead. Stefan pedals away like the devil is after us.

He drops me off at the usual corner, the farthest outskirts of my hood where the chances are lowest he'll be spotted by Mama, or Trey, or anybody worth avoiding. Where before his eyes held wonder and an emotion I dare not think about, his gaze now stares anywhere but at me. Yeah, thought so.

"See ya later, suga." I twist my words to my put-on corner whore simpleton. Men like to think I'm simple and stupid, so I give them what they want. It's what I was trained to do. What I'm paid to do. Stefan nods and turns to go but I stop him with a kiss goodbye. His lips are stiff and unsure when before they were hungry and demanding. I break the kiss with a porn-worthy *pop* and saunter away, leaving him staring after me. It takes everything I have not to flash him a middle finger.

• • • •

I WASH THE SMELL OF man from my skin, as I do every night but for a very different reason. Stefan's scent lingers in my nose and I burn it out with the smell of marijuana. The bathroom window gets stuck cracked open, but I decide to leave it open instead of fight with it. The warm fog fills my mind and settles the unease as it stirs.

Sandy's in my bed. Which means Deshawn's on his shit again. I can't stomach looking at her to see the new damage and so I leave the light off. It doesn't matter anymore. I'll sneak a grand every day, the maximum allowed, and Sandy will be free in a couple weeks. We've endured together for years, we can handle a few weeks.

Stefan's too dumb and innocent to notice before it's too late. By the time that puppy comes barking up my tree, Sandy and I will be long gone.

Twenty-three more names added to my list. More nickels. More broken toys and dirty rocks. One person gave me an engagement ring that was probably stolen. The large diamond flashes on my pinky and brings a smile to my face. I suck in a breath as my finger slips along the edge of a page. The taste of iron coats my tongue. She was the weirdest read of the day. *Sandra.*

"You that boy?" she'd asked me. Mona talks about me. This Sandra knows about me. 8:15 p.m. was her time. I finger through the pages of the book she'd given me. *Bridge to Terabithia.* I remember reading this as a little kid. She looked so sad when she handed it to me. I should've taken the cheap bangle from her wrist that I'd spotted when she approached.

She had purple eyeshadow heavily circling both of her eyes, hot-pink makeup on her cheeks that spread oddly to her jaw. When I read her time, she nodded and said, "Okay, I can do that."

Of all those I've read, those who've believed, those who've scoffed, those who've changed their lives and those who've spit fraud at me, I've never had a reaction like Sandra's. *I can do that.* What did she mean?

Never mind that. If Mona is talking about me to this girl, that must mean she doesn't hate me, right? Yesterday makes two times she's missed coming to see me. Over two weeks have passed without a word from her. I've wandered near those streets but held back, afraid of what I'll find there.

I meant what I said to her. I am falling in love with her. She's a whole lot of woman. Mona's carved out a hole in me and settled in for the long haul. But maybe I was just a friend to her. She kissed me so easily, so passionately, and then she disappeared into the night.

And I haven't seen her since. I'm afraid if I hunt her down, she'll voice my fears. And I'll be alone again. But if she never comes back, if I never go to her, I'll be alone then too. Maybe she's scared to be loved. It makes sense. Or maybe this is some kind of test to see if I'll fight for her.

My feet make the decision for me. They carry me to my bike and pedal me toward that side of town. The new bike I'd purchased after it was stolen the last time I was here is the same model. It's not worth much so I can't fathom why it was taken, but I won't take my eyes off it this time. The streets look dirtier than the last time. The sweet smell I remember is replaced with something hot and sour. I look around for an overflowing dumpster baking in the sun but see nothing.

The liquor store's neon lights flash and buzz in the early evening. Sandra leans against the brick, perched between graffiti and old gum smashed into the cracks. Her face matches the bright colors of the neon above her.

"Hey!" I pedal up to her and seem to have startled her from her thoughts. She jumps sideways with a squeal.

"Um, hi." She chews a yellow painted nail where chipped paint reveals a blackened tip. The matching yellow lipstick gives her a sickly pallor with the vibrant makeup smeared even thicker than when we'd spoken.

"Mona around?"

"Um." Sandra stares at her tall black heels and stomps. She grinds the ball of her foot as if stomping out a cigarette. "Cockroach."

"What?" I look around and am thankful to see the stoop across the street is empty.

Sandra lifts her boot to reveal a smear of bug guts spread on the pavement. "No, I don't think she's around."

Her voice is monotone, her responses lagging and disjointed. "Are you okay?" I whisper at her as if the bricks had ears. *Blink twice if you are in danger.* I remember a line like that in a movie. A cop asking a battered woman who definitely didn't fall down the stairs and walk into a door.

Sandra's head whips up at the sound of tires squealing around a corner. A bright red Mustang flies past us only to stop in a screaming screech of rubber smoke. The sports car slams into reverse and a rolled-down window lines up behind me.

"Well look who it is." The man from before, the one who knocked me out, smiles from the driver's seat. He leans over the gear shifter and gold flashes between his lips. I swallow back the nerves that spike. If he has this car, what'd he need with my bike? I know it was him who took it. Ask him! Just open your mouth and say something!

"You sure get around, don't you, boy?" The lumbering length of him crawls from the suddenly small-looking car and he stands between Sandra and me. "And look, you already got a nice new shiny bike."

Sandra sidesteps toward the alley. I want to tell her to run in the opposite direction. If this goes like last time, that alley's right where this guy's headed, with me in tow. Dammit, just speak up! Tell him to back off! My jaw clenches, my tongue working like it has to dig the words out from between my teeth.

Trey. That's what Mona said his name was. She said he was harmless. Mona. I think of her kiss, her cherry and cinnamon taste. The soft and full feeling of her breasts pressed against me. "Back off, Trey," I growl.

"Who the fuck you think you talkin' to?"

His imposing shadow expands, filling my vision and overtaking my space. I stumble back, falling toward the ground. My head knocks against something solid. Sandra stares down at me with a look of either disinterest or boredom.

"Damn, boy! Watch it, she was just painted!" Trey grabs me with one hand and my bike with the other and drags me away from the car. As I crumple to the sidewalk, the center bar of my bike comes down so hard on my shin that I bite my tongue to keep from crying out. The red paint is pristine and untouched, but he scowls at me as if I'd ripped the door from the body.

His clean white sneaker clomps on the bike, pinning me to the sidewalk. I flinch and squeeze my eyes shut, waiting for the blows. A tug on my hand has me peeking through my lashes to find him grinning wide and smug. He slips the engagement ring from my finger, then releases his hold on me.

"Well now, Sandy. Look what I've got. Come with me, girl. Shh, shh, come now." Sandy's bored gaze widens but she lets him push her into the passenger seat. "Let's go to the pawn shop and then I'll give you a ride home, how's that sound?" Trey's sinister voice turns sweet. As soon as he slides behind the wheel, the tires erupt in a bloodcurdling scream. Smoke billows behind him and the last thing I see before he rips around the corner is Sandra's gaping face twisted in a slurry of emotions.

• • • •

"UM, HEY, STEFAN."

The ice pack I held against my shin plops to the deck, forgotten. I jump to my feet, only to stumble and fall back to my seat.

"M-Mona. Hey, hi. Um, hey."

She's wearing a tight red dress and flip-flops. Subtle dark eyeshadow kisses each eye. Her lips shine clear. A gray sweater drapes over her shoulders. Her large hoop earrings are replaced with tiny white hearts. Her head is bare of any wigs and instead she sports a short pixie cut. The dress has a modest neckline and ends midway down her legs. It's the most I've ever seen her covered. She looks stunning.

"Mind if I join you?" Her voice is different. She sounds less natural and more...refined. But a put-on refinement. As if she were acting. My pulse jumps as sweat beads on my brow. I nod and kick the ice pack out of sight. *Sweetheart* dips and sends it sliding back in front of me. Mona waits for the boat to settle over the swell of a wave before easing onto the deck.

"I...I've missed you." I stare at the pack. A few cubes of ice have broken free and slide side to side with each sway of a new wave. A wet trail forms in their path and they look like crystal slugs dancing between our feet.

Mona says nothing but sits on her knees and picks up the fallen ice, tossing them one cube at a time into the water. The *plink-plink* sound draws a flock of ravenous gulls ever searching for scraps. A few battle over the next cube as it soars through the air, only to flap away empty-beaked and disappointed.

She doesn't ask what happened. She's probably used to random injuries and bruises. The rainbow face of Sandra flashes in my mind and her twisted features stare back at me. Does Mona's face twist like that every time a man drives off with her? Or does she turn on the charm, smile sweetly at him, and press her breasts against him?

The sunset casts an orange glow to the evening and I realize this is the first time I've seen Mona in daylight. She stares at the horizon, her face turned away from me. She knew last time I had a run-in with Trey. Is that why she's here? That was only a couple hours ago. Is she here to tell me to back off and leave her alone?

"Mona." When she turns to look at me, a determined look is in her molten chocolate eyes. I open my mouth to ask what this is all about when she holds up a hand.

"I came by earlier but you were gone. I wandered this boat a little bit." The tone in her voice sets me on edge. My gaze flicks to the upper level, the level of Gramps' old room. The different curtains lining the windows suddenly stick out too plainly. I'd bought them in a hurry a few weeks ago, trying to clean up for Mona. I should've tried harder and bought all matching. Some are blue, some red, some white, one pink.

"That's a lot of stuff you got up there." Her thin wrist gestures to the pink curtain in the window closest to us. The fading light makes the pink glow like a beacon. "Looked like a lot of trash."

"It's not trash. It's the collection from the reads I do is all. I haven't had a chance to go through it yet." I remember every name and face. Save every nickel and the occasional dime. But it's the trinkets I love, the things held by someone while they thought of me. Those mean the most.

Mona's glossy lips part and I wait for an argument to start, although why she'd care is beyond me. But she surprises me by smiling instead. "Well, no matter. Come on, suga. I wanna show you something."

My mind freezes as I watch her. The hammock creaks as it sways, empty for now, but watching us, and waiting. Her body dips and sashays in time with *Sweetheart*. Idly, I notice the thrash of the waves beyond the window and recognize the signs of a coming storm. There's no music but her movements stir an unnamed song through my mind.

The smell of cinnamon and cherries surrounds me. The door at my back seems to tremble as if in anticipation of something. My fingers trace the wood as hers trace her hip, her side, her breast. Red pools at her feet and beautiful bare skin shines before me.

Her lips slide along my neck. A shiver weaves through my being. *I never... I've never...* the words stick in my throat. Her mouth puckers, "shh," as if reading my mind. She uses some kind of magic to remove my clothes. Poof, my chest is bare. Poof, my legs feel the chill breeze from the window. And with a third wave of her secret magic, I stand naked body pressed to hers. My bony and lanky frame feels wrong against the delicate softness of her.

"Ah!" The door rattles as I rear back at the touch of her tongue against my chest. Down and down she licks hot ice into my skin. *Wait, wait.* My throat tightens as hers opens for me. Sensations explode at the slippery feel of her mouth taking all of me. I gasp, choking on air that has grown thick.

I blink and find the wood planks of the ceiling dancing in my vision. Mona appears above me and for the first time, I notice the bite of the hammock's netting into my bare backside. Her knees gouge into my ribs but before I can clear the fog from my mind, a new sensation ignites.

"M-Mona!" I cry her name, head tipping back. Her body takes me deep and my mind falls away to be torn apart by the vicious waves crashing outside. Her hips ride and buck, back and forth, back and forth. My eyes roll back.

"Mona," I whisper, sitting forward and stilling her movements. She blinks and I get a strange feeling as if I'd interrupted an actress on stage. "Please."

My hands frame her face. *Look at me, Mona. Please, please, look at me.* I lean toward her, our lips nearly touching. She stares back at me through her thick lashes with confusion dancing in her eyes. Her delicate brow furrows. Her lips part and a hot pink tongue flashes out to lick along the plump tantalizing flesh.

I lunge for that tongue and capture it between my teeth, sucking it into my mouth and tasting her. She gasps a wonderful sound. Her body returns to its dance but I grip her hips to stop her. And I kiss her. Her short hair whispers against my palms. Her smooth hot back twitches beneath my touch. I pull her close, crushing her tight against me.

The crippling loneliness, the isolation, the pain that has burned me for so long begins to recede a little as we continue to kiss. The two weeks of her absence has left me hollow, listless all over again.

But she's here now. Her warmth is surrounding me, her scent filling up the cabin. I have to make sure she never leaves me again.

"I love you, Mona," I whisper against her lips. Her eyes widen and for a second, it felt as though this was a first time for us both. She smiles sweetly and bats those thick lashes. A hand pushes me back and her hips pump, slow, slower.

My thoughts flash to her little coin purse and I realize she doesn't have it with her. I think of the wad of cash, the stack of foil packets. Jealousy surfaces at the thought that each one of those foil packets has probably been used since then. The slick bare feel of her clenches around me and the swirling thoughts and emotions slam into me in a crescendo. My body trembles beneath her, a forceful release explodes. My jaw clenches, my fingers grip her thighs.

Mona's breath pants against my chest. Her breasts press into me. I wrap my arms around her sweat-slicked back and kiss the top of her head.

Mona. My sweet Mona. How I love you.

He's fast asleep. Like a little puppy, all tuckered out after a long day of play. Either he never suspected a thing, or he's love drunk and doesn't care. Slipping his debit card into his wallet and leaving without him so much as stirring feels too easy. Or perhaps I wish he'd wake up and catch me. See who I really am and what he's really meant to me.

Easy money. That's all this was. I got a little carried away acting like I cared about him and that's why my body's humming from his touch. He was gentle and innocent. Of course he'd be delicate with me. It's been a long time since anybody treated me like I was breakable. Nothing to get myself worked up over. I'm allowed to enjoy myself sometimes too.

I love you.

I smirk at the closed door. Some part of me will miss him and our little dates. When Sandy and I are settled somewhere far from here, building our new lives together, maybe I'll send him a postcard or something. Do houseboats have addresses?

The waves toss and throw the boat angrily. It's almost as if Stefan's *Sweetheart* is thrashing to buck me off. A smile rises at the thought. It would've been fun to experience sailing around on it, just once. With the last of the money to free Sandy, we can do all sorts of things now. Maybe one day we'll take ourselves a cruise.

Between violent waves, I hop from the deck to the dock. That wasn't so hard. Guess I've gotten used to this a bit. As soon as the thought settles, the boat rises, knocking my foot off the edge and sending me flat on my face onto the gull-shit covered dock. I roll onto my back and kick to the sky, whisper-screaming into my puffed-out cheeks.

A swirl of light and dark clouds dance overhead. I watch the whorls a while, almost hoping Stefan will find me. As soon as I get up, I'll be on a new path in life. Sandy and I will be different people. I never even realized it until now. That was the last little show I'll ever put on for a man. From here on out, we're free.

The wind stills the closer I get to my house. Thankful it hasn't started pouring yet, I hurry across the street, leaving behind the clean and quiet as I dive back into the pulsing hood that's always been home. There's no such thing as sleep and quiet here. Dogs bark incessantly. A woman's keening cry sounds from somewhere near. A man yells incoherently.

Normally this time of night grinds on my nerves. Too early for anyone I deal with to go home and too late to hope for anybody to be in any kind of mood that isn't foul. No matter. Deshawn's attitude will perk right up the moment he sees my stack of cash with Sandy's freedom written on it.

I run through the alley and slip in our back door. The TV blasts in the living room but I don't stop to say anything to Mama. I haven't decided yet if I wanna say goodbye to her. With only the cash in hand, I leave without a second glance at my childhood home.

We only have a little extra to get us far from here, but I'll make it work. I can work the streets a bit on my own if I have to. As long as I get Sandy free and can keep her safe, it won't matter what I'll have to do.

Deshawn's house is all lit up, even the backyard light shines like a searchlight through the alley. The sound of barking and yelling intensifies. The clasp that holds his rickety gate in place is rusted and won't budge. Damn. I wanted to avoid bumping into Jeremy and Martin and any other dealing goons.

Whatever. Sandy's probably out on her first trick of the night or she's waiting beneath our spot by the liquor store and about to be picked up. I'll likely have to wait for her return anyway. Maybe I'll go back and get Mama to cook up something good and I'll sneak it for the road. I should've told Sandy about all this so she didn't have to turn one more man, but part of me feared Stefan might've caught on and my little plan to sneak his card back wouldn't go so smoothly.

None of that matters now. She's as good as free. The air is stagnant and the rot of the alley's worth of piled up garbage hits my nose all at once. I gag, breathe through my mouth, and jog for the street and somewhat fresher air. Just before I reach the end, a shadow leaps from nowhere and knocks me to the ground.

"Shit! Get away from me, mother—"

"Shh, shh! Shut the fuck up, Mona!" Trey's harsh whisper cuts into my ear as his sweaty hand fumbles over my face searching in the dark to clamp over my mouth. "I didn't mean to, it—it was an accident. I'm sorry. I'm so sorry!"

Trey's shadow whips above me. In the faint outline of a nearby porchlight I can see his head tossing back and forth as if looking for someone. He's always in a hurry to go places. Hauling his Mustang up and down the street like the cops are after him, running around and knocking people to the ground as if the whole world is in his way. It's not like him to apologize for it.

Unless he's sorry for what he's about to do to me. I bite at his hand but as soon as I open my mouth, he jumps off me.

"Motherfucker!" I yell at him, scurrying to sit up and defend myself. But as soon as I get my bearings, he's gone. What the hell was that about?

Afraid to linger in the dark alley any longer, I run the last few feet to the street and breathe the fresher air. The old men always sitting on their stoop across the way, laughing and drinking and catcalling, are absent. In fact, nobody's out on the street. Nobody lurking at their usual shadow hideouts awaiting a car's flashing lights to signal want for drugs. Nobody smoking on porches or wandering down the sidewalk drunk.

I glance up at the boiling sky and wonder if something major is brewing and I missed the warnings. My thoughts flick to Stefan in his sex coma back on the water, but I shake my head. I don't care what happens to him anymore. Easy money. Easy money, that's all he was. Besides, those boats are designed to survive storms, right?

With a nod to steer myself back on track, I round the corner, intent on marching straight through Deshawn's front door, throwing the money in his face, and taking Sandy no matter what.

"I told you I didn't see nothin'!" Mama's voice cuts through the noise. The yelling I'd heard was a walkie-talkie. Cops cluster on the street. In the flashing lights, I see Mama's face and a few others beside her that I recognize. Dammit. I should've known. It wasn't a storm keeping folks inside, but our monthly run-in with cops bored with nothing better to do than harass people just trying to make a living.

Normally, Sandy, myself, and a few other girls take care of them with a few sweet words and things none of us care to talk about the next day. But I promised myself I'd never do that for another man again. Unless it's for Sandy...

I scan the faces of my friends and family and neighbors all lined up on the sidewalk but don't see her. Good. She's probably with a trick after all. A head bobs in the lit-up police car and confusion halts my nearing steps. From the bushes a couple houses down, I can see there are four police cars. Two is the most I've ever seen. Except when somebody's been shot. Great, that'd be just my luck right when I'm all ready to go.

Wait, that's not a police car. As I crawl closer to get a better look, I notice the car they're all standing around is red and sporty. Is that Trey's? Yeah, figures he stole it. No way whatever he's into made enough to get one of those legally. He's too dumb to know changing the color doesn't do a thing if the plates are the same.

"All right. You're coming with me." An officer hauls Mama to her feet and for the first time, I notice everyone is hunched oddly like they're all cuffed. What the hell?

"Leave her alone, she didn't do nothin'!"

"Don't worry, you're coming too, big boy." The officer laughs back at Jeremy as another cop pulls him to his feet. One by one I watch as everyone is piled into the back seats. As soon as one car pulls off, another drives up to take more people away. I dive into the bushes as a car with the sirens blaring comes racing up the street. An officer barks at the driver to cut the noise and three more people are taken.

It's been a couple years since a neighborhood bust. Why now of all times? Right when I'd gotten a taste of freedom, right when it was at our fingertips. No, no this could actually be a good thing. If Deshawn's busted and Sandy's not back yet, we can run away and use the money for our new lives. If she's busted too, a little bail money gone, but we can still run with a hefty chunk leftover and start anew.

Even if Deshawn was tipped off and got away in time, there's still a good chance Sandy was left behind in the mess. Not likely he'd go to any effort to save her from an arrest. No, he probably sent her to work, then hightailed into hiding. Bastard.

Martin's gentle voice and the words spilling from his blubbering lips have me inching closer to hear him over the din. "She-she just...looked up when he came peelin' 'round the corner and she-she...she just smiled and walked out."

"You telling us she did it on purpose? She wasn't crossing and he came flying through here going lord knows how fast?" An officer bows low to stare down at Martin's hunched figure perched on the curb. His head bobs up and is flashed in blue, then down and is flashed in red.

"You say 'he', but who is 'he'?" The officer jerks Martin to his feet with such violence that he staggers. I want to shout at him to leave him alone. Leave us all the hell alone. I recognize that officer and grit my teeth to focus on right now and not let my mind wander to the last time I saw him.

"You see, Martin, this car belongs to a fella by the name of Michael Franks a few towns over. It was reported stolen a couple months ago. Michael's nice and warm in his bed. So tell me, who was behind the wheel when this nice young lady decided to play a game of chicken?"

"Wasn't like that. It wasn't like that! She was—she wouldn't—"

"Shut your mouth, Martin!" A yell erupts from somewhere on the other side of the street that I can't see. Was that Deshawn's voice?

I crawl forward only to dive into the next house's bushes as a pair of black SUVs silently pull in behind the two remaining police cars. An officer pulls something from his hands that looks like a tape measure but as I watch him attach it to a tree and the yellow tape unravels, realization dawns. A break in the crowd of cops reveals a white sheet in front of the Mustang.

At that moment, a vicious gust of wind barrels through the street, sending the yellow tape from the cop's hands and into the faces of the crime scene team climbing from the SUVs. That same gust gently lifts the white sheet and dances away with it down the road and out of sight.

"Shit. Do we got another sheet around? Well, whatever. They'll be taking more pictures anyway," an officer says.

A dark trail connects the shadowed lump on the ground to the front of the Mustang. Heart pounding and sweat dripping off my brow, I crawl in the darkness, closer and closer, all the while my insides are screaming to run, turn away, dance into the night like that sheet and never look back.

The red and blue lights snap off. For a moment, the neighborhood is blanketed in darkness. There's silence. A bright white fills the night. Flash. Flash. The blinding light embeds haunting images deep in my mind. Purple eyeshadow. Bright pink blush. Yellow lipstick.

Sandy. It looked as if she lay at their feet with her ear pressed to the ground, listening for my footsteps. Listening for me to come find her, come save her, come run away with her. But her face is pressed so firmly to the pavement that it looks strange. As if half of it had been ground down to the nose. One sad dull eye stares back at me.

I shake my head. My mouth works a silent chant over and over. No, no. No! I clutch the money to my chest and run. I run and run until the night swallows me whole.

Chapter Nine – Stefan

I should've known Barry wouldn't leave it alone. What the hell was I thinking going along with something like this? I pace the altar, a cold sweat sticking my shirt to my back. This is so fucking stupid. Standing on a corner is one thing. I get maybe three people at most waiting in line. But this?

"You ready?" Uncle David comes out of the back room, a bottled water in his hand. I gulp down half.

"This is stupid." I start to shake and drop to my knees. Just breathe.

"I'm sorry, baby. You know how he gets when he's chasing an idea. Let's just get through today and then never speak of this again, yeah? Tell ya what, you stay strong for me today and I'll make you a pound of jerky, waddaya say?"

"Promise?"

"Ladies and gentlemen," Barry bellows outside the church doors, interrupting our deal. "I give you, Tod, the Death Psychic."

I wince at the weird title. A line of people rush in the doors and queue in front of me, waiting, staring in wonder.

• • • •

THIS STUPID DEATH PSYCHIC crap is Mona's fault. After she kissed me, she disappeared for two weeks. After she slept with me, I thought maybe she'd disappeared like that again when I didn't see her the following week. But then she didn't come by the next week, or the next, or the one after that.

A few days after I last saw her, my bank called with some "possibly suspicious" withdrawals. I can't believe it took that long for them to notice the money we'd been pulling to buy a few hours of her freedom. Maybe I should check my balance and see how much she end-ed up costing me for a one-night-a-week friendship.

But part of me is too scared to know. Somehow, putting a price tag on our nights together will make it all seem as dirty as I'm start-ing to feel. I fell asleep with her in my arms. And woke up cold and lonely without so much as a goodbye note. Which would have been fine had she come back a week later. Now I feel used. She took my virginity and left.

After the third week, I went looking for her. Not only was she missing, I also didn't see a single person I recognized from previous visits. No Sandra. No laughing drunks on the corner. Not even that jerk bike thief Trey. Anyone I did find acted like they'd never heard of Mona or Sandra.

A month of loneliness went by, one day bleeding into the next. Every week on the nights she was supposed to be with me, I'd revisit that park and sit on the bench where we'd kissed. Sometimes I'd bike past her street, peek into the pink shadow of the neon lights hoping for the silhouette of her.

Mona was the only thing that kept me going after losing Gramps. Growing up without my mom or my grandma, not even a sister, it was a nice change having a woman around. Mona brought a lightness and a sweetness to every day when we were together. It was as if col-ors were brighter and the scent of flowers was everywhere. I was extra careful to keep my face shaved and my clothes ironed, the deck swept and the dishes clean. The mere idea of her presence had me wanting to be better, even if being better meant something as simple as fold-ing my laundry instead of picking the clean clothes out of a basket.

"That wasn't so bad, huh, kid?" Barry slaps me on my sweat-drenched back. Yeah, easy for him to say. So many people. So many smells and sounds. My stomach roils.

"You still owe me beef jerky." I cough, pointing an accusing finger at Uncle David.

He raises his hands in surrender. "As soon as we get home, that dehydrator's getting right to work, I swear."

"At this rate, we'll be able to quit our jobs and have a real go at this!" Barry does some weird gyration he'd probably call a dance.

I've read two hundred sixty-nine people for Barry. I've kept every nickel and the three dimes. It's not even enough money to pay for a meal at my favorite diner, let alone to rent this strip mall church the three times he's made me do this. If his plan was to use me to quit their jobs, I can see why he wanted to raise my rate. But I only agreed to do this if my rate stayed the same. Reading a million people still won't be enough for one of them to quit.

Barry flashes me a sheepish look. "Kidding."

"How much longer?" I groan into the citrus soda Uncle David got for me. After every one of these events Barry puts on, my stomach's in a twisted mess. Heck, before I entered this dinky rent-a-church, my stomach was doing flips and it continued for long after my breakfast vacated. Our third show ended over an hour ago, and I can still smell all those people as if they were standing in a mass under my nose.

"I'm sorry, baby." Uncle David rubs my back in reassuring circles. Barry is scribbling on a notepad, pacing the tiny breakroom with a wild look in his eye. Unease has me gulping more soda. "Slow down or it'll come back up," Uncle David coos beside me.

"Two more days are booked here. But then we've got three more at the other location across town. Good news is it's closer to the dock, so you can run home right after." Barry doesn't so much as glance my way, all business and hyped on the success of his latest fascination. If only I weren't the star of his little show.

After he wore me down and I relented to this endeavor, I'd thought it would be a one and done, it'd be as uneventful as it is when I sit on the corner with my sign, and Barry'd be off on the next big thing. I should've known better. Apparently these rent-a-church strip mall eyesores are *so* cheap if you book several days in a row, and they're a *downright steal* if you book more than one location.

I huff out a breath and Uncle David's rubbing picks up speed. My back has begun to feel numb from the constant rubbing. My hand shakes from the strain of this nightmare. Only a few more days of this and we'll never speak of it again. I stare down at a wrinkle in my pants and will the vertigo to go away.

When Mona stopped coming around, all those feelings of being better in little ways vanished. About all I can motivate myself to do anymore is shave. When I do venture to the laundromat or to Uncle David and Barry's place to do my laundry, the clean clothes go right back into the basket. Everything I wear is rumpled and mismatched. My hair is growing into an unruly mass. Some weeks all I do is sleep and eat when I'm awake. Other times I can't sleep a bit and can't even think about food.

That's why this is her fault. I was in no condition when Barry came by, for the seventeenth day in a row.

"Boy, does it reek in this cabin. When you shower last?"

"Leave me alone. I just wanna be alone!" I curl away from Barry and burrow into the hammock's netting until the rope digs into the side of my face.

"Nope. Can't do it. And I'm keepin' comin' by till you agree."

I look over my shoulder so he can see me roll my eyes. "Why do you care so much? It's just a weird talent, ain't worth no business." Barry smiles wide. I turn away with a scowl.

"So, you ready to tell me her name?"

I mumble, "I don't know what you're talking about" under my breath and Barry drones on.

"Something has you cooped up all over again. After Jeb...after we lost your grandpa, I thought you was never gonna get out of it. Then you had a light shinin' in your eyes. Just like that it's out again. Somethin' happen? She leave?"

I bolt out of the hammock, briefly stagger as Sweetheart dips, then jut a finger in his face. "Of course she left! Everybody leaves me!"

Barry's eyes widen at my outburst. He waits until my breathing levels and the anger leaves. Tears pool in my eyes but I stare at the ceiling and will them not to fall. When I ease back into the comforting embrace of the hammock, Barry's voice turns gentle and soothing.

"Tell me what you love about sittin' on the corner with your sign—what you call it—reading people."

The days have been cold since Mona left. Cloudy. Windy. I feel winter in the air despite it being months away. Barry found me in a pool of misery and hasn't stopped coming by every day since. And each day he asks that same question.

"I don't like people. They hurt me and leave me and use me. But I like reading people 'cause in a way, it's the closest—the most intimate—I can be with somebody without havin' 'em around enough to leave me. But they give me something that's like a symbol of our connection. And maybe, just maybe, the time I give 'em can save 'em from themselves."

I meant it when I said that to him. I love feeling connected to everyone I read without letting them close enough to leave me. I love the idea that giving them their time of death could free them from themselves, their fears holding them to a job or marriage or someone else's vision for their lives. But reading this many people, seeing the crowd piling in the doors and breathing up all my oxygen, it brings back the memories of those times I tried going to school.

Their taunts and jeers, their laughter and cliques. I was never really bullied but I could never fit in with any of them. I didn't want to scream and chase on the playground. If I had a book or a quiet place to sit and daydream, I was happy. The only time I fit in was when I first showed off my talent and my schoolmate, Will, let me into his little gang.

But soon Will was bored with my talent, and kids being kids didn't much care about the false idea of death. And just as soon as

I had friends and was relevant, I was a weird nobody again. Home-schooling with Gramps was a lot more fun anyway, so I stopped going to public school. For so long it's just been Gramps and me and sometimes Uncle David and Barry.

I'm not used to dealing with people. Especially so many. Being around them makes me itchy and nauseous. I'm starting to wonder if keeping to myself isolated growing up may be why it was so easy for Mona to use me like she did. What was I to her anyway? An easy lay and quick money? I bet she used that money for drugs to get high with her other clients and they all sit around and laugh at her easy stupid little virgin.

My fear of being around people must have been so obvious. I lost Gramps and ran straight to her. A random hooker who questioned why I was in the wrong neighborhood. I was so stupid I might as well have painted "I'm a dumbass, take my money" right on my forehead. I bet Mona and Trey took all the money they milked from me and ran off together. That why I couldn't find either of them.

Mona refused to let me read her time the day I met her, and I never questioned or pushed it again. I would go so far as avoiding her eyes and tuning out the time that popped into my head whenever our gazes met. That's how far I went for her sake. Of course she didn't want me to read her. She didn't want to change her life around. And anybody with half a brain can guess a girl like that will die in the small hours late in the night.

Well, screw her. All of these people, I'm helping them. They're lining up to see me and then turning their lives around because of me. She can take the money. I'll be happy if I never see her again. It's these people who need me. I'm not doing this because of her. No, that's right, it's in *spite* of her. I'll show her. I'm worth something to these complete strangers. Even if it's a mere nickel and a trinket. After I read their precious time, I become priceless to them.

Five Years Later

"Have you found him yet? We're running out of time!" I yell into the phone, then mouth apologies into the gaping faces of the crowd around me.

"No, not yet. I have no idea what he'd be wearing! A suit? A robe?"

"Well keep looking!" I hang up and run from the cluster of gawkers to search for higher ground. I spot a rise in the sidewalk up ahead, stairs surrounding a small monument, and I dive through the crowd until I reach it.

This part is the worst. Knowing it's about to happen, knowing I can stop it, but hunting my target down before it's too late amid a city chock full of hustle and bustle. My wrist vibrates. I hold the smart watch eye level to glance at it while keeping an eye on the crowd.

Found him!

Yessica sends me a picture and sure enough, we've got him. I bee-line for her at the other end of the block. I spot him before I can find her. He's keeping his face down and standing close in the group waiting at a crosswalk. He glances up from his shoes to watch as a bus races to beat the turning light and my heart stops.

I thought he was crossing to do it at the bridge. There are so many bridges nearby that it was difficult to find him in a busy city in the middle of lunchtime on a workday. I have so many of my crew stationed at every bridge within a mile of his work and his usual restaurant. I was so sure it was going to be a bridge.

Just as his foot leaves the curb, our eyes briefly connect. *By bus.* The words flood my mind and Sandy's face stares back at me. I freeze under her penetrating stare as the bus wooshes by. My dress flutters in the gust and a nearby teenage boy whistles. The crowd erupts in screams and his eyes slide closed, a smile on his lips.

"No!" I scream, knowing I was too late. Knowing I failed again. I squeeze my eyes shut and wait for the sound of the impact, the screech of brakes, the smell of burned rubber and something much worse.

"Are you okay? Oh my God, oh my God. Did you see that? She saved him!" A woman's shrill voice is the only sound that reaches me.

"Desda!" Yessica's scream knocks the fear straight out of me. I open my eyes and breathe in relief. She's on the ground, her body wrapped around his, and he's in one piece. He stares at the sky and the crowd hunched around them. And then he bursts into tears.

"It's okay, you're fine now. It's all right, everyone. He's with us. Follow me, Mr. Stansfield." I pull him back to his feet.

••••

"WHY DID YOU SAVE ME?" Bob Stansfield is still shaking. The French café we'd rushed him into is empty after the lunch rush. A waiter refills his tea and I hold the cup to his lips.

"That's just what we do." Yessica smiles from across the table. But her attention quickly returns to the tablet in her hands as she makes last-minute arrangements.

"I'm the president of my company, did you know that? I love my job. I think. I mean, I love the money. So much money, I never have the time to spend any. I have a penthouse apartment. And my own driver. A maid."

"I know, honey. I know. Here, have some soup." Mr. Stansfield lets me spoon-feed him. He clutches his suit jacket around his shoulders as if it were a blanket.

"It's everything my father wanted for me. The degree and the job and the salary and the stuff to prove it. You know what I wanted? A farm. Yeah, can you believe it? I wouldn't even know what to do with a horse if I saw one, but I wanted a farm. Plants and animals and a wife carrying a pitchfork, pregnant, posing for a ridiculous family portrait."

Robert P. Stansfield the third has no children. No wife nor ex-wife. Outside of a few high-profile fiancées that went nowhere, he has no one. His father passed away several years ago. His job kept every waking hour occupied. Fifty-three years old. And ready to end his life by bridge, or bus, if one so happens to barrel in his path.

I was sipping a latte and eating brunch when I saw him yesterday. Walking to work, that same dull look in his eyes. *By bridge.* The words flooded my mind when our gazes randomly connected. I jumped up and went running after him from the restaurant. His gray eyes barely registered the bullshit story I wove about missing a meeting with him and needing a business card to call his secretary to reschedule. I knew there was no time to waste. If Yessica hadn't gotten to him in time...her eyes meet mine and a warm smile splits her pretty features.

· · · ·

"YOU SURE THE MOUNTAINS was a good fit for him? I was thinking somewhere more beachy." Yessica's feet are on the dash.

I click my teeth and swat at her ankles. This van needs a good scrubbing. "He probably goes to a beach every year on a company trip and works in his hotel the whole time. Nah, guy like him needed nature. Peace. Quiet. And friendship."

"I didn't even know they had adult camps. That's so weird. Cool, but weird."

· · · ·

"ALL RIGHT, I'M HEADING out, need anything?" Yessica hovers in the office doorway.

I hold up a finger to quiet her so I can hear through the static of the police scanner. She cocks her head in question. I shake mine in response. Nothing. The "off" switch makes a loud snap as I flick it impatiently.

"Y'know, most people would be happy there's nothing going on. I mean, even if there was some guy about to jump off a building, it'd probably be too late for us to get there and stop him."

I give her my usual, "I know, just checking." And push her out the door. Her headlights disappear into the dark and not long after, a new set appears from the opposite direction. I head to the kitchen to wait for them and put a pot of coffee on.

The front door slams shut. Boots scuff on the rug. "Were your eyes even open, old man? That pass was clearly supposed to be a fake. Ain't nobody betting the last shot of the game on that rookie."

"You call me old man one more time, and I'll show you just how far I can shove this old man's boot up your caboose." Jacob's raspy voice saying *caboose* brings a smile to my face.

"See! Nobody says caboose. It's *ass*, old man."

"You two are rowdy as ever." I laugh over my cup of chocolatey coffee as my two partners in crime push and shove their way into my kitchen.

"And Adam's mouth is foul as ever." Jacob pours coffee into his favorite hot-pink mug and sips it straight. He sighs with appreciation. "You make the best coffee, Desda, I swear. Don't tell Ma I said that."

"She use that French press I gave you yet?"

Jacob shakes his head, a twinkle in his eye. "Nope. Can't figure out the pressin' part."

"Yeah, yeah, yeah. Small talk aside, what's the scoop?" Adam plops into a chair next to me, his own steaming mug in hand, his cup full of mostly cream and sugar, with a splash of coffee.

I shake my head, staring down into the dark brown liquid. No blips on our radar tonight means back to our base plan, hoping word has spread enough through the surrounding areas.

"Damn. All right, I've got a friend workin' at the gas station who'll keep an eye out for us. And Jacob has his sister cousin or whoever at the grocery store. So, we hang near the dance club strip and see if we get any leads?"

"She's ma's sister. Club will be too risky. Besides, cops patrol that enough. I say we head to the drop-off spot we been havin' the girls spread rumors about. Sound like a plan to you, Desda?"

The coffee turns sour in my stomach. "I hate this plan. I wish there was some better way."

Adam lays his hand on my shoulder. "I know, I know. We feel the same as you. Candy and Lila volunteered to stay in. They know where to find us when they're ready to be free."

"I can't believe they'd be willing to do this, after all they've been through." Candy and Lila were our first rescues. After they learned what I do at night, they wanted to do anything they could to help. It was their choice to go back. I have to trust they know when to give up. And I have to hope word will spread long before then.

"Mama?" Nettie tiptoes in, rubbing her eyes.

"Sorry, did we wake you? I was gonna come up before we headed out."

"No, it's fine." Nettie yawns and flashes her perfect white teeth. Perfect except for the two missing in the front. I look away. Soon, soon I'll have enough saved up to get those fixed for her.

Her braids fray around her shoulders and her red flannel pajamas hang loosely on her frame. The black silk bows tied in her hair and the sweet way she's rubbing her eyes makes her look five and not the mature fourteen that she really is. Only three years that she's been mine and right from day one, she carved out a hole in me and nobody can tell me she's not my daughter.

She reminded me so much of Sandy the day I set eyes on her. Small, big eyes, wild hair, a love of bright colors. Her mother raised her a lot like me, started her young on the streets, grooming her for a life of servitude with her body. But then her mother died and she was sold to a dealer. Ever since freeing her and adopting her, I've made it my life's mission to free as many victims of sex trafficking as I can. Never again will a girl—or boy—feel like the only way to escape is to step foot in front of a car.

"Jennifer finally fell asleep. Brice been out for a couple hours. Hey, is that my cup?" Nettie plucks Jacob's pink mug off the table and drains the rest of his coffee. He feigns shock with his jaw dropped, then elbows her in the ribs with a smile.

"Thank you for watching over them, baby. Want Jacob to stay with and keep you company?" I stifle a yawn and rise to hit the road.

"Nah, like I said, they out. I can handle it, you can trust me." Watching her rinse out her mug and put it in the dishwasher fills me with pride. She's young but so mature for her age. Smart, too. Testing two grades ahead, reading every book I throw at her and coming back hungry for more. "Stop lookin' at me like that. Don't you got work to do?"

With her hands on her hips, giving me her sassy look, she reminds me of myself back in the day.

"All right, all right, we're going. Call me if you need anything. Don't stay up too late, I don't know when we'll get back." I kiss the top of her head and she squeezes me tight.

"Want me to have a bed made up, just in case you find somebody?"

"Don't worry about it, I already got it ready on my lunch." I turn to Jacob and Adam and wave for them to follow me out the door.

"Desda, shouldn't you take a night off? Let me and Jacob handle it tonight. You haven't missed a night in what, a week straight now? When you sleepin'?" Adam keeps his voice low until we're in the van.

"I'm fine, don't you worry about me." The van sputters to life and Yessica's shoe prints on the dash remind me I'd forgotten to clean it out earlier. "Damn. Sorry about the mess."

"Ain't no mess." Jacob wipes the dusty print with his gray shirt sleeve. "It's fine, see? Adam's right, you should stay in. You already do too much."

"Y'all lay off me. I say when enough is enough. Right now, we got a restaurant to scope out."

But when we arrive, the parking lot is dark and empty. Not even a random car is left behind waiting until morning for its owner. Damn.

"All right, you two know what to do. Spread out, look for any hookers and try to buy one. Let's save somebody tonight."

I park the van in our hidden spot between streetlights and watch as Adam and Jacob split up. When their silhouettes fade into the darkness, I pull out my tablet and sift through my social media profiles, searching for the red flag posts of people sounding depressed, posting frequent pictures of drug or alcohol abuse, ranting about lost jobs or bad relationships.

When nothing new comes up, I rerun my ads for my travel company and target users with traits I found to mean they might be considering suicide. The ads haven't been converting well, which means my criteria is lacking. I switch apps to my list builder to brainstorm possible subjects to target that could help me find more people considering suicide. Before I can add anything useful to the list, my head hits the steering wheel and the first sleep I've had in days claims me.

Barry would kill me if he knew I was doing this. But this little sideshow is just for me, like the old days. The quiet trade from a few people and no more. With Barry, there's always a crowd. With him curating the event, I feel like a phony televangelist or faith healer or snake oil seller. A good ten percent of those who show up hand over a coin and a rock or shoelace or half a pair of broken scissors and once I give them their time, brandish me with the label of fraud, then leave with a snicker.

Here on some random street corner in some random town for a couple hours by myself, and I'm just another hobo except you get a reward when you give me change. And it's way better than a smudged windshield from a newspaper scrubbing. At least most patrons tell me so.

That song, you know the one, something about living like you're dying and riding bulls and such. Well, with my gift of their time of death, people take to this mindset and lose all inhibitions. With the exception of their time—then they become paranoid, have a sweating breakdown for that entire minute, and if they've survived through it, live life even harder. Every day that they survive past their time pushes them harder to embrace life.

Is it today? Tomorrow? Next week? In fifty years? Nobody has ever known. But now that I know the time and give away such information so cheaply, the fear of death is stronger, yet people are simultaneously freed from it.

Live like you're dying save for one minute every day. People would almost kill for that kind of freedom. I've had people want to kidnap me with plans to sell me on black markets or monopolize my ability and turn it into a much more profitable business. That's what Barry says anyway. After he got wind of that plan, bodyguards have been at every show since. How we can afford them, or how he figured out those plans existed in the first place, I'll never know.

I have read so many people, hundreds of thousands, maybe even millions by now, that I had to upgrade from my collection of notebooks documenting each person I read and accept new technology. Barry hired a secretary who enters the info into a spreadsheet live as I read each one. How we can afford to pay her, I'll never know.

When I do the private little street corner gigs alone, I still jot those in a notebook for myself.

I don't set up shop on a corner with my sign this time. Instead, I roam around the filthy Chicago streets and look for people who could use this knowledge. The sun is setting, casting orange light on the windows of the gray and beige buildings around me. Barry's tour at the event center was this weekend. I don't know how he advertised beyond the local brochures we put out, but many of the people I read weren't even from Chicago. Some of them came fresh from the airport, pulling their luggage and families along in the huge line.

"Could you spare a dollar?" the man asks, liquor on his breath.

I smile at him and take his outstretched hands in mine. "How about if you give me a nickel, I'll give you twenty bucks and the best knowledge of your life?"

"Yeah, yeah, sure. I got somethin'." The man, late fifties, gray and black hair, sunburned face and layers of smelly clothes, begins to sift through each coat pocket until he hands me a dime. I pull a dirty scarf from around his sweaty neck and stuff both it and the coin into my pocket.

His eyes are rheumy and gray in color, his teeth yellow and few. "What's your name?"

The man grips my shoulders, swaying. The crowd shifts around us, smirks on their faces that a homeless drunk has a tourist in his clutches.

"Benjamin." He nods, his head bobbing up and down with conviction. "Benjamin Theodore Smith. Can I have that fifty now?"

It was a twenty, but I don't correct him. "10:46 p.m. is when you're gonna die."

Benjamin stands still, his breath whooshing out and in. Out and in. "What?"

"I don't know how, I don't know what day or year or month. But your time of death will be 10:46 p.m." I pull a fifty from my wallet and push it into his hand. He takes the bill and looks between me and President Grant.

I walk among the bustling crowd, whistling. As I cross the street, I look over my shoulder for Benjamin. He's standing where I left him, slack-jawed and staring at me. Another man in a similar getup who'd been lounging against a building slips up behind Benjamin and yanks the bill from his distracted fingers. He blinks, smiles at the thief, then turns and walks away.

"Hey, man, I didn't—" I can hear the other homeless man yell as he jumps back. Benjamin just keeps walking, a skip in his step. He'll go on to do great things, I can feel it.

As I round the corner, dusk arrives, casting the busy streets in the closest to darkness that the city lights will allow. Horns and sirens continue to blare. Suits of all shapes and sizes storm past, ears lent to another's voice on cell phones and headsets and earpieces, their words yelling into the air and demanding control of the conversation.

There's so much noise. So much chaos. If only these people had come to my event, they would be saved from their busy and loud misery. But not a single face do I recognize. I stop and lean against a building, taking it all in. A woman stands beneath an awning over the door beside me.

"But you said if we...you promised the promotion to me. Why did you give it to him? After what we did... Please, Mr. Wi—but, but my husband. My children!"

The woman stares at her phone with a look of horror etched into her pretty features. Auburn hair trimmed neatly at the shoulders, green eyes, navy blue designer pantsuit.

"What's your name, miss?" I step under the awning and reach to take her hands in mine. She backs against the door and tucks her phone into her purse, pulling the purse tightly against her chest. Her eyes narrow.

"I can help you. I can save you," I reassure her. I attempt to make my voice soft and soothing but have to nearly yell over the city street cacophony.

"Amber Reese," she says tentatively. She leans forward and looks up and down the sidewalk, as if searching for escape. I stand off to the side of the stoop to give her plenty of room to leave.

"Miss Reese, did you happen to see my event this weekend?" I ask, even though I know she didn't attend. I hand her the folded up brochure from my pocket. Barry insisted on sending out the thing to drum up walk-ins despite him promising this would be a limited number event. I read something like a thousand people because of this brochure, when I'd planned to only read maybe five hundred.

Amber skims the brochure, then looks at the doctored photo of me and back to my face. "You can tell when I'm gonna die? For a nickel and a—" She looks down at the words, squinting in the dim light from above.

"Trinket. Doesn't matter what it is. For a nickel and a trinket I can tell you when you'll die."

"Uh-huh." She remains looking skeptical but digs through her purse. Along with the money, she places the cracked cap to a tube of lipstick in my hands. "Have at it then, Death Psychic." Her features screw up at that title, and I wince, still hating the phrase.

"11:17 a.m."

She blinks rapidly. "Like, *tomorrow*? But my children..."

"Maybe tomorrow, maybe fifty years from now. I only know the time. And I've never been wrong—"

"Not in a million reads. Yeah, it says that." She hands the brochure back and takes a step as if to leave. But then her face crumples and she collapses to her knees, wailing sobs screaming from her.

"Hey! What are you doing? Get away from her!" a man's voice yells from the crowd rushing by. A few other voices join in. I back away from Amber and into the rushing foot traffic.

"Watch it!"

"Hey!" the voice calls after me, but I can't see who's yelling. I turn and run.

There's no sound coming through the adjoining door between my hotel room and Barry and Uncle David's. Grateful they're still out on their date, I faceplant into the stack of crisp fluffy pillows. Sixteen names added to my journal. Sixteen new faces and times to forever remember. Eighty cents added to the little coin purse in my suitcase. And sixteen trinkets piled into the box to ship back home before we head off to our next stop in Ohio.

. . . .

PEOPLE ENTER THE OHIO event center; we're in some no-name town and the crowd is smaller than it was in Chicago, but not by much. There seem to be more locals than the last few events, at least. I stare out at the waiting queue of people ready to get their second chance at life.

This is worse than stage fright. I don't think most people with stage fright vomit before going on stage, nor do they probably have stomachs full of antacids, ibuprofen, and Dramamine. I stay seated as the red rope is pulled aside by the hired security guard. The massive room spins and the faces swirl as they get larger.

So many strangers. *Think of the names. Think of the new things you'll get, the eyes that will see you for a few seconds, they'll really see you.* I hold a large breath in until the first person kneels at my feet. She sways and hums.

I glance into her face and she bows as if I were some kind of royalty.

"Name." Another hired security guard belts out from behind my shoulder, making both me and the woman jump.

"R-right. Um, it's Nessie Van Dyk. Uh, here, is this enough?" Shaking, she places a nickel and a small porcelain figurine on my palm, taking special care not to touch me. I've received one other of these before, a Hummel figure with a little girl and two geese. This one depicts a cluster of kids all leaning forward as if running off on some adventure.

"Miss Nessie." I take her cold hands in mine. She nods once, biting her lip, and bends close. "8:39 p.m."

"Next!" the guard bellows. I can't tell whether Nessie or I screeched, but too soon another person gathers Nessie from the floor and ushers her out a side door.

A woman is pushed forward in a wheelchair. The man behind her looks radiant, as if he'd just won the lottery. The woman, on the other hand, looks like she has a closer relationship to death than I could ever have. Her head is wrapped in a scarf that I imagine hides a lack of any hair beneath it. Her eyes are hollow, sunken, dark. But there's a glimmer of hope shining deep in their depths.

"Hi, Bridgett Newman," she squeaks. The man behind her has a tarnished-looking wedding band that matches the one barely clinging to her own finger. I have to rise from my throne to reach her proffered hand. It feels as if I'm shaking hands with the air. My heart sinks. I love reading people because it gives them a renewed sense of embracing life. But she is the sickest-looking person I've ever read. It feels as if I'm announcing when her suffering will be over instead.

I kneel before her and grasp both her frail hands in mine. They're cold. Her husband starts to kneel beside me but a growl from the guard stops him.

"Please, don't look at me like that. I hate when people look at me with pity like that. Don't worry, dear." Bridgett cups a hand to my cheek. For some odd reason, tears pool in my eyes. "I'm cured. I'm finally in remission. Just gotta recover from the last rounds of chemo. So tell me, what's my time?"

I blink. A strength enters her voice, and her eyes harden. I'm reminded of her husband's behavior. He's already won the lottery, but she's stuck scratching her ticket. I smile warmly but an empty pit forms in my stomach. "10:13 p.m. is your time."

"Thank you, thank you so much!" The man speaks over her words that are lost to my ears. "My turn! I'm Neil. Neil L. Newman. The L doesn't stand for anything."

"Oh, um, 6:09 a.m. is your time." I stumble back to my throne.

"Here, take these." Their wedding bands are dumped in my palm along with two shiny nickels. I open my mouth to protest but the man is already wheeling her away. Her eyes are locked on my outturned palm and the rings perched on it, her face twisted with distaste and maybe even determination.

"Next!"

"19:40." Military time. Which means the man—Henry Jay Wilcox—won't be dying in the US. But I don't tell him anymore as his scowl has my throat seizing.

I watch as he scoffs and stomps toward the exit. I glance to the corner of the makeshift altar to see Uncle David whispering in our secretary Belinda's ear. He catches my gaze and flashes a thumbs up.

So many people. So many people.

"Keep it moving!"

I jump to standing and a hush befalls the first half of the line. The guard's walkie crackles and he barks something into it. A cold sweat coats my skin.

"Hi. My name is Rena Linslow but you can call me Lin. I like horses and fast cars and lollipops. This one's my favorite. You got change for a dime?" A little girl bounces from one foot to the next in front of me holding out a hand curled around the stick of a sucker. An older version of her scowls behind her, piercing me with a look of irritation or hatred or probably both.

"9:03 a.m." I croak as my throat squeezes and my stomach pitches.

"Break!" the guard bellows, and more appear from the shadows to push the crowd farther back. Uncle David sidles up to me, reassuring hand on my back and a bottle of water held out in the other hand.

Barry rushes up, his large frame towering in my view. "It's a little soon, Stefan. You take that pill I gave you? It shoulda helped with the motion sickness by now."

"But we're not moving. I think it's something else, Bear. Maybe we should see—"

"He don't need a damn doctor. Hell, I bet there's one here now. He's fine. You fine, right?"

I nod and sip at the water. The walkie pops and I jump.

"What's going on? I paid good money to be here!"

"Brief intermission. Stay back!" the guard retorts.

"Next!" Barry yells and pulls Uncle David away. Just a few more. Just a few hundred more.

Bridgett remembers the day she met Neil. He was kayaking the same river, bundled up in the same filthy yellow life jacket. She followed the instructor's guidance with ease and she realized she was a woman born for life on the water. But Neil looked like a cat, far too close to the enemy and practically hissing at the tiny waves that lapped his boat. But when they attempted the first tiny rapids, Neil took to it with surprising dexterity while she, on the other hand, somehow found herself upside down and spinning.

Before she realized she was even underwater, the man she was laughing at for his fear of water only moments before had dived into the murky depths to rescue her. All the while the instructor sat in his boat paralyzed while watching the waves assault her.

One year later, she and Neil were happily married and exploring the country together. Hiking up mountains, biking off-road trails, kayaking calmer waters, spelunking dark caves. She and Neil hadn't found a natural environment they didn't jump to explore. They planned to continue their adventurous lives for a few more years before trying for children.

She expected the doctor would give her the dreaded news that she couldn't. Or maybe it was Neil who wouldn't be able to. She hadn't expected the c-word. She felt fine, she lived a healthy life. How could cancer have snuck up on their happy lives and spray painted "stage three" all over everything?

Just as suddenly as she had learned to smile after a hard childhood of neglect and loneliness, the cozy blanket of happiness was ripped off her. She knew she would beat the cancer. Her survival chances were high and her body immediately showed improvement after the first round. But the damage had already been done. Her ruminating thoughts sour her mood as she watches Neil through the window while he hobbles up their front walkway.

Bridgett listlessly stares as Neil lugs in groceries. She longs to feel the sun on her skin, the cool water of a river or lake splashing on her face. She should be free to do those things again, once her strength returns. But Neil sold all their supplies. Their RV, gone. Camping supplies, sold. Her kayak, given away. He quickly found a home to settle in closest to all her doctors. He even quit his remote job and found something with great medical benefits but was only a five minute drive away, "just in case".

She can't so much as get the mail for Neil's fears the sun's rays will somehow reactivate what the chemo obliterated. She can't enjoy sweets or the cancer will reawaken and feed on the sugar. The outside world is filled with carcinogens, so never mind a simple drive through the countryside.

"You're too close to the window!" he scolds her as he shuffles in with bags filled with dry and "safe" foods. "And what are you doing out of your wheelchair? What if you'd fallen while I was away?"

He drops the bags as if she had in fact fallen and flees to her side to push her back into that blasted chair. Her back screams from all the sitting. Her lungs ache for fresh outside air scented with flowers and car exhaust and too much perfume. Neil doesn't see her anymore. He sees glass in the shape of her, so delicate and fragile.

She loved Neil so much before. But now, her heart is cold. She wants to love him again, to explore with him again. But when he looks at her the way he is now, as if his entire world is in her lap and she must carry it, all she wants is to run away. Free herself from his obsessive control, and free him from his fear of losing her.

Her chest aches at the thought of hurting him after he's done so much. The thought of living the rest of her life like this, the decades she's been granted stretched before her but living in fear of Neil's next obsessive attempt to protect her, makes her wish for the strength to stand up and run out the door. Run and run until the weakness of her body makes her succumb to the death Neil and her doctors and her own body fought so hard to thwart.

Bridgett stares at the dinner Neil prepared and wonders if she'll know what flavor tastes like ever again. Even as her taste buds have likely returned, nothing she's allowed to eat has any flavor. By next month, he'll read some new diet that cures cancer—despite hers already being cured—and she'll endure something even more heinous to the palate.

"Can we go for a walk?"

Neil smiles warmly at her. "Of course, sweetheart." Her heart dances in excitement. His hand covers hers. "Once the sun has gone down. And after your time, of course."

"It's going to rain tonight," she whispers to her dinner plate.

She's made up her mind. No longer can she live like this. Neil shouldn't have to either. She made up her mind some time ago. The last straw was that death psychic. Whether it's real or not, Neil believes her death will come at 10:13 p.m. She can't go to sleep until after the time has passed. She can't go for walks—or he walks while she's pushed—until her time has passed. She only agreed to spend the thousands to make the trip because she thought it would earn her freedom. In her mind, she could be free to live life again, so long as she was careful around 10:13 p.m.

Bridgett smiles to herself remembering the man who approached her after they had their times read. Neil went to pull the car up for her and the man slipped out of the building. He gave her the idea to do this. What was his name? If only she could remember. If only she could thank him for giving her the courage she needed. He set her on the right path and once Neil goes to sleep, she's going to start walking down it.

"What kind of kinky shit are y'all into?" The dark-haired woman scoffs as she looks around the van at each of us. Jacob shifts uncomfortably beside her and Adam stifles a laugh from the passenger seat.

"We're here to save you, hon." I twist from the driver's seat to pat her knee.

She stares blankly from my hand to my face. "Y'all some kind of Jesus freaks? Look, I appreciate the thought, but I don't need saving. I got work to do, so if you'll excuse me." She rises from her seat, reaching for the door handle.

"What's your name?" Adam asks her with his deep and gentle voice. He's supremely handsome and his face and kindness stop her retreat.

"I'm Rhiannon. But you can call me Ann."

"We can free you from this life, Ann. We can help you start over, go anywhere, do anything." Adam's hand waves in the air as if to reference the entire neighborhood. It's a lot like the neighborhood I worked as a kid. Even though the houses are older and the streets filled with noise, everything is cleaner. No bottles line the gutters, no scent of rot permeates the air. There's probably a city official claiming to give this area a facelift. Instead of randomized busts like my old neighborhood, I imagine these residents are plagued with city ordinance violation fines to clean up, repaint, remove broken-down vehicles and the like. As if a clean front porch scares off drug addiction and child abuse.

"I chose this life. I don't think there's anything wrong with what I do, thank you very much. Now, let me get back to work." Rhiannon raises her chin. She's wearing nice clothes—a black satin dress with a short hem, moderate black pumps that I'd bet anything have memory foam inserts inside. Tasteful makeup and light perfume make her seem more likely to go on a date at a dance club than to be working the corners and turning tricks.

"If you have children, we can save them, too. If you're afraid your pimp will find you, we can protect you. You'll be safe if you come with us. This is what we do." Jacob's gravelly voice brings a protective, fatherly feel to the operation. With his age and his sparse words, coupled with Adam's sweet and soothing ways, and my presence as a woman who's endured it, we form a comforting dream team that make even the most terrified and abused victims happily accept our help.

So why won't this Rhiannon woman? What do they have on her? Maybe Nettie should come on a few runs with us, maybe a young girl would help stubborn victims like Rhiannon to see that we can save her.

"My pimp? That's a gross word. Yes, there's a man I give a little of my money to so I can throw his name around for protection. And yes, when money's tight, I go to him. But this money is mine to make. And this life is mine to lead. I'm not some ignorant little girl who doesn't know any better. I chose this and I'm happy. Now, goodbye." Rhiannon throws open the door and rushes out into the night.

"Wait!" I leap from the van and jog a few paces to catch up to her. Adam and Jacob sit in the van, stunned, their jaws dropped open and their pink tongues illuminated by the overhead interior lights. "I was like you, only a few years ago. My mama had me working the streets from a young age. I didn't care about getting myself out. I wanted to keep working so I could free my friend. Only I was too late. But it's not too late for you. We're offering to save you, your children, your friends. We can save everyone!"

Rhiannon's long, straight dark hair billows softly around her. Her bright blue contacts glint in the streetlight glow. Plum lipstick covers her thin lips that are turned up in a half smile. "I'm sorry that happened to you. What you're doing is a good thing for the folks who need it. But I'm not one of them, sweetheart." She squeezes my shoulder and her nails are perfect French tips.

"Please, we only want to help! Haven't you had a dream to be something else? We can help you!" Rhiannon saunters into the night as I call after her. I can't lose another one. Not like this. There has to be something they have over her, some reason she's too afraid to come with us.

"I am working on my own dreams, my own way." She whirls under the streetlight to face me. She looks like a beautiful actress on stage. "I do this because it's easy money. I do this because I love the company of men. And some women. I'm working for that big house on the hill and the money for the degree that will get me there. But I'm doing it my way."

Her silhouette fades into the night. Her voice calls from the darkness. "Keep doing what you're doing. I'll spread the word. Just remember, not all of us need help. You can't save everyone."

• • • •

NETTIE MEETS ME AT the door when I return home alone and empty-handed. "Nobody again tonight?" She asks from the kitchen as she makes me a cup of my favorite coffee, a mocha with more chocolate than coffee.

"No, but I ran into a woman who said she'll spread the word for us." I don't tell her I lost her, that I couldn't save her. Rhiannon. I'll have to ask Candy and Lila to keep their ears open about her in case something happens that'll open her up to being rescued. "Anyway, how are they?"

"Brice isn't doing so great. Heather called from her sister's up in Maine. She sounds good. Almost hyper, she sounded so happy. She's workin' at her sister's hobby shop and took up knitting. She say she feels like an ol' lady now."

My chest warms at the news. Heather had been in it for five years until we saved her. She'd been a victim of her own doing, addicted and selling herself to pay for coke, crystal, anything she could get. The rehab we'd sent her to helped, but being away from her connections, being with family again, that's what she needed. Maybe that's what Rhiannon meant. She was working for herself. Could it have been an addiction she wasn't ready to kick?

"What's going on with Brice?"

"I don't know. He wouldn't come out of his room for dinner. He took the tray I left for him but I don't know if he ate any. Ain't even come out for the bathroom once today."

I sip from the cat-shaped mug and watch as my little girl gets to work reheating me up some dinner. She's a great cook. And she's patient, kind, amazing with our rescued patients. My shoulders loosen with every sip of the mocha she'd made me. I wouldn't be able to do all this if it weren't for her.

"Thank you, Nettie. You're such a good kid."

"I know. How'd you get so lucky?"

I laugh. Nettie's wearing fluffy orange and black striped footie pajamas. Her hair is wrapped in a vibrant neon-orange scarf. She whistles as she reheats the food.

For a moment, everything is right in the world. A content sigh escapes. Through the kitchen window, I can see the branches dance and sway against a moonless sky. The evening was unseasonably warm for this late in autumn. Nettie's pjs have me sweating just looking at her.

"Mama." Nettie turns around, hand on her hip, spatula in her grasp. "When' the last time you slept?"

I look away. "I napped in the car while Adam and Jacob were out searching."

She puts a plate in front of me. Steamed broccoli, chicken piccata, mashed potatoes. "I asked when the last time you slept, not napped. Napping ain't sleeping."

"Thank you for the food, sweet pea." I moan over a bite with great enthusiasm. She rolls her eyes and refills my mug. "You keep spoiling me like this and I'll start to think I need to tip you."

Nettie pins me with a look, plops in the chair across from me, and waits. I huff a breath between bites. "I'll get some sleep right after this, okay?"

"Promise?"

"I promise, baby. Why don't you go up and get some sleep yourself?"

"Nope. I'm waiting right here till you done. I leave now and you'll be doing the dishes and suddenly you'll be cleaning the whole kitchen. Then making breakfast. Ain't happening. I'm waiting right here for you."

After dinner, I settle under my blankets and give Nettie a thumbs up as she leans against my doorjamb. She nods to my side table light and with a smirk, I reach over and click it off. "Happy now, Mother?" I tease in the darkness.

"Goodnight, Mama. No getting up. Even if you have to pee. Hold it till morning."

I stare at the darkness above me and listen to the sounds of my daughter turning in for the night. She taps softly on a door down the hall and wishes Brice a good night. Her door squeaks and the house fills with silence.

Brice is a young twenty-two-year-old who was taken as a young boy from his parents at the park one day. He'd been sold and used and turned to drugs to survive and endure. He scrounged up enough to hunt down his parents. Only to find his mother had committed suicide a few years after his abduction. His father died from a heart attack a few years after that. He'd clung to the dream of being reunited, only to realize he'd never see his parents again.

It's no wonder he hasn't shown much recovery in the couple months he's been with us. After we sent him off to rehab, I thought we could track down other relatives and get him started on his new life. But he wasn't so much as speaking by the time rehab was through with him. And so he's stayed with us, going to routine therapy but not doing much else.

Sandy's face flashes in my mind. I won't fail. I'll do everything in my power to save Brice. And Rhiannon. I may not end suicide and sex trafficking, but what I'm doing is real. These people will go on to live lives they were rejected or turned away from. And maybe a few of them will join my cause. Maybe one day the actions I take will help and inspire the right people, put the right things in motion, and the future will become a whole lot safer and brighter.

I wait for the thrum of caffeine to rush through my veins and give me my second wind so I can check my laptop for new leads. But my heart rate steadies, softer, softer now. My breath leaves my body in a deep whoosh. Brice has us, he's got family now. He'll be okay, someday. Rhiannon isn't ready for us yet. She's got herself a Sandy she's trying to save, or a kid, or an addiction. I'll keep cracking at her until I save her and whoever else I need to save. For right now, this bed is sinking beneath me and my constant rushing thoughts are nodding off one by one.

Dammit. Nettie gave me decaf again, didn't she? That girl...my lips groggily turn up in a smile. That sweet, sweet girl. I fall hard into a deep sleep.

Bang-bang-bang! My eyes fly open as my heart leaps in my throat. "Fuck. Fuck." I pant as the adrenaline surges through my veins. How long was I out? I fumble on the nightstand for my phone. Three hours. I'd only just closed my eyes.

"Mama?" Nettie's voice calls softly from the hallway.

"Yeah, baby?"

"It's all right, B. Don't you worry none, go on back to sleep." Nettie's voice sounds farther away. Light pools under my door from what looks to be Brice's room.

Bang-bang-bang! "Holy—" The banging I'd thought was the remnant of a forgotten dream echoes through the house. Who in the hell could that be at this ungodly hour?

"Stay here." I toss the words with barely a glance in their direction as Brice and Nettie stare wide-eyed at the darkness of the stairs that leads to the front door. The house is eerily still as if holding its breath. I rush down the staircase and notice the steps are oddly silent despite their usual creaking protests. Blackness greets my peering gaze from the other side of the peephole, and the only sound beyond the pounding in my ears is the dead click of the porchlight switch when the light fails to illuminate our late-night visitor.

Bang-bang! I jump back at the sound of the fist smashing against the door and clasp a hand over my mouth to stifle the shriek that gurgles up my throat. It was only a matter of time. I shouldn't be surprised somebody figured out where I live, where I take their forced whores and their burned-out ready-to-end-it-all spouses. Is it an angry pimp? An abusive wife looking for her husband? A pedophile in search of his favorite toy?

Rage fills me at that last thought. My teeth clench and my nostrils flair. I glance at the stairs and am thankful to find them empty. Nettie must be with Brice, keeping him calm while also readying to protect him. I fumble in the darkness underneath the entry table and find the handle of one of my many protection pieces.

With a quick glance at my nightgown, I grope for the coatrack behind the door and throw a coat on, slip the gun into the pocket, then take a stance in a lowered position. My lungs suck in air and adrenalin rushes through, readying me. I roll my neck and shoulders, then, in one fluid motion, I unlock the deadbolt and yank the door open wide.

Chapter Thirteen – Stefan

*"*S*till no sign of Bridgett Newman as the search continues. Join us tonight as we speak with Bridgett's husband about this touching case."*

"How long has it been now, Brad?"

"Well, Linda, the police have been searching for two days. Our thoughts are with her family and friends in these difficult times."

This is why I hate the news. It's always doom and gloom but with one happy story thrown in as if it provides some kind of balance. I'll never understand how anybody can watch the stuff. The waitress pours my third cup of coffee while eyeing me hard. I fidget with the sugar packets, my knee jiggling beneath the table.

"Buddy, there you are! Why always this dump, huh? No offense, ma'am." Barry hobbles from behind the waitress and tips his trucker hat toward her.

"Mm-hmm. What'll it be, pops? Four slices o' pie or we playin' healthy tonight with only three?" Her name tag says Brenda. She's the same waitress every time. I adore her. But I can never remember her name.

"Shucks, you know me. Your pie is all I dream of each night, my darlin.'" Barry grabs his hat, clutches it to his chest, and bats his eyes at her from his side of the booth. Brenda walks off with a *humph* and a particular extra sway to her hips.

"I'm gonna tell Uncle David." I chuckle into my coffee cup. The porcelain is cracked, thin brown lines running along the side and around the small loop of a handle. One ill-placed tap on the table and hot coffee will erupt in our laps.

"Hey, I'm on vacation. I deserve extra pie!"

"It's not a vacation if it's work," I mumble.

"Yeah, yeah. Anyway, what's her time?" Barry leans forward, my coffee trembling in its cup.

"I told you before. I haven't read her."

"The hell not? You come in here every meal you get, and you're tellin' me you ain't read her, not once?"

I nod, not looking up from my cup. "Seems too personal somehow."

Barry sighs and makes a show of sitting back, throwing an arm over the booth, and turning his attention to the news.

Aside from an old man who I'm pretty sure lives here, we're The Corner Café's only patrons at this hour. The thin windows lining the small restaurant are fogged up from the rain. The window next to me has a tiny trickle running along the inside. I brought a plant in once, named Bob, and put it at the end of the stream to catch the rain. Nobody ever bothered with it and now I watch as the rain collects in the dry soil. When I'm on long tours, I return to find Bob half dead and have to order a glass of water to dump on it if there's no rain in the forecast.

"Y'know they tried reaching out to us."

"Who?" I look up from Bob's yellow-streaked leaves just as the waitress sets pie in front of Barry and today's soup of the day in front of me. Cheesy potato. Not bad, although I was craving the chicken and dumpling.

Barry stuffs his face with lemon merengue as he juts a thumb at the TV.

"The news?"

Brenda gives my coffee a warmup that I immediately chase with four packets of sugar. Still too bitter.

"That station, yeah." His mouth is full of fluffy merengue. "AB...CP...what'er it is. I recognize the man, Brad whoever, they said wanted to meet with us."

I say nothing. This isn't unusual. With a tour that has just gone international, I suppose it was only a matter of time before my hometown news would want an interview.

"They want info on that missing woman."

"Bridgett Newman?"

"That the cancer one?"

I nod and sip at the soup, burning my tongue.

"How'd you know her name so easy like that? Hey, darlin', get me some blueberry, would ya?" Barry yells over his shoulder toward the counter, not even bothering to check if the waitress is there to hear him. She gives me an eyeroll, clutches her chest in mock heart attack, then shakes her head.

I don't bother reminding him the news was covering the story as he walked in. But that's not how I remembered her name. I remember all the names and faces of everyone I've read. The first time I heard her name, I immediately remembered the frail woman with the dark-circled eyes that held the tiniest shimmer of hope.

"Well anyway, I told 'em to stuff it. 'Less they wanna interview about your special talent, to hell with 'em. Ain't got time for it. On the road in a few days, who wants to talk about some dead girl?"

She's not dead, she's missing. 10:13 p.m. That's her time. And 6:09 a.m. is her husband's. I hope she is dead. She looked miserable.

"Where we going this time?" The TV is changed by the cook to some sports game and my question is lost to the roar of a crowd thousands of miles away.

"Herm?" Barry slurs around a mouthful of blueberry. The waitress puts a peach cobbler in front of him without him having to request it. He turns the mass of himself in her direction, quirks a brow, and shovels a mouthful of peach in with the blueberry.

"Thought you should have a little more fruit in your diet," she says with a smirk, then places a turkey sandwich in front of me. "Here, honey. You're 'bout to vibrate on up out of here with all that coffee in ya. You need more'n soup."

"Thank you, ma'am," I mumble to the sandwich. There's tomato and lettuce, a large glob of mayo, a drizzle of mustard. Just how I like it. And a pickle speared with a toothpick on top. A foreign warmth floods my chest.

Plant watered, belly full, Barry's word vomit of this tour's itinerary flooding my mind, and I finally get to flee the bright buzzing lights of the diner. The dank night swallows me whole and I hug the shadows on my leisurely stroll back to the harbor.

Sweetheart is bobbing in excitement as I approach. Anticipation spikes as I stare at her dance. It'll be a nice steady rocking to put me to sleep tonight. It's hot, humid from the earlier rain, and the smell of the water whooshes in with an occasional splash as *Sweetheart* dips and bucks over a swell. My hammock sways and sand pools beneath my eyelids.

But I fight sleep. On the road again means more time away from the diner, nights in unfamiliar waters. No nights in *Sweetheart* for a month. No turkey sandwiches and warm feelings in the chest for a month. I hope the waitress—Brenda—will water Bob. I try to soak up the smell of the water, the feel of the heavy air in my lungs, the slosh of my full belly with every dip and bunt.

A month.

* * * *

"CLOCK'S TICKIN'!" I startle awake to the deep bellow. Barry. Shit, what time is it? I scramble to brush my teeth, toss the toiletry bag in my luggage, and scurry to get ready for the trip.

"Almost done!" I holler as I do one final pass through everything I'd packed. My special treasure box. Clothes and other essentials. Wait, socks! And underwear. Shit! I toss handfuls and stuff them into the already overpacked and tiny suitcase. Like a cartoon character, I hop on the thing to smoosh it down enough to zip closed.

"I've leavin' without you!" Barry's yell fades as if to make good on the threat. I roll my eyes knowing this trip means nothing without me.

I grumble on my way out. "I said I'm—" But then my foot slips on something and I find myself staring at the ceiling. "Ow! The hell?"

A folded piece of paper clings to my foot just as Barry screams incoherently. I stick it into my pocket and run after his receding outline in the distance.

Once settled into the plastic chairs in the terminal and waiting our turn to board, I finally relax. We made it two hours before we have to board but Barry still screamed and cussed at Uncle David and me like there was a fire only we could put out once we got there. Now that we're here, I can see what had him so excited.

"What?" he says over a mouthful. I grimace and look away without responding. The sound of children crying and businessmen yelling into their phones dulls beneath the noise of Barry's wrappers. Plastic crinkles as his hand snakes into chip bags and candy pouches. His lips smack with every chew of everything he can get his hands on from the short distance between the security checkpoint and our terminal.

I pull out my headphones to drown out the noise with music, only to grasp a piece of paper instead. Oh, right, I forgot! The noises fall away as the guitar and drums of Mudvayne's "Happy?" fills my ears. A contented sigh escapes.

The paper looks like a thick cardstock folded in half. Somebody must've put it under the entrance door to the main level's living area. Probably notice of late dock fees or something. No other reason to be so official with that kind of fancy paper. I scoff, then shake my head at Uncle David's curious glance. With disinterest, I unfold the paper.

Stefan,

I can't believe this boat is still here. It looks exactly like I remember it. I hope you still around, living on it and I just missed you. A lot has changed since the last time I saw you. I've heard some rumors about a Death Psychic. Guess that means you musta kept on with that death time stuff. Maybe you don't remember me, but on the off chance you do and care to catch up, email me.

~~D~~Mona

Mona! A "D" is scribbled out before her name. She must have changed it. Maybe that means she's working somewhere else under a new stage name or whatever it's called. Or maybe she got away. The letter is signed with an email address. Mona came to see me! When? How could I have missed it? How long has the letter been there? If I hadn't slipped on it I wouldn't have found it until we got back. Or I might never have found it. The headache I've had since I fell was worth it to finally have a way to contact her.

It's been so many years now. Six? Seven? I can't help but wander over to those dark and filthy streets in search of her when I have a bad day. Just seeing where that bright neon used to flicker in the night brings warmth to my chest and lifts my mood. I start to enter her email into my phone but am interrupted with a harsh nudge. Barry yanks the earbud from my ear to inform me with barbecue chip breath that the plane is boarding.

Once settled into my seat, I try again to enter the email, only to be halted by the captain asking that all devices be powered down.

"Come on, let's play!" Barry spills over onto my seat. It's gonna be a long flight if I have no way around him to get to the bathroom for over twelve hours.

I don't wanna. I shake my head.

"Gonna be a long trip if you don't feel like talkin'. Come on. 12:06."

I sigh and tuck my phone back in my pocket. "A.m. or p.m.?"

We're in coach and the mother in the window seat has turned her head slightly, listening. The baby in her arms stands then drops, stands then drops. With each jump, her wrists slam onto the armrests, red marks that'll turn to bruises glow bright on each arm. She's wearing an off-white three-quarter sleeve shirt, a decorative button at the end of each folded cuff. The button closest to me hangs on by a few thin threads and clatters against the plastic armrest as the baby twists abruptly to smack the seat in front of it.

"P.m.," Barry says on the other side of me.

"Naalie Gonzales. Denver Massachusetts. Braden Hostel. Amber Smith," I mumble, eyes locked on the button.

"I don't get how you do that."

"He's a savant, Bear." Uncle David's red mouth and gray beard curve when I turn to peek at him filling up the aisle seat on the other side of Barry.

"Baby, you know I don't know what that means."

"Think of it as part of the ability. How can he know the time anyone will die? I don't know the answer to that, either."

"That's you?" The mother beside me, her baby smacking the window and screeching, turns abruptly to face me. I stare at the floor around her knees.

"Shore is, madam," Barry tells her, pride puffing up his chest. "Don't work on babies though."

It does work on babies. It works on anything with eyes, actually.

"Read me. Oh, please, please read me."

"That'll be—" Barry starts to ramble off the fee, but I hold up a hand and face the woman.

Fear fills her eyes. Her hair coats her scalp, unwashed in who knows how many days. Her fingers clutch the onesie of the baby in her arms. She's panting suddenly. In anticipation? Excitement? No, she's trembling in terror.

"What's your name?"

"Misty Belrose—I mean, Misty Jonston. I'll pay. Whatever you want. Please read me. I heard about you. My hus—ex—he had a friend. You read him once. He was a corporate CEO or something, I don't know." The baby twists again, this time to pull at her hair. She lets him tug, pulling her bun out in chunks. "Ouch! But then, after you read him, he quit. Gave away his car, everything. Left his girl-friend and just...went off into—sit still!—the mountains or lake or something. He seems so free. I want to be free. Please—" The baby lands a hard smack on her nose, her eyes water but she doesn't look away.

13:45 fills my mind as I stare into her brown eyes. 13:45. Her accent sounds like she's southern American. If her time is in the twenty-four-hour notation, she's not dying in the States. Her baby has plopped into her lap, satisfied with his collection of her hair, and gnaws on his fist. Reaching for her wrist, I finger the loose button. It relents with a gentle *pop*.

"I'll take this as payment." Her head cocks as I fondle the button, a smile forming on my lips. "13:45," I tell her, grave in my delivery.

The baby returns to the window, smacking and screeching as his mother's face contorts with every emotion. Her gaze drops to the floor. "What does that mean? Thirteen?"

"Military time, madam," Barry offers.

"Military?" She looks at me, confusion knitting her unkempt brows.

"The twenty-four-hour clock is used by many parts of the world. The US only uses twelve, hence a.m., p.m.," Barry explains.

"So, Manchester..."

I nod. We're landing in Manchester, England, where she must be headed. We're on the next flight to Tokyo after a brief weekend tour in Stockport.

"So I'm going to..."

"Don't worry, madam. It could be years from now. See, how it works is, the time you're given is what your obituary will say. So, if you're only here visiting and end up dead, your obit would get print-ed by family back home in the States, yeah? So, don't worry. Sounds to me like you gotta make home somewhere else than the States 'fore then." Barry sits back, content with himself after his monologue.

But if she's here visiting family it could be a different story. I thought the time printed in the obituary was the time I was reading people, but after my grandpa passed and the time they printed was different than the time I knew he'd passed, I knew my assumption was wrong. Plus, in most cases, a time is never mentioned in an obit. I suspect it may actually have to do with the time zone someone will be in when they pass. But I don't tell Barry or Misty this. I've only read a small handful of people with military death times, and I've yet to come across one I've read who's passed to figure this out.

The mother nods, an absent look in her eyes. Her baby tugs at her shirt and she opens her blouse to feed him. We turn away out of respect and let her feed and process the news in as much privacy as this tiny plane can offer.

I wake up a couple hours later with my head resting against the mother's. She and her baby huddle together in slumber. Sun rays streak through the clouds as day begins to break. The cabin fills with dusty gold. Snoring in various tones surrounds me. The plane bucks in a small battle with turbulence, then steadies. My stiff neck and back creak. My heart yearns for *Sweetheart*.

I ease my head away from Misty's and reach for Barry's old wristwatch. A gasp behind me makes me jump and grasp his arm with too much force.

"Ah! Careful now, all ya had to do was ask!" Barry's thick voice grumbles as I startle him awake.

"What time is it?!" Misty's breathy question comes out as a plea. The baby stirs in her arms.

"Five. A.m., madam. It's only morning." Barry's voice is softer, soothing.

"Right, right." She nods and I stare at the filthy blue fabric of the seat in front of me. From the corner of my eye, I see her fingers raise and curl as she counts. We've only been on the plane for a few hours.

The time I gave her will come an hour and sixteen minutes before we're scheduled to land in Manchester.

She leans to look out the window, clutching the sleeping baby to her chest. I want to tell her not to worry, she won't die in those waters below us. Barry, Uncle David, the stewardesses who I accidently caught eyes with, all have different times. But I say nothing.

"Have you heard of Last Chance Travel Agency?" Misty says to the window.

"Pardon?" Barry leans forward. "Boy, am I hungry. When did they say would be breakfast?"

I shrug, staring at the mother.

"They say they can save you. From yourself, I mean. You take a survey and bam. Here's the place and that's where you'll stay, give me your money. Don't worry, it'll all be better after. Bon voyage!"

I wonder if Misty is waiting for me to say something, but I don't know what to say. I've never heard of it. That's what I should say. That's what she asked me. Just say it, dammit! Before I can utter a sound, Misty clamps a hand over her mouth, quieting the sobs that rack her.

"I'm sorry. I'm so sorry, my sweet Jackie." She strokes the baby's forehead. His eyes blink open. His head turns toward me and I quickly look away before our gazes meet.

Chapter Fourteen – Desdamona

I settle into the rocking chair and watch the morning sun peek through the dark looming clouds. The wood screeches as my head tips back.

"Dammit."

The chair came with the house. And just like the house, it had more *character*—according to the realtor—than it did function. I'd spent half the sleepless night sanding and hammering and gluing. The damn thing screamed at me as if it wanted to continue sitting out on the porch, empty, waiting for its long-dead owner to return.

I feel stupid. And foolishness makes me itchy, makes me want to be productive to avoid thinking about it. And combing the streets for a week straight after chasing a nightmare all the way back home last week has me drained. More so than usual.

About a month after our late-night visitor, I had a dream about those streets. Sandy was standing *there*. That awful spot where so much of our youth was taken from us. Her face was painted up in all those colors she liked to wear. She looked at me and said one word. *Come.*

I felt it. The pull to saving somebody. Normally it happens during the day. I catch someone's gaze and a voice fills my mind, telling me the way they plan to end their life. And then I feel a pull toward them, a thread ties itself around me and the person ready to throw everything away. I can't function until I save them. Much the same way when I see someone working the streets. When there's a soul to save, we become connected. The moment I woke from that dream, I felt that string tying me to someone, pulling me back to the hell I once called home.

But by the time my plane landed and the Uber dropped me at the curb on the nicer street nearby, it was as if the thread snapped as soon as my heels hit the ground. The sidewalk was filled with people shopping and laughing. The streets were lined with nice cars and shiny bicycles. I stood on the nicer side, the side that was always so bright and untouchable back in my youth, and I stared across the street into my past.

I saw the litter in the gutters and the lowrider pulling up to the curb for me. Or Sandy. Sometimes we would take turns—rock, paper, scissors—deciding who would take the Chevy and who would sidle up on the Harley. The neon lights would buzz and the neighborhood bumped with a never-ending energy.

A florist's box truck obstructed my view as it stopped at a new traffic light and my gaze was lost in a field of tulips and a laughing white family frolicking carelessly in the rows of oversaturated color. The truck cruised away at a safe and slow speed. My Uber driver pulled into the slow and steady traffic just as I had reached out to climb back in.

He'd dropped me off at the wrong place. There was no liquor store with neon lights. No trash heaps rotting in the hot sun. No car on jacks surrounded by brown paper bags with empty bottles inside. A boutique in a new strip of little shops and cafes sat where Sandy stood in the dream only nights prior, beckoning me, staring into my soul and demanding my presence.

There were townhouses where my house once stood. The nicer side of the street threw up all over the neighborhood, spreading its cinnamon and perfume smells, its fresh paint and new polished wood. Valet signs stood where once there were parking meters and bus benches. Flowers grew everywhere—everywhere!

I rock in the chair and strain to hear the morning birds sing their little tunes over the protests of the chair. What was that dream about? What was Sandy—or my subconscious—telling me? I'd flown all the way there only to find nothing from my past. My childhood home, the liquor store, everything but the street name was different. Gentrified. It was as if Sandy and I had been erased. Painted and built over.

Perhaps it wasn't someone I had to save, but someone I had to say goodbye to. Am I ready to say goodbye to the person I was? I'd wasted so much time that I could've used saving others. So much money I could've put to the house and Nettie and Brice and Rhiannon. The trip was so pointless I didn't even get the chance to see my old friend, Stefan.

That poor boy. I owe him so much. If it weren't for his trusting ways coming into my life when he did, I'd never have been able to build this life. His boat looked the same and sat in the exact spot I remembered it. At least that part of my hometown hadn't changed. But he wasn't there. And like a fool, I'd left a note instead of leaving well enough alone.

What if he hates me for all I took from him? What if he won't so much as give me the chance to make it right? What if he's got himself a wife now and has to explain who the hell Mona is and why the hell she's leaving notes on his boat? *Don't worry, baby, she just some whore who stole from me. It was before I met you!* I shake my head and kick at the porch, sending me back sharply in the rocking chair. A loud *pop* of angry shifting wood startles away a small flock of birds from the apple tree in the front yard.

Yessica's Pontiac turns onto the street, announcing its presence in the quiet neighborhood with its squealing belt. She pulls in the drive, shuts off the engine while half out of the car, then kicks the door behind her like it was a stray dog at her heels. She flounces up the steps and opens her mouth to speak. I brace myself for her usual morning diatribe. No, I haven't slept. Yes, I tried. Yes, I realize it's bad for me.

But to my surprise, Yessica twists on her heel and plops on the porch swing opposite me. I send her a quizzical look, then feign nonchalance and rock back. The chair shifts beneath my weight and pops. I launch to my feet in fear it's about to collapse, a yell clambers up my throat in the process.

"Damn chair. Firewood all it's good for anyhow," I mumble and invite myself to join Yessica. The porch swing offers a squeaking protest albeit much, much quieter. She scowls into the light part of the sky and for a moment, I fear her look will send the sun scurrying back behind the hills.

She huffs. Sighs loudly. Taps her foot. Jiggles the swing side to side, then front to back.

"Girl, will you just say it already? Ain't like you to be keeping them lips shut."

Yessica's dark brown eyes flick to mine, then back to the rising sun. "Have you...checked the emails this morning?" Her usual loud voice is nothing but a gentle whisper.

"I have not." I wave a hand to the rocking chair failed project and the mess of equipment piled around it.

"Well, there's, um..." She clears her throat, then repeats her fidgeting from before. I elbow her right as the front window beside us illuminates. A lanky shadow sluggishly crosses in the beam of light and clanking soon follows. My stomach growls in anticipation of Nettie's delicious cooking.

"A death threat."

"A who now?"

Yessica all but throws her phone at me. I skim over the email sent to my travel business's email address. We don't get many emails from actual people, mostly promotional garbage from hotels, airlines, cruise lines, and the like. The sender used a free online email system and left it anonymous.

I know what u did. U took her from me. I got people. U gonna get urs

I scoff and toss the phone back to Yessica. "That all?" I hold open the door for her and she launches into her plan to track down whoever it could be by asking all the women we've helped recently.

"Can you think of any ladies we've helped who talked about a bad marriage? Jealous boyfriend? I'm so amped up I can't think straight." She launches into curses under her breath as she pours coffee for us both.

"*¡Hijo de la chingada!*" She keeps her cursing in Spanish as I'd asked her when my baby's around. Nettie pours goop into the Belgian waffle maker and my mouth waters.

We've had nothing but happy clients. While some went on the trips we sent them on and returned with a new outlook on life, others have come back and made minor changes, only to revert to some of their old ways. At least according to the follow-up we do, checking in to see how they're doing after nearly ending their lives and throwing everything away.

Sometimes they need therapy, a shoulder, an extra push to change. I have a team of psychologists, psychiatrists, life coaches, and such at the ready for those moments. But this email didn't feel like someone unhappy with our involvement in trying to change their life around. And it didn't sound like someone who's angry that we prevented a loved one's suicide. *U took her from me.* No, it sounds more like...

The hair stands on the back of my neck. That email was worded as if it had come from a trafficker in a rage that we'd taken his slave from him. My night work has zero connections to my business. I don't even send the traffic victims anywhere under any of the company's travel accounts. It's all kept completely separate so my business could never be tied to the work I do with Jacob and Adam.

There's no way. How would anybody ever find the company email address and my link to Last Chance Travel Agency?

"This *perra* make it sound like he's salty we didn't let his woman off herself. I can't think of anybody who'd make a death threat. This is fu—ahem, ridiculous."

Nettie's gaze whips up to meet mine, her eyes narrowing at Yessica's words. I kick her under the table and smile sweetly at Nettie. "It's nothing to worry about, baby. Go on, take that to Brice before it get cold."

"Mm-hmm." She lays the sass on thick with a smirk. She plops a plate each in front of us, sucks her teeth, then saunters out of the room with two other plates in her hands. I stifle a giggle at her acting so mature and annoyed like she's the mom while she's wearing fuzzy pink footie pajamas and a matching bunny-eared hat.

I point at Yessica and give her the eye. She mouths *sorry*, then digs into the breakfast. The waffle sucks up all the moisture in my mouth as I mull over the email. I work at it like cud and will the sick feeling in my gut to fade enough that I can at least get one meal in me today.

"Who eats waffles dry?" Yessica scoffs and I realize I never added syrup. My phone vibrates.

Stefan: Mona? It's Stefan.

Stefan: Mona? It's Stefan.

Mona: Hi, Stefan! I see you got my note.

Stefan: Yeah, I'm sorry I wasn't there. When did you drop it off?

Mona: Oh, I can't remember. Doesn't matter now. How you been? What you been up to?

Stefan: All right I guess. Doing that reading thing still. Nothing new. What about you?

Mona: Well, I moved south. Was passing through when I stopped to see you. Bought a house, big and ugly and perfect in every way. I gotta daughter now. You would like her. She's kind and sweet, just like you. Name's Nettie.

Stefan: That's nice.

I read over our conversation from last night. Mona. She has a daughter.

"We made the news!" Barry suddenly exclaims, fist slamming on the table. A hush befalls the restaurant. I barely have the energy to glance up from my breakfast, I think something they call bangers and mash maybe. I tried to order what I thought people ate here, trying not to be so obviously American, but with Barry's outburst, my efforts are clearly in vain.

Mona and I were up late last night catching up. Well, late for the time here but I guess it was only the afternoon for her. Shit, she probably wonders why I stopped responding after what would be dinnertime for her. I didn't get the chance to tell her I was in England.

"Really? What's it say!" Uncle David is practically vibrating with excitement. He and Barry remind me of a couple of schoolgirls texting a crush. It's taking everything I have to keep my eyes open. Jet lag really is a nightmare. I thought we would get one day of trying to adjust before the show starts tomorrow, but of course Barry would have none of it. Uncle David was too pent up to see the sights and now here I am, three hours of sleep if that in me and eating breakfast when I should be settling in for the night in *Sweetheart*. That mattress was deep and soft and everything I hate about beds.

Barry holds his phone in my face and a blurry image of a man floats in front of me. I rub my eyes and the image clears. Benjamin Smith. I'd recognize him anywhere. He looks a lot healthier, cleaner, and happier in the photo than when I read him. 10:46 p.m. is when he's gonna die.

I nod. "I remember him. Benjamin, 10:46 p.m." The headline above the image reads *Death Psychic Gives Local Man Second Chance*. A smile splits across my face. It's hard work giving people their own second chances at life all the time. Feels good to get a little recognition.

"We are gonna be booked solid. Anywhere we wanna go, just say the word and I bet they'll drop a royal wedding to fit us in!" Barry belly laughs, earning scowls from the people around us. I swear I hear someone whisper "Stupid, loud Americans."

"What's it say, come on, read it already!" Uncle David tries grabbing the phone from Barry's hand but he snatches it back.

"All right, all right. Hold onto your britches, honey bunny. Let's see. 'Local man Benjamin Theodore Smith says he was going to kill himself when a kind stranger stopped him, said a few words, and changed his life forever. "I was standing right here, on the edge of this very bridge. I was gonna do it. I was gonna jump and end it all. But then this man, I'll never forget him. He was beautiful and wearing all white. He said he could tell me when I was gonna die. I thought that was weird considering that's what I was trying to do. But then he said 10:40 p.m. I can't explain it but one minute I'm about to take my own life, at peace with death. And then this prophet, this angel, comes out of nowhere and tells me when I'm gonna die. I knew if I jumped I wouldn't die then but much later or I could have become a potato the rest of my life. So I climbed down and he wrapped his arms around me, took the scarf from my neck and wiped my face clean and he said, and I'll never forget it, 'I have now blessed you. Your life will forever be filled with positivity, luck, and love.' And he was right." Smith tells *The Chicago Tribune* that he had been homeless for ten years and made the decision to end his life after reconnecting with his adult daughter, only to be rejected.'" Barry pauses and sips his coffee.

"When did you read this fella?" Uncle David asks, toast mush in his mouth.

"When we went to Chicago that first time, I think. Sure as hell didn't happen like he said. He got the time wrong too."

"Don't matter none. This is great publicity!" Barry waves the phone in the air. "We gonna have to change up your wardrobe a bit."

• • • •

I THOUGHT HE MEANT I was going to need better clothes than the old things I've had for the last ten years. Maybe he thought we were going to become a sought-after show with countries warring for an appearance and my wardrobe should reflect a cleaner image. I sure as hell didn't expect this crap.

"Who the hell he s'pose to be? Ginger Jesus?" A teen boy sneers. The guards at this show don't bark at the crowd's every twitch. Somehow the lack of force makes me more anxious than the hollering beefy guards back home ever had. I stare into my white-clad lap. This is getting foolish. White linen pants and gauzy shirt and some weird wooden bird pendant have me feeling like I'm about to try out for a movie.

My breakfast thoroughly retched out in the bushes and my churning stomach pumped full of pills and my pits stinging with sweat have become almost familiar. No matter how many shows I do, no matter the millions read, this part never gets easier. A sea of faces stare at me and see this thing that my ability has become. A parlor trick, as Barry called it the first time he found out about it. Sitting in front of all these strangers and I feel like I'm pulling bunnies out of hats while people laugh and jeer and throw garbage at me.

"First in line," the guard says with a cheerful lilt. The crowd surges forward.

As each person passes, a coin is tossed in the coin collection plate held by a hired hand dressed similar to me, but it's a woman and the white clothes are tighter, skimpier. The trinket is placed with great care into my hands, we embrace, I get their name and give their time. The trinket is taken from me by another white-dressed woman and is placed somewhere out of sight. Then the next person is up.

Three hours in and the pills have taken effect. Barry upgraded from motion sickness and antacids straight to the good stuff, anti-depressants and anti-anxiety pills pump through my veins and cast a strange net over my head. The mass of noise, stink, and flesh melts into a soothing, undulating wave of kindness. Each person comes before me and I see them and only them. I hear only their name, smell only their breath and body.

A golden light embraces the crowd. The sunlight streams through boring plain windows and kaleidoscopes into a beautiful array of color, stretching red, blue, green, gold across the people at my feet. Their voices dull and eventually all fade but one. All other noise around us becomes lost in the ocean. This person before me smells of sweat and bergamot.

"Peace be with you, Great One." The young man bows low. I bow my head and smile. The ocean parts for him and welcomes another.

"I-I expect you knew I was coming. But um, anyway, I've been a member of your following since the beginning. I'm a Top Fan on your page! Do you remember me? Of course you do, I'm sorry. I'm just so nervous. It's Samantha. Neely, that is. Sam Neely. This is my grandmother's ring. Will you accept it, oh Great One?" Sam falls to her knees before me, her hands outstretched in offering.

I take her gift and warmth fills my chest. "Look at me, Samantha. Your time of death is 9:51 p.m." She falls to my feet and weeps. Her tears trickle between my toes. I feel the tip of her tongue trace a metatarsal bone.

The ocean waves come crashing all around me. A guard silently ushers her away and I stare at the shiny strip of saliva left on top of my foot. The din of the crowd assaults my ears. The colors meld into a crescendo so bright, the back of my eyes burn.

"Break!" Barry calls, and Uncle David collects me before I can slide from the chair onto the floor. The chair's red plush suddenly feels offensively garish as I stare at it with hatred, all the while three large bodies haul me from the massive room.

I dry heave the last foamy drops left in my stomach, then sink into the cool rough fabric of the private bathroom's floor. Who the hell puts carpet in a bathroom, anyway? The carpet tiles are worn down to the white plasticky underside. Bare floor is visible in the shape of shoes in front of the toilet. My cheek is caressed in the heel of one shoe-worn spot.

"Much better than it has been. You made it almost all the way through without needing a break this time. Proud of you, kid." Barry's muffled voice reverberates through the door. I croak out a request for water and a cool rag. My request is either immediately fulfilled by one of the many skimpily dressed women or I passed out as soon as I'd said it, but I open my eyes to a woman's outstretched hand offering a bottled water.

"There you are, Great One. Your power takes so much out of you. Let me help you be more comfortable." Too weak to argue, I take the help offered and lean on the tiny woman as she guides me from the bathroom floor to a seating area with an old leather sofa. Her dark hair and pale face wavers before my blurry eyes and I pass out again.

"What the hell is with this Great One nonsense? You hear all of them calling him that? Tell me this isn't your doing."

"Of course it ain't! I woulda come up with something much catchier than that cliché crap!"

A cool, wet sensation spills across my brow.

"Look at this! That explains it."

"Ugh, where am I?" I moan when the bright light sears into my eyes and forces me to squeeze them shut again.

"Hey, there you are. I was getting worried. We're still in the back. You were only out about ten minutes. How d'you feel?" Uncle David's voice is close. He must be the one rubbing the cloth over my forehead.

"Like death." My lips stick to my teeth, and I cough until water is tipped into my mouth.

"Looks like you got yourself a cult following, oh Great One." I hear Barry's voice from somewhere across the room. He laughs his belly laugh. If I had the energy I'd bark at him that I was against the stupid white getup from the start, but then he rambles on about some Facebook page. "Says here it's the official page for Tod The Death Psychic. I'm gonna have to look into this. Looks like we got a fraud pretending to be you. I'll sue 'em!"

"Now, now, let me see that." There's a swap of gentle hands to rough hands as Barry takes Uncle David's place mopping my brow. "No, see, it says it's the official *fan page* for Tod The Death Psychic. Looks like it's a bunch of people's testimonials how he changed their lives."

A fan page?

"How many likes?" The rag is mashed over my nose and I grunt, drawing Barry's attention back to me and my pain.

"Wow, um, 304,000. That's, that's a lot." *304,000 people.* All liking this fan page, all claiming I changed their lives. The headache begins to melt away and I can finally smile. People see me. They remember me. They care about *me.*

"That's amazing. Can I see?" I sit up, the room only offering a tiny spin before settling. Thousands of familiar faces stare back at me, reminding me of all the shows we've done, all the hands I've held, all the trinkets I've been gifted. All the headaches, the vomiting, the sheer terror before every show. It was all worth it. Just for this.

Fraud!!! I can't believe all of you people buy into this crap. This man is a disgusting money hungry fraud and should be publicly hung!

It's not his fault you were too weak to change your life around with the wonderful gift the Great One bestowed upon you.

Wrong. I never should've wasted a nickel on this fraud. My wife bought into that crap. And look what it got her!! I know he was responsible, I just know it! Give me back my wife, you monster!

An article is attached with the latest update on the Bridgett Newman missing persons case. It's awful that she's been missing so long, and her husband hasn't moved on, but I can't fathom why he'd think I'd have anything to do with it. I've read millions, odds are lots of them have gone missing or will go missing. Maybe her husband was abusive, and she ran away in the middle of the night. Easier to blame me, the guy who saved her, than it is himself.

I forgive the simple-minded grieving husband and scroll through more testimonials. People leaving their terrible jobs and miserable marriages and going on cruises and eloping. There's so much amazing happiness in my hands that I completely forget about the headache and sick feeling in my gut.

"Oh Great One. Here's some juice." The brunette reappears and holds out a cup to me as she bows low. The cup is white and filled with a fragrant fruity mix and decorated with a tiny yellow umbrella. I sip the liquid and am reinvigorated enough to return to the show to read the remaining hundred waiting patiently for my return.

Stefan: Mona, I had the most amazing day! People's lives are changed because of me. I'm helping people, really saving them!

Mona: That's great! I'm happy for you.

Stefan: I'm going to Tokyo next. We're in Stockport in England, did I mention that? We've gone international!!

Mona: That's great!

Stefan: Everything okay?

Mona: Bad day for us here. But we'll get through it. Gotta go. It was great catching up.

James stares at the loot. He can't believe it went so smoothly. He hardly even planned it out. He showed up, waved his gun around, demanded all the money in the gigantic safe, and then he was off before anybody could flash a badge in his face. All within minutes of stepping off the plane from seeing that death kid and getting his time read back in Stockport. He'd had to get a passport and everything. He'd never stepped foot outside of America until then. He bought the cheapest tickets and left all his worries behind.

He's still not sure if he believes in all that but like Macbeth, the knowledge fills him with confidence as he flies around curved roads and down steep hills. He can't remember what state he ended up in, what those cheap plane tickets said about his return trip to America. He hopped off the plane, grabbed a rental, bought a gun, and drove to the nearest bank that didn't have a security guard parked outside.

After he finds a good spot to lay low, he'll check online for videos to figure out how to get into the fat stacks of cash without triggering the ink bombs and dye packs. Then, the world is his. He was desperate to pay off his credit cards and student loans and that hefty mortgage. But now, who cares about credit when there's so much green piled around that he can hardly shift gears?

James tries to drift around a corner the way he'd seen on TV, turning the opposite direction and sending the car's rear into a screeching slide. But the little rental sedan sends him fishtailing instead. He throws his head back and laughs as a semi blares his horn and swerves around him. He doesn't bother looking in the rearview to see if the trucker makes it by okay. Maybe he should toss a bag of cash out for him, just in case?

"Nah!" James yells and cranks up the volume on the radio. A slow '70s tune comes on. He smirks and mashes buttons while beating his foot on the pedal, wondering if the thing will drive faster if the floor is out of the pedal's way. The radio gives him the perfect tune, AC/DC's "Highway to Hell". He turns it all the way up and is disappointed when the decibels aren't hurting his ears.

"Damn cheap cars," he mutters. The road forms a tight turn ahead according to the sign he flies past. James shuffles in his seat and readies for another try at a drifting turn. But before he reaches the curve, a bag of cash falls into his lap. A thick stack of the money gets wedged into the steering wheel.

The car is airborne and the scenery is breathtaking. James hollers Dukes of Hazzard style out the window. He feels the drop in his stomach and his eyes flick to the radio's clock. 1:17 p.m. He won't die until 4:50 a.m. He smiles as the ground comes up fast to meet him. Right before impact, everything seems to freeze. Bags of cash fly around him. One bag tears open and blue dye splatters his face. He feels like laughing but his breath is lodged in his throat.

James stares at the bright blue sky. A cloud briefly blocks out the sun before disappearing entirely. A bird circles high overhead and the shadow of its wings dances under the vibrant rays. The flashing of light jars him fully awake. James opens his mouth to laugh and jeer at the world that has kept him in line all his life. But his lips are stuck to his teeth. He's desperately thirsty.

Another bird joins the first. He smiles at them and their simplicity. Eat, shit, fuck, die. Humans aren't much different. But he's freed from that bullshit. No longer does he have to stay in line and follow orders. Paying bills and saying "yes sir" is for chumps. Not for the likes of him—men freed from the fear of death. He tries to sit up and count the cash that survived the crash but can't seem to find his arms.

They must've fallen asleep as he lay there unconscious. James waits for circulation to return. What should he do first with his money? New clothes, new car, new house? Probably should make good use of his passport before he's tracked down. There were probably security cameras at the bank and he didn't bother with masks or stealth of any kind.

A bird lands on a strip of metal lying above him. How strange, the metal trash is the same color of the rental car. The bird squawks at him. He cocks his head and the thing flies away, back to circle in the sky. The sun sits lower. It shines right into his eyes and no matter how he turns his head, he can't escape it.

He tries again to move but his body doesn't so much as wiggle. He feels tired. And so damn thirsty. With nothing left to do, he stares right at the sun and watches as it oozes toward the horizon. Someone will be coming for him soon. Someone will help. They'll be glad to help and leave the cops out of it in exchange for a bag of cash or two.

James smiles and waits. He won't die now. That he knows for sure. The sun blinds him until there's nothing but darkness. Or no, maybe it's nighttime now. Yeah, that makes sense. It must be night out. He must've fallen asleep again.

The sound of the birds grows close. But then the caws fade as if someone is slowly turning down the volume. James can no longer hear as his wristwatch tick-tick-ticks.

The birds gather close and give a test sniff.

The minute hand shifts, 4:50 a.m. The birds dive in.

Chapter Sixteen – Desdamona

"Anything?" I stand in the doorway of the office for the travel agency. The floorboards creak and bow under my feet. I toggle my weight between each foot with a frown. This house needs so much work, so much time and money I don't have to spare.

Yessica shakes her head and makes like she's refreshing the webpage. Her Facebook profile photo reflects on her reading glasses. I smirk and plop into the ratty wingback chair across from the folding table we use as a desk.

The formal dining room serves as my makeshift office. Travel agency by day, sex traffic busting headquarters by night. Red and gold wallpaper lines the cracked walls in patchy strips where my picking and peeling failed to remove it before I'd given up completely. Three walls have tall windows stretching a foot shy of the floor up to the eleven-foot ceiling, making curtains impossible to find. The sun streams through the room, illuminating the dust dancing in the stagnant air.

Another hot day. The heat sticks to my skin and taunts me with another thing wrong with this house. No central air conditioning when I'd bought it and our last window unit finally bit the dust last month. Yessica's newsfeed scrolls by in reverse on her glasses. I notice she feigns typing with one hand as she scrolls.

"Mama?" Nettie's head pops in the doorway and my eyes land on the loose hinges where French doors should be hanging. "We're gonna go for a walk."

Yessica stops fake typing and peers over her glasses. The bun on her head lets loose a stray curl. One perfectly drawn eyebrow quirks upwards.

"We?" I lean forward in the wingback chair, much to its protest. Is there anything in this house that doesn't scream at me when I move? Brice stands in the hallway, his head down, one toe kicking at a loose baseboard. It taps against the wall and a piece of insulation floats onto his hair from a hole near the crown molding.

"Hey, Brice, right? I don't think we've ever met. I've heard a lot about you." Yessica rises from her desk chair and makes like she's going to shake his hand. Brice peeks up through his thick lashes, then drops his chin to his chest while backing toward the front door slowly.

She glances at me and I shake my head. With a shrug she sits back down and returns to her fake working. Nettie offers a sad smile, then turns to Brice and lays her hand on his shoulder. He smiles so sweetly at her my heart skips a beat. I creep into the sitting room and watch through the front window as they head for the road.

Brice is only a couple inches taller than my Nettie. He's pale, so pale that the sun has already given a red hue to his bare arms. His curly blond locks flop with every awkward step. Nettie turns to him laughing and he looks at her straight on, his bright blue eyes flashing.

"My God," Yessica whispers beside me, scaring the crap out of me.

I lay a hand over my thundering heart and count my breaths. "Girl, don't be sneaking up on me like that."

"Sneak? How could anybody sneak with the floors sounding like they're dying?" She elbows me before bending close to the window to peer under the overgrown tree limbs in the front yard. Brice and Nettie disappear around the corner. "Oooh, aren't you excited, Mama?"

I nibble on my thumb nail. "Excited for what? It's just a walk." It's the first time I've seen Brice outside of his bedroom except for the few times we've bumped into each other in the hallway as he darts back into hiding after leaving the bathroom. He was wearing the red and blue striped tank top I bought him when he first came to stay with us. His hair looked swept back with a little product in it to control the waves.

"Just a walk. Ha! Denial, Mama, that's what that is." Yessica claps like an excited schoolgirl. "They in love." She sings, spins, points at me, and claps again.

Laughter fills the old house as YouTube entertains my bored employee. I chug water in the kitchen and count each drip from the leaky tap. Drip. Drip...drip.

"You gotta see this!" Yessica chortles. She's no longer hiding that there's no work to do, and I'm too bored to send her home early.

The shrill ring of my cell has me jumping and sloshing water from my glass. I plop the cup onto the counter and race back to the office, diving for the cell where I'd left it on the corner of the desk. Yessica covers her mouth to stifle her laughter, turns down the volume on what sounds like a cat compilation video, and waves me to answer.

"Yes? Yes, hello, Last Chance Travel—"

"Mama. You can see it's me callin'. We walked to the gas station. Y'all want anything?"

Nettie. Damn. "Surprise me." I hang up and plop into the chair with an aggravated huff. I've half a mind to start working on that stubborn rocking chair again. It's the peak of summer, which means overall depression tends to be lower. Our business of hunting down potential suicides sometimes slows a bit this time of year, but usually we stay just as busy as any other small online travel agency. At least great weather means tonight's prospects should be better.

Yessica's hooting laughter draws my interest, and soon I find myself huddled up beside her, watching videos on her phone of cats fighting dogs with light sabers. She holds her phone between us with one hand and scrolls through Facebook on the laptop with her other hand. An ad pops up on her phone, so we both turn our attention to the laptop to catch up on gossip on a string of comments about somebody getting divorced.

She clicks through the comment strings with the juiciest gossip like, *"I heard he was caught cheating with three women at the same time!" "That's crap and you know it. You shouldn't spread such awful things online." "Everyone knows your husband's the real cheater. Way to project."* But I'm more interested in the people involved. Is nearly single Cindy feeling like life is too much to handle? Is the possible cheater divorcee Charles about to give up and end it all?

All too soon she's moving on to something else. Another video plays and her eyes are drawn from the laptop newsfeed but her fingers idly scroll. A sponsored post pops up with a familiar face staring back at me.

"'Scuse me a minute." Distracted by a singing cat and a talking parrot, she trades seats without looking up at me or questioning my insistence. The ad reads "Tod The Death Psychic Official Fan Page: Want to change your life around? All it costs is five cents and an item of personal significance. Join us and meet the Great One at his next stop! First in line tickets for the Dallas tour available now!"

Stefan's face stretches in an odd smile in the grainy profile photo. The picture looks like it was zoomed in and snapped in a room full of people based on the collection of outstretched hands at the bottom of the image. A dark head of hair kneels at his feet as if he were some kind of royalty. My nose wrinkles. So he's doing a tour nearby soon, is he? A skim through the comments reveals praises that make Stefan—or Tod, as they call him—into some kind of prophet. But one comment catches my eye.

"Fraud. You'll get yours!"

The front door bursts open and thundering steps trample through the house. "Mama! Call the cops, somebody out here!"

Yessica and I bolt for the door. Smoke billows across the lawn behind Nettie. "What the hell?"

Brice is white as a ghost and pushes past us. He flies up the stairs and the slam of his bedroom door soon follows. Nettie stands in the street, on her phone despite telling me to call. The source of the smoke is Yessica's little Pontiac. The thing is engulfed in flames. Nettie points and yells into her phone as I jog down to meet her.

"He ran south two blocks then turned west. He's wearing a dark blue sweatsuit with the hood up. Yeah. Light brown hair. White. Medium. Um...maybe five...nine? Mama," she turns to me, hand over her brow, shielding the sun, "how tall is Brice?"

"What? Er...I don't know, five eleven, I think."

"Yes, five nine or so. He was a little shorter than my friend, he's five eleven. Okay, okay. Yeah, thank you."

"My car! What the hell is going on?" Yessica screams on the front lawn, whipping her head between us on the street and what's left of her cute little car.

. . . .

"A MIDDLE-AGED WHITE guy with light brown hair? It doesn't ring a bell, honestly. Could it have been a kid? You said the guy's hood was up and she only got a quick glance, right?" Adam scratches his scalp vigorously, a sign that he's agitated.

"Yeah, Nettie said his hood was up but he looked old. To her middle age would seem old. She guessed forty. I can't think of anyone we've come across who meets that description. Heck, the last middle-aged guy we worked with was Bob Stansfield, and he's backpacking through Nepal as we speak. I can't think of any pimps that match that description, can you?"

"It could've been mistaken identity. A random act of violence. Mid-life crisis, maybe?" he offers. I pick at the pizza we'd ordered but my stomach is in knots. Adam wolfs down his third slice.

"Mid-life crisis? He'd just buy a Corvette he can't afford, not light up somebody's car. And in the driveway in the middle of the day, no less. Sounds personal to me. Like somebody gotta bone with that Yessica girl." Jacob shakes his head as he wipes his fingers clean on a paper napkin before folding it carefully and tucking it beneath his plate.

Nettie went upstairs to comfort Brice as soon as the police were done taking her statement. The house smells of burned rubber. Yessica's burned Pontiac was towed away an hour ago and she went home, shaken, but just as confused as the rest of us. I glance over my shoulder to make sure Nettie hasn't come back down for seconds.

"I don't think it was random. Or that it had anything to do with Yessica. Had the van or my car been parked closest to the road, I think it would've been just as likely to get torched. No, somebody's out to get us." I tell them of the weird threatening email Yessica had found.

"And you think this has to do with us, not your travel business?" Adam leans forward, his arms folded on the table. It wobbles beneath his weight. Another thing that needs fixing. Dammit, not the time!

"The way it was worded. It said we took *her*. I don't know anyone who'd be angry that we stopped their girlfriend or sister from committing suicide. No, I'm almost positive this is a pimp after us. We must've taken his star girl." I shrug but the motion betrays the tremor that racks through me.

Adam taps a finger on the table. "But who? We haven't exactly been fruitful in our efforts lately. Mostly older women are afraid they're about to be offed for not being useful anymore. I can't think of anyone we've saved that could've stirred this up."

I look over at Jacob but he stares at the floor, nodding solemnly without any contribution. "That's not what I'm worried about. Who, why, when. This person, they emailed my *business*. They showed up at my *house*. They shouldn't have been able to find us here, or my business. They follow us here after saving a night worker, okay. That explains the car. But there's no sign out there saying we do business out of here. It's registered to a PO box, not this address. There's nothing connecting this house to the agency. So how does that explain the email? How could a pimp make the connection?"

"Somebody following *you*," Jacob pipes up. His words are sure. His head bobs as if listening to Sunday's sermon.

Chapter Seventeen – Stefan

The tour to Tokyo was brief. I suspect Barry might be jumping on this international tour idea too soon. The turnout was mostly middle and high school kids, curious to see what a death psychic does. Plus, he didn't research the equivalent for a nickel and now I have a small collection of one yen coins. The only trinkets I received were snacks from the local vending machines near the small building Barry rented. I think the request for trinkets got lost in translation somewhere along with my stage title of a death psychic. I'm pretty sure the food given was in the mind that it was some kind of offering to the dead.

Barry cut the tour short and dragged us to some new *primo* rental spot just outside of New York City. I've lost count how long we've been jumping from city to city, state to state, and country to country. Is Mr. Howard, my dock neighbor, still taking care of *Sweetheart*? Has that waitress watered Bob? Have the neighborhood kids who show up when I do my impromptu readings forgotten all about me? Have all the trinkets from this long drawn-out tour finally arrived back home? Has Barry's plethora of hired goons added it to my collection without breaking anything?

Annoyed with my thoughts and anxious to get this over with so we can finally go home, I stop waiting for Barry to let me know when they're ready to go. We're always early. At this rate, we're not even going to be on time. Maybe this last-minute booking didn't get enough online reservations? Maybe Barry's hoping if we drag our feet, the impatient crowd will stir interest in people walking by who'll just decide to hop in line and have their lives turned around by yours truly. It wouldn't be the first time he's tried something ridiculous on a whim. Case in point, the garish messiah-esque outfit I've been sweating in for the last hour while stewing in my thoughts and waiting to leave already.

"Barry? Uncle David?" I call through the connecting doors between our hotel rooms. "You guys about ready?"

"Give us a minute, will ya?" Barry barks through the door, but the worry in his tone has me on edge.

Without waiting for permission, I try the handle and find it unlocked. I barge into their room. "What's taking so long?"

Barry is bent over the side of the bed, his lower half hidden behind the mess of blankets piled high. "Nothing, nothing. He's fine."

As I step farther into the room, Uncle David's feet come into view. He's lying on the floor, half propped on his elbows while Barry fusses over him.

"Hey, baby. I'm fine. Just fell outta bed. You know how he gets." Uncle David offers me a half-smile, then turns to Barry where an odd soothing look takes over his features. "Help me up, would you, Bear?"

With a strange gentleness, Barry helps Uncle David to his feet before urging him to sit on the edge of the bed.

"We're gonna be late, you guys." I stifle the urge to tap my foot as I think about all my fans waiting to see me. Uncle David doesn't even look dressed yet.

"You two go ahead. I think I'll sit this one out, if it's all right with you."

"I'm not leaving you here alone," Barry whimpers. I quirk a brow at them.

"It's only a couple hours, I'll be fine."

I resist the urge to roll my eyes. They were out on another date late into the night again. Sometimes I swear Barry drags me on these tours as an excuse to travel the world so he can take Uncle David on only the best dates. Mona flashes through my mind at that thought. Whenever I used to think about her, anger and sadness would fester. But now that we've reconnected, I feel excitement and yearn to see her again.

The last we talked, I told her about our international tour. I thought she would be happy for me. But then she said it was a bad day for *us*. Who is us? I thought it was her and her daughter. I guess it makes sense her daughter has a father, I just assumed he wasn't in the picture or Mona would've mentioned him by now. But maybe I was wrong. Maybe there is a man in her life and he found out about us talking.

Stefan: Hey, Mona! It's been awhile. How are things?

God, I sound so formal. Like an estranged sibling beating around the bush and about to ask for money. Barry flies around the hotel room in a mad rush to get ready while stopping every few minutes to fluff Uncle David's pillow or refresh his water on the table beside him.

"Quit fussing over me and get out of here already!" Uncle David throws a pillow at him and it smacks the back of his head. I roll my eyes and refresh my phone to see if Mona's texted back yet. Still nothing. Where was it she said she was living again? What time is it there? I look through our messages but only see that she said she moved south. I start looking through time zones on a map and calculating from the time in New York when Barry starts dragging me out the door.

He's silent most of the way there, his jaw grinding back and forth. Just as we're about to enter the building through the back, roars of the growing crowd already assaulting my ears, Barry yanks me to a halt.

"What time? Just tell me his time. You know it, so spit it out already!" Barry shakes my shoulders, a frantic look in his wide eyes. Sweat beads on his forehead.

"Uncle David? It's not right. I—"

"To hell with coins and knickknacks! I know you don't need that crap, so tell me!" His fingers dig into my shoulders and I turn my head in confusion.

"Why didn't Uncle David really want to come?"

"Never mind that! When? Nine a.m.? Three p.m.? When, boy? When!"

"11:14 p.m., okay!" I shout into his shiny face and rip myself from his meaty grasp. A sick feeling coils in my gut as I stare at him pacing and whispering to himself.

"Yeah. Of course. Yeah, that makes so much sense. Only a little over an hour before me. Yeah, yeah. I couldn't last long without him. That makes sense. Okay," Barry mumbles, nodding.

He must think he'll die of heartbreak whenever Uncle David dies. Maybe they had a big fight and he's afraid they're done for. Yeah, right. Uncle David loves Barry too much. No matter what dumb thing Barry's done now, he shouldn't worry so much. Uncle David probably just needs to calm down, but he'll be back on the tour.

"That's something I would do, isn't it? I knew it but...I didn't know it could predict that way too..." Barry's mumbling continues but I tune out, no longer afraid but mildly annoyed I got dragged in the middle of their little spat.

· · · ·

I'M SITTING IN MY USUAL throne, shipped place to place to coincide with this new image we're going with, and Barry hasn't said a word since we came in. By now, he'd be clucking over whoever's in charge of taking down the names and times. But the woman—dressed in skimpy white—looks between Barry and me with wide and frantic eyes.

I open my mouth to tell her what cloud document she should use to start notetaking but the bile rises in my throat. I choke it down with a bottled water another woman hands me. Barry palms me more pills. The room looks like it used to be a roadside convenience store, now with pews made out of zip-tied plastic chairs lining either side of the makeshift aisle.

The chairs look brand new. As does the crisp white paint and shiny posters of ads plastered with my face that line the walls. I shift in the plush throne and wonder if there's a bathroom somewhere. My breakfast of sugary coffee foamed out of me in the parking lot after Barry's outburst. I glance over my shoulder at him and he offers a distracted thumbs up as he stares at his phone.

I check mine again. Still no Mona. To keep my stomach settled as I wait for the pills to kick in, I reread our messages and look for where it got derailed. But I find nothing that clues in to why I haven't heard from her. The shaking in my hands begins to still. The glaringly white room softens. The imposing wall of muscled guards with cackling walkies and tight white shirts begins to look reassuring and comforting. The din of the crowd beyond the doors sounds less like a protest and more like a chorus.

My head falls back into the plush throne. Mona. The feel of her lips on mine that night in the park. The taste of cherries and cinnamon. The sensations of *Sweetheart* swaying as Mona's hips rock slowly. My heart swells with anticipation. I want to find her. I want to see her again.

"Mr. Great One, sir?" The crowd appears at my feet. A teen boy kneels at my throne. Outstretched in his hand is a little toy car. I take the proffered trinket and think back to those days reading at home when toys were the trinket of choice my people bestowed upon me.

I place my hand on the boy's head. "Your time of death is..."

"Fraud! Fraud! You're a fake! Lies! Lies! You'll burn in the lake!" The chorus beyond the doors is singing a song I've never heard before. I cock my head and strain to listen. "Fraud! Fraud!"

The boy's head swivels toward the door. "Don't worry, oh Great One. We believers don't listen to those fools! We know your wisdom is infinite!"

The boy's face swirls before me. I blink and shake my head to still the vertigo. I lean forward and peer into his eyes as they run away from his face. "Your time of death...is..."

What was his name? Did I get his nickel? What happened to that car he'd given me? I blink and an elderly woman's hands are grasping my own. I hear a time like an alarm clock sounding in my head but the noise is distorted as if I were under water. Where is Barry? Barry? I turn to look for him but the room spins.

"Keep it moving!" The water forms ripples around the words. Who said that? Who's yelling?

"Your time of death is..." I peer at the man before me. His lips are curled in a snarl. Sweat coats my skin and my white linen shirt clings to me. How can I sweat under water?

"Your time of death is..."

"Looks like I beat the devil," the man says. A woman screams.

"Get down!" The water ripples around the yells. The man's trinket is a gun. I turn to the guard over my shoulder to reassure him. We've had a few trinkets that were guns, knives, shuriken and the like. But the guard is running through the water. The man is still smiling that sinister smile at me.

"I beat the devil!" the man screams. I need to ask his name before I read his time. Have I been asking their names? The poor woman taking the notes, she has to be so far behind.

The guard lunges for the man. The gun fires. A beautiful display of red leeches into the water. I lurch forward and vomit all over my feet.

• • • •

"YOU OVERDOSED HIM BECAUSE you were worried? He nearly died because you were worried? You knock over a glass, trip and fall over your own feet when you're worried. You don't accidently give someone way too many pills! Jeb would be so disappointed—"

"You think I don't know that? Of course I know that!"

"That aside, we have much bigger problems, gentlemen. While no one is at fault for what happened at the scene of the crime, the issue at hand is the chaos this is causing. I can do my best to explain this to the detective, but I wish you'd sought my counsel before now. This is some hefty PR you're asking."

"Wait, crime? Don't you mean accident?"

"Er, no, Mr. Williams. The vic—ahem, the man succumbed a few moments ago."

The strange conversation pulls me out of a wonderfully deep sleep. The rocking sway of *Sweetheart* stills and I realize I'm in a bed and not back home. Begrudgingly, I peer from one bleary eye. The bright white sears into my skull. I groan but the dryness of my throat makes the sound empty. I try to swallow but find my tongue swollen.

The bright white of the room from before? It feels like ages have passed since I fell asleep. Are we still there? Have they dragged me to some back room to recuperate? How long have my fans been waiting?

"I don't suppose you've been monitoring the news on your tours?" I don't recognize the voice. Barry and Uncle David's voices mumble something incoherent in response. Is this one of the guards speaking?

"I thought that might be the case. Well, as you can see..."

I squint into the room but am puzzled by my surroundings. Instead of a couch in a makeshift breakroom, I find myself sprawled out on a small bed surrounded with knobs and buttons. A drop ceiling contrasts against drab beige walls. A washed-out blue curtain billows against a blast of disinfectant-stinking air.

"*Riots erupt after a peculiar visitor makes a stop in New York City. One is dead, dozens are injured, and property damage estimates are still climbing. Anita is on the scene. Are you with us, Anita?*"

"*Hi, Leslie. I'm here at The Loft Event Center where a special event was scheduled earlier today. Tod the Death Psychic, as he calls himself, claims to know when a person is going to die. Supporters of this psychic schedule to meet him months in advance and have to travel sometimes as far as to the other side of the world for the opportunity. I'm here with Ashleigh, one of the locals who came to protest today's event. Ashleigh, you have not met Tod the Psychic, have you?*"

"*No, only those who've paid the entry fee get to meet him. His face is plastered all over, though. And I'm not a local, my team and I have been after this guy for a while. His tours are so hush-hush that it's been next to impossible to track him down. We had to pitch in several thousand for a ticket here today just so we could get the location and details. Several thousand! His posters claim it's only five cents, but that's a total lie. This guy's a complete fraud!*"

"*And what does your sign say?*"

"*It says, 'A nickel isn't worth the eternal fire!' God did not intend for man to know when he'll die. That knowledge is for God and God alone. Anyone buying into this crap is selling their soul to the devil!*"

"*So you believe Tod can tell when you'll die?*"

"*Of course not! If he could, do you think he would've let Isaac kill himself like that?*"

"*Was Isaac a part of your group?*"

"*No, I've never met the guy. It's awful what he did and how he did it, but maybe now people will see how dangerous this Tod guy is. Look around you, this town is literally on fire! Everywhere this guy goes, chaos follows. That's why it's so hard to find out where he's gonna be next. This guy's a fraud and he knows it!*"

"Okay, I get it. Turn that off!" Barry yanks at the remote that's attached to my bed and mashes buttons until the screen goes dark. "Oh, you're awake. Hey kid, how you feeling?"

"Stefan? Stefan! I was so worried!" Uncle David elbows Barry out of the way. My head throbs as I peer through the bright light from one figure to the next. A man in a dark blue suit hovers in the corner whispering with Barry. He's shaking his head at whatever the man is saying. The man crosses his arms and gives a stern look as if Barry had asked for a cookie before dinner. Then he turns to the window and points through the open blinds. Barry flashes a worried look in my direction before closing the blinds and thankfully shutting out much of the light.

Uncle David pushes a button, likely summoning a nurse. His sweaty hand pets my forehead. I try again to say something but my lips cling to my teeth.

I cough out the raspy words, "What...happen?"

"Somebody didn't read their prescription instructions, that's what," a woman's voice answers from the doorway. "Hi, honey. I bet you feel like death. Don't worry, we've pumped out all the yucky. If you miss several doses, you can't make up for it by taking it all at once, okay? I know you've been traveling around through a lot of different time zones and that can get confusing, but we don't want to see you back here for this again, do we?"

The dark round woman looks like an angel. For a moment, I feel as though I'm meeting my grandmother for the first time. A plastic bendy straw is tilted to my lips with one hand while her other hand works with buttons on a machine with a clear bag of fluid hanging from it.

Uncle David hovers on my other side casting shifty stares to the whispering duo in the corner. What the hell is going on? The thought fades as cool water floods my enflamed tongue. I furrow my brows and squint at Uncle David, but he only shifts from foot to foot and looks over his shoulder.

"I'll be right back with a menu. I bet you're good and hungry, aren't you, sweetie?" The nurse pats my knee after adjusting my bed to sitting up. When she turns to leave, she looks back and gestures for Uncle David to follow her.

"He's still outside waiting. Are you ready for me to send him in now?"

Uncle David glances first at me then at Barry, who's still in a heated whisper debate in the corner. "No, not yet. Let me get with our lawyer first."

She shrugs then leaves the room, closing the door behind her. I fumble for the cup of water and down the rest of it. Barry stomps from the corner to my bedside, grabs the container on my tray, and pours more water into my cup. His hand shakes and water spills down my front. I notice then that my gauzy getup has been replaced with a hospital gown and my arm is taped up with a clear tube running from it.

"Oh, oh, damn. Lemme find something to clean that up with." Barry rushes to the cabinets on the opposite wall but returns with only a few small sheets of paper towel. I pull the blankets up to cover the cold wet spot on my belly, then stare pointedly between the three men.

"I'm so sorry, Stefan. I gave you too many of the wrong pills. I shoulda been paying more attention." Barry's outstretched hands holding the paper towel drop to his sides.

"So, that guy at the throne, that was a hallucination?" My voice is still raspy and everyone has to lean in to hear me. They exchange worried looks.

"*Sweetheart*, listen, what happened wasn't your fault. It was nobody's fault, you understand me? That man..." Uncle David takes my hand and strokes the back with his thumb. I pull away and make like my IV is itchy. "He was troubled. He chose to end his life and make a spectacle of what we're doing. He was a deluded protester, nothing more. I don't want you concerning yourself about it anymore."

"Sir, you can't go in there! Sir!"

The door flies open and another strange man barges in. The middle-aged man has sandy-blond hair that's as unkempt as my own. His haggard face is unshaven and his clothes look wrinkled and stained with dirt and grease. "Detective Landers, Chicago PD. I need to ask you all a few questions."

"You're a bit far outside your jurisdiction, Detective. Why don't you give me a call and we can set up a meeting at a more reasonable time...and place?" The blue-suited man holds out a card to the detective. My angel nurse is gripping the gray rain jacket of Detective Landers and is tugging him backwards toward the door.

He lets her pull him away from my bed but before his face disappears from view behind my parted curtain, Detective Landers sends a look of pure hatred at me. My mind flashes to the man at the altar and his sinister smile. My stomach churns and I erupt in a coughing fit that has Uncle David and Barry flying to my side.

Chapter Eighteen – Desdamona

The night breeze billows through the trees in my front yard and brings with it the scent of the neighbor's beautiful flower garden. A pang of envy stirs as I picture what a similar garden would do for my ugly front yard. Aside from a few mature trees, the remaining land is dead grass and overgrown weeds.

The porch swing offers a much quieter protest than the rocking chair I've since given up on. I look over at it and again contemplate burning the thing. Exhaustion settles in my bones but my anxious mind is screaming. I think of the poor woman upstairs curled up in her bed and of my Nettie, who's likely sitting in her bedroom with her ear to the wall, listening for our new patient to so much as whimper. Then Nettie will swoop in with kind words, cocoa, and a heating blanket.

I should feel grateful that another victim is off the streets. I should be happy that Rhiannon led this woman to our pickup spot in that part of town. I'd gotten the call only a few short hours ago that one of my part-timers has someone. I have numerous people paid to take turns sitting in different locations wearing the same getup. My girls working the streets will send unwilling trafficked victims their way. If they sit with one of my part-timers and say the code phrase "How are Stacy and the kids?", my person will call and either Jacob, Adam or I will rush to the scene.

That was the plan anyway. We'd rush in, corral the victim into our getaway vehicle, and before her pimp or anyone else can take notice, she's on her way home to me and my protection. Melanie, who is upstairs and tucked in after a long bath and big dinner, was the first we've saved this way. If it's working, maybe I won't have to spend nights prowling the streets with Adam and Jacob trying to save every street worker we come across. It's better this way. Sooner or later, our three faces were bound to be recognized.

I should be happy this plan is working. But maybe we're too late. Maybe whoever set fire to Yessica's car will come here looking for Melanie. I reach under the blankets piled in my lap and stroke the cold steel of the barrel. Rhiannon brought Melanie to me. Candy and Lila are spreading rumors about our pickup spots. It's working. I should be happy.

But it should be Rhiannon in that bed. And Candy and Lila should be well on their way to rebuilding new lives by now. I can't stomach the thought of them still out there, still doing those miserable things. Candy and Lila, they were raised in it like me, like Nettie. I stayed in for Sandy. Candy and Lila stay in to help our cause but know they can leave when they're ready. But Rhiannon, she outright refused. I have to find her again. I have to figure out how to save her too.

The front door creaks open but in the dark, I can't see as Nettie steps out to join me on the porch swing. The swing dips toward her as she sits beside me. But then I realize little Nettie weighs next to nothing and the swing wouldn't dip toward her.

"It's Melanie." Brice's voice sends my heart into my throat.

"Boy, don't you be scaring me like that!" I lay a hand over my heart and count my breaths. It's been so long since I've heard him speak, so long since he's said anything to me. But his words have me shaking off the thought. "What is it, she all right?"

I start to rise but Brice lays a hand on my arm. "Yeah, Nettie's with her. It's just...it's been awhile, you know?"

His voice is soft but it's so nice to hear. It has been some time since we've had another patient here. I imagine right about now, Melanie is sobbing into Nettie's shoulder and telling her story while Nettie rubs her back.

"You two should get some sleep. I'll go in and be with Mel." I pat his knee but he puts his hand on my arm again. Puzzled, I sit and wait.

"Thank you."

"I know, baby." I try to rise but he stops me again.

"I can't go back in. The things she's saying...I can't listen. Or the nightmares..."

"Okay, okay, baby. We'll sit out here a while longer, okay?" I shift some of the blankets onto Brice's lap, careful to keep the gun hidden on my thighs. The breeze whips through my hair. I suck the scent of roses and irises and peonies deep into my lungs.

"How much longer?" he whispers.

"Hmm?"

"Till I can get over it. How long did it take you to get over it?"

My heart plummets. I reach for his knee, then think better of it and lace my fingers in my lap instead. I watch the road for any movement and feel reassured at the weight of hard metal beneath my hands. "There's no such thing as getting over it."

I rock the swing and tip my head back. The chains creak under the weight of what I'd imagine is Brice's shoulders drooping.

"All that's happened to you, to me, to Nettie and Melanie, you can't get over that. None of us ever will. It's like a backpack. All those mean and nasty feelings you got twisting inside you, all of that is inside that backpack. You and me, we got five hundred pounds of ugly stuff on our backs.

"If I were to put five hundred pounds of books in a backpack and put it on your back right now and tell you to go run a mile, could you do it? Hell, no. Course not. Not even a bodybuilder could do that on a whim. But if you put that bag over your shoulders and never take it off, you know what happens then? Every day, you can take one more step than the day before. Sometimes, you'll be too tired and can't even get off the floor. And that's okay. One day, one more step and one more, soon you'll be walking around with that backpack on and you won't realize it's there.

"Is it because you got over it? Did it magically disappear, lose weight until it was nothing? No, it's still five hundred pounds of ugly. You open it up and look inside and everything's still there. All that changed is you got stronger. You figured out how to take the next step with all that weight holding you down. I carry my backpack with me everywhere I go. Sometimes, something happens and it gets so heavy I can't even stand up all over again. But I know all I have to do is take one step. It doesn't get easier, *you* get stronger. You're already so strong. I've seen you grow so much already. And when your bag gets too heavy again, Nettie and me are right here when you're ready to try walking."

Brice is silent for a long time. My analogy has helped a few people who've had it really bad, like Brice here. Like Melanie upstairs. I can't help but wonder if it would've given Sandy any solace. Maybe nothing would have. Maybe she did what she did because there wasn't any other way that she saw herself getting out. Or maybe if I had robbed Stefan sooner rather than dragging my feet out of a delusion of love, maybe I would've gotten to her in time. It could be her sitting right next to me, helping me rescue others like us.

My throat squeezes. Brice's subtle sobs reach my ears and his sorrow has my own tears rising. I can't undo what Sandy did. I can't change that I took so much from Stefan for selfish reasons. But maybe I can save Melanie and Brice and Rhiannon. I can make up for my wrongs a little at a time. My guilt is the heaviest book in my backpack. It's time I stopped ignoring it and learned how to carry it.

Stefan: Hey, Mona! It's been awhile. How are things?

I stare at the text message. Was there ever any chance, had my life gone a bit differently, that he and I could've been together? Would he have looked my way if he didn't have money to burn or if I was never forced to work the streets?

Mona: I need to see you.

I send the message before I can reason my way out of it. I've been saving up for a long time to earn back the money I took from him. I've held on to it for too long now. It's time I eased some of my guilt.

The bright light of my phone illuminates the dark. Brice lays his head on my shoulder and we sway until his hiccupping breaths turn to gentle snoring.

Stefan's text is almost immediate. *I'm going back home. Be there in a few days. Just got out of the hospital. Gonna recover for a bit. When can you come over?*

Mona: What happen? You okay?

Stefan: Long story. I'll tell you when you get here. When can I expect you?

The porch light flicks on. I quickly reply. *Soon. I'll let you know.*

Nettie's head pokes out the door. She peers through the overhead light and smiles when she sees Brice asleep on my shoulder. "Mel's asleep now. I was gonna make a midnight snack. Hungry?"

I smile at my sweet girl. She shifts in the doorway and a loud thud jerks Brice awake—she must have kicked something over. I open my mouth to request some of her special peanut butter cookies when the look on her face has a chill running down my spine.

"No! She was fine, she was asleep, I swear! Mel!" She yells and disappears from view. The screen door smacks shut. I leap up to chase after her, terrified that it's happened again. Brice is frozen on the swing, terror etched into his sleepy features, and for a moment I'm torn between the one who needs me now and the one who may have just refused my help, permanently.

Sandy's hollow one-eyed stare flashes through my mind and it's the last thing I ever want Nettie to see. I ignore the pain that rises from turning my back on Brice, and the guilt from thinking of my daughter before any thoughts of what Melanie may have just done.

"Nettie! Don't go in there!" I scream as I bound up the stairs. *Please, please don't let Nettie see.*

D*evil in disguise.*
    Fraud.
Snake oil only five cents!
A nickel isn't worth the eternal fire!

The chants and taunts echo through my pounding head. The brightly colored posters waving over the crowd outside the hospital plagued my dreams last night. I want to go back to the days when it was just me, a box, and a sign for a couple hours and for the fun of it.

I stare into the coffee-stained wood tabletop. Why didn't I pay attention to the plane, the terminal? These protests and what that man did...it never occurred to me to even look up until I stepped off the plane. I wasn't back home in Indiana, but far from it. I thought Barry would let me recover at home. Not send me straight to a tour in Dallas, Texas. How much longer until I can see *Sweetheart* again?

After the hospital, Barry hadn't said much, and he and Uncle David have kept to themselves. I tried to do the tour, to act like normal, but I barely made it through an hour of reading before my stomach was having none of it. I should've said something before running off during a break, but I know Barry wouldn't listen and would just pass me more pills.

"Oh my God, hi! It's been so long, how have you been?" A lithe blond jogs up to the table and sits across from me.

Her face is unfamiliar. I've not read her yet. Brown roots, shadowed eyes, smile plastered on with layers of lipstick. *1:19 a.m.* Nope, I've never met this woman.

"How is everyone? Stacy, the kids? You haven't aged a bit since I last saw you. What's it been, ten years? No, had to be..." I watch her chin, avoiding her eyes, and try to make sense of her rambling.

I tune out. Ten years ago I would've been a kid. Well, a teenager, but still. Movement over her shoulder catches my attention. A looming shadow hovers just beyond the café door, watching this strange woman with intensity. A couple exiting hold the door open for the dark figure but he makes no move other than to angle to the side for them to pass.

"It's you, right?" The woman leans forward and whispers before loudly launching into another rambling of nonsense.

"Oh my goodness, is that Elizabeth? What on earth, come here, you!" Another stranger appears beside my table, a middle-aged man dressed in an unassuming navy hoodie, much like mine. I pull the hood down further, covering my eyes and hoping this mistaken identity will get forgotten with whatever reunion is going on.

A peek through my hair dangling at the edge of my hood reveals the strange woman across from me hasn't moved. She's looking between me and the other man who stands awkwardly holding his arms out to her. With an irritated huff, the stranger scoots into my side of the booth, forcing me to hug the wall.

What the hell is going on? All I wanted was a few quiet minutes and a hot mocha before facing Barry. Was that so much to ask? Of course it was in a big city like Dallas. What was I thinking?

"How's school going? Are you still going for...what was it, don't tell me...to be a teacher, right?" The man leans forward, holding the woman's arms by the wrists as he nearly yells in her face. But then he pulls in close, whispering. I find myself edging over to catch what he says to her. "He's still there, stay calm. Help is on the way."

"Thank you." The woman nods, tears forming in her eyes. I look away. Still clutching each other on the table, they launch into a painfully loud conversation so forced, it's like two people auditioning for a play without a script or having any idea what the play is even about.

My coffee has gone cold by the time I take my last sip and the two haven't quieted down much. Barry is probably looking for me.

I should go. Just ask them to let you out! It's not that hard! Heart pounding, palms sweating, I lean over, mouth open, ready.

"I was looking everywhere for you guys! So sorry I'm late!" Another stranger appears tableside and forces her way into my solitary time. This woman forces the first woman to hug the wall much like me. "Wow, this place is crowded."

I blink in confusion. Aside from a small handful of people based on the noise level, this place seems fairly empty for a big city café in the middle of a Saturday. The third woman joins in on the weird forced banter except she sounds more natural and at ease. I thought the man and the first woman might have been father and daughter, both being white with fair hair, but this second woman has me second-guessing the situation.

"Adam," the latest stranger says softly enough I nearly miss it.

"Yeah, we good," the man beside me replies, his voice losing its theatrical performance.

"All right, honey, we're gonna take a little walk. I didn't catch your name, Mr...." Silence befalls the table and I realize she's addressing me.

"Stefan." It comes out a croaky whisper.

I risk a glance at the second woman and gasp at the sight of her. Light black skin shines in the glow of the sunlight reflecting off windshields beyond the windows of the café. Deep chocolate eyes pin me with intensity and authority. Her chin raises as I stare and I find my gaze tracing high cheekbones, proud eyebrows, and a large mouth of plump lips obscuring a flash of white teeth. She looks young, really young. Behind her tough demeanor is a look of worry hidden in her gaze. Staring at people all day for hours, I've started to pick up on a few things. And that fear and worry in her eyes gives me a sudden fierce urge to protect her.

"Stefan, come with us, won't you please?" Her teeth flash in a warm smile. There's a gap in the front where her front teeth are missing.

The middle-aged man beside me loops his arm around my shoulders as if we were old friends, and I'm ushered out a side door behind the young woman and the blond one. Her small arm glistens around the shoulders of the blond woman as she hugs her close, much the same as the man is doing with me.

So caught up in the strange feeling of protection am I that it takes a moment for my anxiety to kick in. We round the corner into the alley behind the café where I imagine bags and bags of wonderful-smelling coffee beans are unloaded at 4 a.m. on dewy mornings as city sounds begin to echo along the small expanse of graffitied brick.

"Woah, buddy. Calm down. We're the good guys. You're safe now." The man's arm leaves my shoulder and snakes around my waist. I realize then that my entire body is vibrating. The 105-degree temp feels as if it has plummeted to zero. My teeth chatter as a bright blue florist van comes into view, its side door open with another strange woman seated inside.

Only then do I notice how the woman in the van and the blond are dressed. Both are wearing thin strappy tops almost like bikinis paired with tiny miniskirts and impressively tall high heels. The woman in the van has faded pink hair and dark bruises on her cheek. Oh, God. I'm in the wrong place, indeed.

"No, no, please. Please, no," I'm chanting, but my trembling body has no fight. The blond woman sits beside the other woman in the van, both silent. The worry-eyed woman pulls me to sit beside her in the back row. She turns to me and tries to cup her hands around my face, attempting to tug my hood out of the way. I twist away and lean over the backpack I've clutched to my front since I first sat down with my coffee.

"Baby, calm down. You're safe now. No one will ever hurt you again. We'll get you to safety. Come on now." She smells like lilacs fresh off the vine. I'm crushed against her pillowy chest and suddenly we're driving away in the van, the middle-aged man—Adam—in the passenger's seat, some other random stranger driving to God knows where.

"What's next? How do you know Billy isn't following us? What if he finds me?" The blond twists around and grabs at the worried young woman beside me, pulling her away from rocking me. I gnaw on my nails.

"Yeah, what about my baby? You said we'd get my baby!" The bruised woman twists around to yell.

"Jacob is heading to the daycare right now. Even if anybody shows up, we got you. You are safe now, you hear me? I'm not letting anything happen to you, never again." She chokes on the last word, then turns back to me, arms wrapping around and holding me tight. "You hear that, baby? Go on and let it out, you're safe now. You're safe."

The van is silent for several minutes while I try working my jaw. Why the hell did I think I could handle something as normal as a run for coffee by myself? Words continue to fail me and my shirt sticks to my back. The van stops beside a colorful building with plastic slides fenced off beside it. I hang my head and focus on dislodging whatever's stuck in my throat.

"Hurry on, Jacob will go with you." I keep my face buried in my hands as she rubs my back and barks orders at the others. Doors open and shut and open and shut. Soon, we're on the road again but with a young quiet child seated in the middle of the two ladies of the evening.

"Adam, Jacob, where we at now? This isn't the way."

Blood fills my mouth as my teeth gnash flesh where once was nail.

"He's not one of 'em." It sounds like the man from the café, Adam.

"What do you mean?" she asks beside me.

"Miss here, went up to him 'cause of his blue hoodie thinking he was me. He's not one of 'em."

Silence fills the space. My heart pounds.

"Could be a plug. They been on to us, Nettie. Knew we shoulda switched pick-up spots." A thick gravelly voice speaks up. Jacob, the driver, I assume.

"Naw, he's no plug. He's in just as much trouble. Boy, you're still shaking. Come here, let me see you." The young woman, Nettie, takes my hands from my face, gently tugging until I release my teeth from my bloodied fingertips. I twist my head away. "What's got you so scared, baby? You need somewhere safe to go? We help people get to safe places so no one can ever hurt them again. You need someplace, don't you?"

"Nettie, he's a plug. We can't take him, it'll ruin everything, then nobody will be safe!" Jacob twists in his seat, pinning me with a steely gaze. He's older and I wonder if he's Nettie's grandfather.

Nettie leans forward. "Honey, you were supposed to sit with the man in the dark blue hoodie with the bright orange backpack. Not this—"

"He got a backpack too, though. I didn't remember the color they said, I just saw some guy alone in a blue hoodie and thought it was him. Maybe y'all should wear a flag or something." The blond speaks without turning around. She puts her face up to the glass and peers through the dark tinted window. "You sure Billy won't find us? Can we hurry up?"

"Mama, I'm hungry."

"In a minute, baby." The bruised woman pats the little girl's hair. Her head barely reaches the top of the bench seat in front of us. I wonder if she is filthy and covered in bruises like her mother.

"Enough of this!" Adam suddenly speaks up and hops out. I let out a squeal as the side door flies open. The women and little girl jump. "Give me that!"

My backpack is ripped away from my lap and its contents dumped on the gray carpet at my feet. A few of the day's spoils stare back at me. A dog collar. A keychain of a feather. A single glove. Army men. Quarter machine rings. Hard candy.

"You homeless or somethin'?" Adam asks me, holding up my tin full of nickels.

"Mama! I'm hungry!"

My face burns. I can't shake the shame from seeing my spoils ruled off as the collection of a homeless man. Why can't I speak up? Why can't I say the simple words, "Take me home, there's been a mistake"? I rummage through the pile and hand one of my brochures over. Unsure what to do with me, they continue on, the awkward exchange keeping the van silent the rest of the way. I let my fear keep my lips glued for another thirty minutes as the van heads to the outskirts of town.

A dilapidated but sprawling Victorian house in the middle of suburban neighborhoods sprouts up, black, peeling, ugly against the backdrop of clean square lawns and cookie-cutter houses. Adam and Nettie argue over me as Jacob ushers everyone else behind the massive and heavy-looking front door of the creepy hulking house.

I fidget with the zipper of my backpack. The front door opens and the scene pouring out of it silences the rushing of my thoughts. A stretcher appears in the doorway, two men and a woman, all EMTs, surround it. A small dark-haired woman lies limp under a thin white sheet. But it isn't this strange scene that stills my mind. It's the woman who follows out the door after them.

Mona! She looks older and a little different with a full head of thick, wavy hair and not the pixie look I'd always seen her with years ago, but I'd recognize that beautiful face anywhere. The fake overdone spray tan is gone. In its place is a natural healthy glow. Her nose and cheeks are dotted with freckles. Were those always there? She's wearing cozy-looking cotton pajamas and her arms are squeezing around herself. She nods at something one of the EMTs says to her and the woman on the stretcher reaches a weak hand toward us.

"She's still...she's okay! Mel!" Nettie screams beside me and all but tramples over me to fly out the van's side door.

Adam reluctantly offers me a hand as I stumble out. "She overdosed a couple hours ago. We got the call to pick up you guys right at the same time. Look, I know it looks scary but trust me, you'll be safe here. That girl tried to take her own life. We didn't think to check her for drugs. We're gonna have to check you, though. And the others."

He keeps rambling but I tune him out. Mona keeps getting larger until I realize my feet have moved me closer to her. The stretcher moves to the street beside the house where an ambulance comes into view. Nettie jumps into the back with them and Mona is close on her heels.

"Mona!" Her name erupts from my throat. The sirens and the birds and the wind stills as her eyes lock with mine. My anxious heart quiets but begins pumping in excitement and anticipation. All this time, all these years. Tears fill my eyes.

"Mona!" And I'm running to her. In my head, we're in a flowery meadow and she's in a flowing dress and we're running to each other. But Mona looks through me rather than at me. No, right, of course she doesn't recognize me. It's been so long since she's last seen me. I've grown from that young boy.

"Stefan?" Her voice is weak and faraway. I stand in front of her but her eyes remain distant.

"Yeah, hi! It's been—"

"Ma'am, we have to go!" an EMT calls.

The chatter inside the ambulance and the sirens and the scene around me comes crashing down. Crowds dot the surrounding streets. Faces fill every window. There's so much noise that her lips move but I can't process her words until long after the ambulance disappears around the corner.

The siren wails get louder as if the ambulance were doubling back and not driving farther away. The chatter of the onlookers grows to a cacophony that has the birds screeching louder to overcome. My stomach pitches and I fall to my knees.

"Woah, there. Come on, let's get you inside. You hungry?" Adam tugs on my elbow.

The contact sends a shock through my body. I bolt upright and run, only to stumble and fall forward, landing hard on my backpack. The impact sends the jar of nickels straight to my stomach and the coffee from earlier spews from my lips.

"Hey!" Adam jogs toward me.

I grab the small fruit tree beside me and use it to climb to my feet. The world tips beneath me but I run. My bag thumps against my stomach but I run.

Her words dance through my frantic mind. As if I were the mailman here to shoot the breeze and interrupted her soaps. As if I were a Girl Scout selling cookies and she didn't have cash handy. As if I were a beggar on the street and she didn't have a spare nickel.

"Not now, sorry."

Chapter Twenty – Desdamona

The house smells of sweet and smoky meat. The oven door hangs open as Nettie broils a spatchcocked chicken. She hums as she dances over pots and pans on the stove. Steam billows around her. I stare at my hands and try to remember to breathe.

"Mama?"

Melanie lying on the floor motionless, that needle sticking in her arm. Nettie staring at her limp body with that look on her face. That look I never wanted to see on my baby's face. And Brice. Back in his room, back to being silent, back to starving himself. And now this.

"So, who was he?"

We'd gotten back late. The newcomers were already settled in their rooms. Adam and Jacob had ordered pizza and made sure everyone was cared for, with new linens and toothbrushes. They're good people. I have to remember to thank them. Adam is still here, dozing on the couch, up late waiting for us to return. And then up even later when the smoke started. Nettie and I haven't bothered to sleep.

By now, I'm sure she'd normally be fussing over the daughter of one of last night's new arrivals. But she's rattled from Melanie's overdose. Everyone is up in their rooms, napping after a late lunch. The therapist is on the way to onboard our latest while checking up on Brice's regression. And Nettie's cooking far too much food, which she does when she's stressed. And I'm doing what I do best, absolutely ly nothing while the house around me goes to shit.

"Mama?"

This is my life. My livelihood. I am supposed to save people from working the streets and stop people from hurting themselves. I devote every single moment to it. So why do I keep failing? Even when I do manage to bring people here, even then I'm not strong enough to keep them safe. I can tell when someone is going to attempt suicide and how they plan to do it. How did I miss it with Melanie? Why did it have to be Nettie getting hurt because of my failure?

"Mama!" Nettie's hand slams on the table in front of me.

I yelp and lurch from my chair. "What? What is it? What's happened now?" I stumble for the front door, afraid to see what else of mine has been put to flame.

"No, Mama. Sit down. Everything's okay. You were just spacing out is all. I was trying to talk to you." Nettie gingerly leads me back to my chair where I collapse. A glass of water is pressed into my shaking hands but my stomach protests after one small sip.

"I'm fine, baby. Just tired."

Nettie's eyes are sunken and underlined with shadows. Her lips are chapped, and her nose is red. Her once delicately coiled and pressed baby hair now stands out at odd angles from her fretting fingers. A pot on the stove begins to boil over and she rushes to snap off the burner. She places both hands on the counter and inhales deeply.

"Mama, I know you still think I'm just a kid, but you don't have to—and you can't—protect me from everything." Nettie turns to face me, and the look on her face makes me feel like I'm the child.

"I know, baby. You do so much to take care of everyone, I just don't like putting more on you is all."

"No, you don't like asking for help. You think you can save everyone, but you can't even save yourself!" Her voice cracks. My eyes widen at her. She's never raised her voice at me. Or anyone, that I've ever heard.

"I can't ask for help? What do you think Adam is here for, huh? What do I pay Yessica and Jacob for? I have plenty—"

"Those are employees. It's different and you know it. You take it all on yourself and still beat yourself up when somebody makes a choice of their own free will that you don't like."

I rise from my seat and feel the heat of embarrassment and anger rising. "Oh, so I should've just let Melanie overdose and die on my floor because she *chose* to put so much mud in her? I should let everybody who wants to die, do it?"

"Not everybody, but yes! This isn't just about Melanie. You blame yourself for what she did like you can protect everyone. The world isn't yours to save!"

"Hold on just a minute, missy! I am trying my hardest—"

"To save the world! You're so obsessed you won't sleep. You hardly eat. You're wasting away and making everyone worry sick and you don't even care. You don't even see someone if they aren't one of your potential victims needing rescue. That poor guy looked so happy to see you and you barely even acknowledged him!"

"Woah, woah! What's going on in here?" Adam storms into the kitchen, rubbing the sleep from his eyes.

"Nothing. I'm gonna go take a nap." Nettie stomps from the room without a spare glance back at me. Just as she turns from view, I catch sight of glistening tears in her eyes.

"Sonofabitch." Adam sits in my chair. I hadn't realized I'd sat back down but somehow in the chair opposite where I last was. He scrubs a hand over his face. "What was all that about? I've never heard y'all fight."

"Yeah, well, we don't. Usually." I reach for the glass of water for something to do, only to remember it was across the table. But the glass is nowhere to be found and a puddle of water is left in its place. "What am I doing?"

Adam rises to sit beside me. His foot kicks something beneath the table. I watch aimlessly as he sweeps broken glass into a dustpan, then throws it in the trash. He turns off the oven before sitting beside me. His hand is cold as it wraps around mine.

"You're amazing, Desdamona. You know that?" His fingers stroke the back of my hand. "I've never met another woman like you. I'm in awe of you every day and I love the work that we do together.

But Nettie's right. You're overdoing it. Have been for some time. You can't save everyone. At least not running on fumes like you are."

I stare at our linked hands, noting his still lingers. "What did she mean? What poor guy was she talking about?"

Adam's brow crinkles. "It's a long story. We picked up someone we thought needed saving, but I don't think he was one of our usuals. He had issues for sure. It was when the ambulance was here and...well, he ran off. It's fine, though. He was just some confused kid. He called you Mona."

My heart stammers. A strange kid, who called me by that old name? The only one who still calls me that is Stefan. But he should be way up north on his houseboat or maybe touring the world doing that death psychic thing. It couldn't possibly be him, could it?

"Where are you going?" Adam's worried look stops me as I rise. I look down at our hands. The memory of that special night in the park with Stefan surfaces. I have to find him. If he was here last night, he couldn't have gotten far.

"I need to...go for a drive. Clear my head."

"Okay, I'll come too."

"No!" Adam blinks in surprise at my outburst. "I mean, no...I'm worried about everyone here. Can you stay with them? Please?"

His face softens and he offers a lopsided smile. "Yeah, of course. I wasn't thinking. I'll stay and watch the place. Don't worry, no one's setting fire to anything else as long as I'm around."

My eyes roam over every out-of-place shape as I drive. Adam's words float in the back of my mind. He's getting too close, too comfortable. His words have worry rising. He's a great employee but I'm not interested in having a man hovering around, protecting me and mine. My fist clenches on the steering wheel. A mop of reddish hair tufts out of a hoodie and I slam on the brakes.

A pale white girl whips her head in my direction and jogs a few paces to put distance between us. Dammit. What the hell is wrong with me? I should just text him. Obviously. But when I pat my pockets for my phone, I realize I must have left it behind. I drop my head and my forehead smacks the steering wheel. A horn blares behind me.

"All right, all right, I'm moving!" I pull over to the side of the street and park. The car flies around me, the driver's middle finger waving out the window.

Tears well. The dancing flames on my porch flash in my mind. "DIE" scorched into the front porch where I rock with Nettie on sleepless nights. The porch of my home where I bring countless people to recover and escape. And someone has it out for us. For me.

You can't even save yourself!

Dammit, Nettie. For a girl so young, she's far too wise. Could it be Stefan behind it all? No, Nettie said he looked excited to see me. But that word was burned on my porch a few hours later. There's no way my sweet and innocent Stefan would do something like that. But then, who?

I'll figure out who's behind it, Nettie, just you watch. I can save myself and everyone else. Sandy's face wavers in my mind but I shake the image away. No. I need to focus. Who could have it out for us? Who could be against us and know not only about my business but my rescuing night workers?

Rhiannon?

She outright refused our help. She showed zero interest in being freed from that life. No, no, it couldn't be her. But what if that's the reason she's afraid to come with me? What if whoever has her in their clutches is trying to scare us off the scent? It makes so much sense. It's gotta be something to do with her. I have to find her.

The evening hours bleed into darkness. I prowl the streets, one eye out for a lanky, sweet man with brown-red hair, and one out for long dark hair sashaying behind a confident young woman. The street names blur. Where was it we last saw her? What's the most likely hotel Stefan would go to?

My head bobs with exhaustion. I shake my head and slap my cheeks. She has to be around here somewhere. I'll find Stefan and Rhiannon and save them all. I can do it. I have to do this. My eyes slip closed.

The van rocks and bounces beneath me, lulling me into a deep sleep.

Chapter Twenty-One – Stefan

"Yo, you need a bump?" A blurred figure steps in my path. I paw at my eyes, but the image before me doesn't clear. I shake my head at the man, and the earth pitches beneath my feet.

"Yeah, whatever, man." His voice pounds into my ears as the earth collides with my face. His chuckle fades into the night. The hard and wet cement tastes earthy and metallic beneath my parched lips. The sky above swirls and spins. My eyes squeeze shut and attempts to open them go unheeded.

"Not now." Mona stands on Sweetheart. *She's leaving me.*

"Go away," she screams at me. I chase along the dock, but she drifts farther and farther away. A crowd forms around me, all familiar faces. Everyone I've ever read appears beside me. One by one, they all jump into the lake and disappear into the murky depths.

As each one of them jumps, they look at me and ask, "Who are you?"

I shove through the crowd and run toward Mona as she chants the same question at me. I try to tell her who I am, but the words jam in my throat.

"Who is Tod? I don't know you. Go away." She turns toward the horizon where flames dance in wait for her. Sweetheart *speeds away. The bodies of all those who've jumped bob to the surface and float after the boat.*

"Who are you?" Their rheumy eyes lock on me.

Mona shoves me awake. I lurch upright to a blindingly bright day. My jaw aches from the stiff sidewalk. My shoulder tingles from how I'd lain over the curb. Where the hell am I? My feet lag beneath me as if they've yet to get the memo that I'm walking. The cement greets me once again.

Is Barry looking for me? I vaguely recall the pestering vibrations of my phone in my pocket all through the night. But my hand trembles so violently that I can't manage to worm my way into the pocket.

I stare into the sun. My eyes water. Then the sun begins to rotate around me, faster and faster. My stomach turns in sync.

The moon eclipses the sun, a dark shadow spreading over the swirling dance above me. Just as the moon blacks out the sun, it speaks.

"Hey, sweet thing. Come with me, baby." The moon grows larger until its lips are a kiss away. I fall back into dreams of Mona.

"Ooh, where you find him at? He's cute. I've got first dibs!"

"Back off, Sheila!"

"What's wrong with him?"

"Withdrawal, looks to me."

"God, from what? I never look that fucked up, even off meth a couple days."

"Pills, I bet anything. Give 'im space. And pass me that hype kit when you done."

I wake up drenched through my jeans and sweatshirt. Salty sweat stings my eyes. My teeth stick to my lips. The smell of something sour and rotten fills my nostrils and my stomach protests. I dry heave onto bare floor where carpet underlayment staples dance beneath my nose. The room I'm in is filled with the remnants of some kind of party. Sleeping forms dot the floor and furniture. A frail-looking woman is curled in the fetal position beside me. A small zipper bag is at her fingertips. A tourniquet that is a pale sickly yellow color is wrapped around her arm and the skin below it looks swollen to almost purple.

I pull at the strap. Her arm flops to the floor in a thud but she doesn't wake. No one around me so much as twitches. The walls are cracked and broken through in spots, offering peeks into other rooms. Through a hole behind the tourniquet woman, I can see into the kitchen where a man and two women take turns bending over a table. The sound of snorting fills the house.

The bare subfloor is sticky beneath me. I sit slowly upright, but the room starts to spin. I fall back onto a pile of ashtray-stinking pillows and blankets. There's an old, tattered sofa likely pulled from a dumpster lying near my feet. Four people pile haphazardly over it with knees and elbows jutting out everywhere I look.

"Hey, sleepyhead!" One of the women from the kitchen emerges with a box of something in her hands. She's pale, sunburned, and a mess. Her clothing looks like it came from the same dumpster as the couch. She smells like ham and onions. Her bleached blond hair looks to be held in place with grease. "Hungry? I got donuts! They're day olds, but still good. You get first pick. Sprinkles? Glazed? Oh, I know. Here, chocolate glazed and cream filled."

When I make no move to sit up or take the proffered pastry, she bends down and shoves one end at my lips. Like a starving stray, I devour it, viciously biting at the donut until something hard catches between my teeth.

"Ow! Damn, you sure is hungry. I knew it." She shakes the finger I'd bitten. "I thought you mighta been a goner. We got one of everything you could ever want so you don't gotta feel like that never again, yeah? Tell Mama Bear, what's your poison, sugar bear?"

I stare blankly at her. Even if I could figure out what she's talking about, my withered tongue wouldn't be able to utter a sound.

"Gary Bear?"

"Yeah, Mama Bear?" The man from the kitchen bends low to avoid hitting his head as he crosses into the room. The towering figure smiles broadly down at me and I swear his eyes glow red. "Uppers, downers? I know, how 'bout a couple z-bars, kid?"

My mouth works but no sound emits. I shake my head.

The woman returns with a glass of some kind of liquid. I try to turn away, but she and that big man surround me, holding my head and pinching my nose. A burning liquid fills my mouth. Vodka?

I cough out the fiery liquid. "No. Mona!" I collapse back into the woman's lap.

"Mona?" The man's big brow crinkles. "Well, I can get you the morphine but who cares about the other stuff?"

The room grows dark. The sound of bumping music jars me from a vivid dream of the last glorious night I'd spent with Mona. I find myself in a bedroom, or what looks like it might've once been a bedroom. The same pile of blankets are pooled beneath me. A man and woman are propped against the wall behind the door. The man slams into her and she moans obnoxiously as he grunts in tune. A dresser beside them rattles from their motion and threatens to crumble from the assault.

Her eyes catch mine. "You can be next if you want."

I shake my head. Surprised to find the ground sturdy beneath my feet, I stumble from the room, squeezing out the door that the couple promptly slam behind me. The sleeping people from before are now alive and gyrating to the music. There's powder on a small table in the living room and a zipper bag that I recognize is the centerpiece for a group of people I've never seen before. A needle is passed around the circle. Where the hell am I?

Their eyes all land on me. Their eyes glow red and their smiles become vicious. I cry out and curl into a ball. "Stay away from me!" But my words are lost to the music that seems to come from nowhere and everywhere.

"Sugar bear, baby, you okay. You safe. Here, feel the ground beneath you. Feel how strong and sturdy it is? Yeah, yeah, just like that."

I rub the ground at her urging, feeling foolish and terrified. How the hell did I get here? Am I still in Texas?

"My...my phone." I fumble for my pocket, but the shaking starts again.

"Oh, here. I switched it off, thing was goin' off and drivin' us all nuts." The woman digs in my pocket, then hands me the phone. I stare at the smudged screen as it lights up with the starting screen. Has Barry called? Has Mona texted?

Sixteen missed calls, all from an unknown number. Three voicemails. I skim through the list, but Barry's number isn't among them. Maybe he called from a phone at the last touring spot? The woman holds up the zippered bag for me, but I shake my head and hit play on the first voicemail. In a far corner, a woman with pink curly hair stares at me. I shudder and look away.

"Hello, this is Detective Landers. I need to speak with you immediately regarding the missing persons case of Bridgett Newman. Please call me back immediately. This case is of upmost importance. Failure to return my call may result in a warrant for your arrest. Call me back—immediately."

My heart pounds. Detective Landers? Wasn't he the one who showed up at the hospital? His look of hatred flashes in my mind. I listen to the rest of the voicemails, all from him and with the same message. That's a lot of *immediately* in such a short voicemail. I scan the missing call list and all of them are from an unknown number. Another scan of the voicemails confirms the Detective didn't provide a number to return his call, immediately.

If I walk out of here, am I going to be arrested? All for missing a few calls? Desperate, I dial Barry and turn away from the pestering of a different woman as she tries pushing a liquor bottle at me.

When he answers, I'll apologize for running away. There's surely another tour nearby set for tonight, so he can't stay mad at me if he wants me to come back. If anybody can find me and help me out of here, it's Barry. The phone goes to voicemail, but the inbox is full. Barry never misses a call. I try again.

Again, he doesn't answer. Panic starts to set in. Could they have arrested him, too? Think, think! Bridgett Newman...Bridgett...time of death 10:13 p.m. She looked sickly but I remember she mentioned something about being in remission. That was her, right? I've read so many over the years, I can't exactly remember those kinds of details anymore. But she must have run off somewhere to enjoy the rest of her life after I granted her that freedom. If I explain that to the police, will they let Barry go?

"Was's this?" Mama Bear slurs as she staggers from foot to foot in front of me. She fingers through one of my brochures. "Tod, the Death Psychic? You're a psychic…of death?"

"Oh my God! It's the Great One!" A scream erupts from somewhere among the cuddle puddle of people draped around the couch. I blink and a small crowd has gathered around me.

"Um, hi. Yes, that's me." My sheepish voice is lost to a growing assault of excited whispers. I nod toward the brochure that this Mama Bear woman is holding, but whatever she'd done with that zippered bag must've kicked in because she sways to the floor. People step around her until her form disappears between a cluster of legs.

"I applied to be one of your helpers. Fucker said I wasn't pretty enough. Sorry, I mean, your boss, I think? You think I'm pretty, right? Can you get me the job?"

"What's my time?"

"I heard about you. How much is it? I got something, hold on."

"Hey, when am I gonna die?"

My heart begins to pound harder than it has in a long time. By now, the pills Barry would give me would be kicking in and this crowd of strangers would no longer terrify me. But as I sit huddled at their feet as they stomp impatiently in front of me, I can feel sheer flight-or-fight panic setting in. I slap my hands over my ears and hum to drown out the noise. Attempts at calming breaths fail as foul air is sucked into my lungs.

Breathe. These people know you. They love you. They need your help. Look at them, drugged out of their minds. They're desperate to be saved. Only you can set them on the right path. I chant over and over to myself, willing my racing heart to settle.

I peer through one eye at them. They're all waiting for me, as if I were a magician on stage and they'd all paid their last dollar to be here. Their hands are outstretched, clutching their offerings and awaiting my caress. Tentatively, I reach a shaking hand out to the nearest person. His hands are clammy. He kneels before me and his eyes look at me with such adoration and hope that the fear melts away.

"What is your name?"

The man sniffles back tears. "Henry Huntsman." In his hands he clutches a zipper pull and a penny.

I scoop his offerings from his oily fingers. "Your time of death is 1:41 a.m."

Another person stoops before me. One by one I read these strangers I was so terrified of before. They're human. They're down on their luck or running from the very responsibilities that my power can free them from. They offer me all that they have. A pile of clothing and various debris forms beside me. Some offer their last drugs that I happily take off their hands despite having no idea what to do with them. Nickels, pennies, and dimes fill all of my pockets.

"Your time of death is 7:17 a.m., Ashley." The woman sobs as I say her name. She kisses my hands. One of my followers helps her to her feet. All around me, the seemingly endless party looks as if it has ended once and for all. Those I have read are washing dishes that are mostly broken. They're sweeping the floor with a tattered old broom or straightening old frames with no pictures inside.

Unsure how to move on with their lives yet and still coming down from their final highs, the crowd shuffles around, looking for purpose. Ashley bows low and backs away from me as another person kneels at my feet. Before I can read them or ask their name, two people surround me and effortlessly lift me to me feet. I'm sat with great delicacy on the sofa. My collection is brought with great care to pool on the floor next to me.

"What time is it?" Ashley whispers to the followers who hold her elbows as she continues her backward bow out of the room.

"Seven oh...three," one of them answers. A man I've not read yet. Oh, wait, his name is Wilson. He's going to die at 3 p.m. on the dot. Ashley freezes in the doorway to another room.

"Ashley? Come on, it's someone else's turn." Wilson urges her from the room.

"I'm gonna die. I'm gonna die in like, ten minutes! I don't wanna die!" Ashley's bloodcurdling scream reverberates against the thin windows in the house. Like a flash mob, everyone around me freezes.

"I don't want to die." Wilson looks back at me, terror coating his eyes.

"Please, no!" someone else screams in another room.

I watch motionless and in horror as the scene erupts around me. Chaos unfolds as Ashley collapses to the floor in the fetal position, screaming into her knees.

Some join her in screaming paralysis. Others tear out their hair and wail with faces turned to the sky. A blur of motion streaks past my eyes as another person runs through the rooms, gasping for breath and chanting, "I can't breathe, I can't breathe!"

My heart palpitates. This is the chaos I cause. This is the result of the information that no one should be burdened with. This is the fear, the panic, the total separation from self that Barry would protect me from seeing. My eyes flick toward the front door.

I stagger to my feet but the moment I step toward the door, Mama Bear—Phillis, time of death 5:31 a.m.—grabs me by the shoulders. "Help Ashley. Help my baby. She's scared out of her mind! Change her time! You can do that, right? Please, hurry!"

"I-I can't. I'm sorry. I have no control over it."

"Then...what do I do? My baby, she's so scared!"

The screaming should be deafening. My fear of people should be paralyzing me right now. But the people all around me are a mirror image of all my fear. Where I've been afraid of them for their smells and sounds and their rejections and cruelty, these people now embody the sum of all that fear. As if I have passed this off on them, and once their times are purged from me, the fear has transferred.

Has everyone succumbed to the fear like this? What about all those testimonials on my fan pages? All those people freed from the lives they were trapped in, were they the minority? Is the fear only part of it? Everyone I've ever read never hung around long afterward. Are there stages of acceptance, like grief? Or is this the consequence of facing mortality under far too many drugs?

I grip Mama Bear's arms. "Give me a hand."

We create a makeshift podium of milk crates and a TV stand turned on its side. Standing up there, watching the chaos I've created, confronting the fear I've passed on like a virus, I feel every bit like the fraud those protesters claimed I was. I suck the stink of the house deep into my lungs.

"Come, my children!" A voice I've never heard erupts from my throat. The hellish wails and screams cease immediately. Eyes accumulate around every doorway. People crawl to cower before the podium. Mama Bear chews on her fingers and places a hand on my lower back, her eyes locked on the shivering form of her daughter curled up in the corner.

"Save us, Great One!" A chorus of voices echo the phrase. I raise a hand and silence befalls the crowd.

"Death is not to be feared. I am sorry I have scared you with this knowledge. My gift is one of fear. I believed I could free people of their fear. That I could gift the world with this knowledge and together we would rise above the misery we humans have created. I realize how foolish my dream has been.

"I grew up isolated, unsure how to befriend anyone, join others, become one of you. I wanted more than anything to be normal but I didn't know how. When I lost the only family I ever knew, I wanted to die. The only thing that kept me going was my love for a woman who barely knew me but let me hang around anyway."

I'm relieved when this earns a few chuckles. The cluster of eyes pinning me in place have begun to lose their fear. Some eyes have regained a glossy glaze. Ashley had crawled to sit at her mother's feet. Phillis strokes her hair and smiles back at me. She nods for me to continue.

"I...I don't remember where I was going with that. I guess I wanted to get close to people—close to you, but this was the only way I knew how. Your times are real, but that doesn't mean I had any right to give you such heavy information. Everywhere I go, chaos has followed. That alone should've clued me in that what I've been doing is wrong. But I ignored it. I was chasing a connection that was never there. I'm sorry for causing you to be afraid. Now I just...I want to go home."

My voice seizes in my throat. My knees grow weak and I stumble from the makeshift podium. The crowd doesn't even notice. A cuddle puddle has formed all around me. My cheeks flame with humiliation at all of the things that I've done, all of the fear that I've passed to others under the excuse of connection. And the one person I wanted to see most, I treated her worst of all.

I want to go home. I want to curl up in *Sweetheart* and sleep until the world forgets about me. But that won't fix anything. I need to see Mona. And I need to go to the police and free Barry, clear up this misunderstanding. Maybe there's even a way I can help find Bridgett Newman.

Tiptoeing around everyone to make my way to the front door has me hopeful when they don't stir. Perhaps they'll forget all about me. Perhaps this whole thing will be ruled off as a hallucination. Maybe one or two will turn their lives around now, but maybe not. My heart aches as I cast one last look at them all before heading out the door.

The sun is searingly bright high overhead as I walk toward the sidewalk. The neighborhood is quiet, the houses lining the streets are colorful, small, homey. The house I walk away from fits in perfectly among them. Its burgundy siding is clean, its windows are streak-free. No one would ever guess what goes on inside. And maybe nobody really cares. If they keep quiet when they're supposed to and keep mostly to themselves, maybe that's all anybody can ever ask of them.

"Wait!" Phillis calls from the doorway. I block out the sun with a hand to my brow and turn toward her. "I want to go home, too, for what it's worth."

I nod, not quite sure I understand.

"Thank you. I'm not sure what good it'll do, but thank you. Ashley's calmed down. I think they all liked your voice. It's cool what you do. A little scary, though."

"Yeah, it is. I think I'm done now. I'll be seeing you, Mama Bear." I turn back down the sidewalk and breathe in the scent of crepe myrtle and dry Texas air. The sun beats on my back and for once, I don't miss the chill air off the water as it blows across *Sweetheart*'s deck.

"Don't you want all your stuff? You earned it!" Phillis calls after me.

Without looking back, I hold my hand up in goodbye. "Keep it!"

Chapter Twenty-Two – Desdamona

"*It's your turn,*" *I groan as the car pulls up to the curb. Sandy stares blankly at it. "Did you hear me? Come on, I did the last one. Rock, paper, scissors?*"

She continues to stare ahead. I watch in confusion as another car pulls behind the first. Then another. Soon, faces fill the windows. Who are all these people? Just as I open my mouth to ask if Sandy knows, the street opens up, a crater forming in front of the line of cars.

"Stop! You're gonna die!" I try to run as the cars slowly begin to drive but my feet are glued to the filthy pavement. A funeral procession of sorts follows before us, one car after the other driving by. One by one, the cars plummet into the dark, gaping hole in the earth. As each car passes, the faces of all the people are laughing at me, their breaths fogging up the windows.

"Sandy! Help me stop them!"

"It's your fault," she says. I turn to stare at her. Why does it feel like a century has passed since I've heard that sweet voice?

"What?"

"You killed me," she says with a broad smile.

"You killed us all." Mel steps from a moving car to stand before me. The car crashes into the pit.

"You killed me." Rhiannon steps from the next car. Her hair sways behind her, then billows in the wind from her car as it disappears into the abyss.

I watch in horror as Nettie steps from another car. Her sweet face is twisted in rage. "It's your fault. We're all dead. Because of you!"

"The world is going to end, what don't you understand?"

"Ma'am, please calm down. We're here to help you. There's no need to be frightened."

"Frightened? More like paranoid from withdrawal. The drugs are to cope with this knowledge. These aren't some drug-fueled delusions!"

The remnants of the death dream fade. I open one eye tentatively, unsure who's in my bedroom and why. Wait, when did I get home? But my room isn't my room. Everything is drab, gray and beige. There's a speckled blue curtain circling around the bed I lie in. What the hell happened?

"Excuse me!" I yell through the paper-thin fabric, and the argument beside me quiets. The curtain is flung aside. A nurse with an irritated look on her face sees me and forces a smile.

"Good morning. I'll get the doctor."

I'm left staring where she left the curtain parted. A woman in a matching bed beside me offers a half-wave. "Hello, I'm Cassy. Did you know the world is gonna end?"

I nod at her and try to keep my eyebrows from rising. "What time is it?" I say as calmly and slowly as possible.

Cassy smirks. "Two in the afternoon. They brought you in late last night. Boy, can you sure snore. That must be some good sleeping pills you take. Can I have some? I won't tattle, I swear. I just need some sleep. It's scary knowing the world is gonna end and everybody just stares at you like you're crazy. Crazy Cassy, that's me."

"I don't take anything, sorry. Just haven't slept lately." I stare at the boring ceiling tiles and count the beeps of the monitor attached to me. An IV drips into my arm. I shift my legs and confirm my fear. A tube runs between my legs. My face twists in disgust. I've got to get out of here. I don't have time for this.

"Yeah, who can sleep in this world. It's like nobody believes that it's ending yet everybody subconsciously has to know it, right? I mean, just look at this shit." Cassy holds up a beige device wired to her bed. A TV somewhere on the other side of my half-drawn curtain blares the news.

"Fires and rioting continue in many areas across the country after the disappearance of the Death Psychic cult leader known only as Tod. Followers believe the leader may have been kidnapped. Sources confirm, however, that the psychic was last seen here, at this Dallas event center where he ran off in the middle of a planned tour visit. Business associate and family friend, David Williams, is urging supporters to reach out via social media if Tod is seen."

"Thank you, Celine. We've followed this Death Psychic before, haven't we?"

"Yes, Andrew. In fact, this psychic has frequently made headlines in many parts of the country and in the world. His brochure claims he can tell a person the time they will pass away. Followers after meeting with Tod have been known to riot, cause public nuisance, and have been arrested for disorderly conduct. His followers have reported feeling freed from conventional fears of death and no longer wish to behave among society. Most recently, one of the protesters from a group against the psychic infiltrated the group and committed suicide in front of the leader."

"That's terrible. Our thoughts are with the surviving family. Tell me, Celine, this psychic's services are advertised as cheap, correct?"

"That's correct, Andrew. His brochure claims the price is five cents, but there have been claims that tickets can run into the thousands. Investigators are looking into possible fraudulent activity, but my sources at the police department say this traveling team has been difficult to pin down due to the frequent unscheduled tours that only elite fans have knowledge as to where they may pop up next."

"Thank you, Celine. Perhaps the investigation spooked this Death Psychic. Viewers are encouraged to call in with any tips if you see this man. He was last seen wearing white pants, a white long-sleeve shirt, and a wooden beaded necklace."

"Turn that off, please." My stomach roils. It's all my fault. Stefan is missing because of me. The world has gone to shit because of me. He must have had a tour after he came to see me, and I caused him to run off. Everything I do, everything I try, and I make it worse. The world is literally on fire because of me.

Cassy sees the look on my face and switches off the TV. "Hey, I know it's scary, but I'm here. It's okay, it'll all be over soon, so you don't have to worry. What am I saying? I'm piss-scared and I've had years to get used to the idea. I'm sorry, I'll shut up now."

"Cassy, talk to me about something else. Distract me. Why are you in here?"

"Swapping war stories, huh? You know those kooks you see on the corner with signs, 'The End is Near!'? Yeah, that's me. Uppers to start my day to spread the word, downers to try to sleep at night. You know Elvis died with like fifty pounds of shit in him? Yeah, mixing uppers and downers will do that to ya. That's me. Every once in a while they gotta clean me out. Then I'm good as new. I was on my corner, spreading the good word. Then everything kept coming up and nothing would stay down. Went on for too long, knew what it was, and checked myself in. But they're holding me now. Been in one too many times, think I might be a danger to myself, you know the drill. Bitches keeping me from my pills. Don't they know the world's ending?"

She flashes an infectious smile. I smile back at her. She chuckles. Laughter bubbles up and pours out of me. I laugh and laugh until tears stream down my cheeks. My side protests from my deep belly laughter. Cassy stares at me like I'm the crazy one. The laughter turns to sobs.

"Aw, there, there, love. I'd come comfort ya but, you know." She holds up her hand high enough for me to see the restraints holding her to the bed. I laugh and cry harder. I'm in the room with the crazy lady. This is it. Hello, rock bottom.

"I used to be normal, you know. Had a career, tons in student loan debt, big ol' expensive house, fancy husband. The whole freaking works. Then one day, I'm walking down the street, enjoying a croissant and whistling. Bam! Some sucker knocks me over the head, takes everything worth anything. I mean, that's what I get for wearing Gucci, amirite? I wake in the hospital, they tell me I was dead for twenty minutes and that it's a miracle I'm unharmed besides the lump on the back of my head. I don't remember much about being dead, being beamed up to the sky and whatnot, then getting beamed back to my body is about it. But ever since then, I've known when the world is gonna end. It's soon, but I won't tell you how soon, 'cause I don't want to scare ya. Anyway, that's my story. Oh, and husband left me and took everything 'cause now I'm crazy. There. Now you know everything about me. So, what's your favorite color? Wait, what's your name?"

I rub the goosebumps that have risen on my arms. A near-death experience and now she has a new ability? Like me and Stefan. I stare back at her and she winks. Her hair is pink with gray and black roots. It stands out in a matted mess around her head. Her face and arms are tanned from a lot of sun exposure, but she has a farmer's tan of pasty white upper arms and shoulders. Her eyes are a pale grayish blue and her round face looks friendly.

"I believe you," I tell her. I sniffle and wipe away the tears that have begun to dry. "I'm Desda, glad to meet you, Cassy. Thanks for the distraction. I had a near-death experience once, too. When I was a little kid. Ever since, I know when someone is about to commit suicide and how they plan to do it. I've managed to stop a few but not enough."

Cassy stares at me, her eyes wide and her brow furrowed as if I might be the one mixing drugs. "For reals?" Her voice squeaks.

I nod, then plop my head back on the thin pillow. So, the world really is ending. Did everything I've worked for mean anything?

"Cassy." An older man walks into the room and offers her a nod. "Ms. Des—Dessed—" He pulls the curtain all the way open.

A bright sunshining day is illuminated beyond a tiny window. The room is otherwise unremarkable.

"Desdamona," I inform him. The doctor's name tag reads Dr. Linslow. He pulls at something on my head and peers underneath. "Stitches look good. You were asleep when they found you. Do you often have trouble sleeping?"

"I sleep like a rock, when I can. I run two businesses, so sleep doesn't always get penciled in."

Dr. Linslow pecks away on a tablet while nodding even though I've stopped speaking. I risk a glance at Cassy, who offers a thumbs up and an unnervingly large smile. I have no idea what that means.

"Okay, I'm going to prescribe you a sleep aid. Take once per day at bedtime. Get some sleep, and no more driving for a while, all right?"

His words give me pause. No more driving...that's right! "The van! I forgot I was driving, what happened to my van?"

The doctor frowns at me, wrinkles appearing all over his face. "If I recall, the report mentioned the van needed to be towed. You weren't severely hurt but responders did note they had to use the jaws of life to get you out. I don't know the details other than that."

I fall back to my pillows. Just what I need right now. That van had the basic insurance, basically coverage in case someone or something gets hurt. My handy blue van is totaled. Is there anything I haven't destroyed yet? Maybe I should hunt down Stefan and we can run away together.

"When am I gettin' outta here, Doc? I'll be good this time, I promise!"

"Not gonna be easy this time, Cassy. You were found passed out in the river. You're lucky you didn't drown. Until I know for sure you weren't trying anything dangerous, you're staying where you are."

"Ah, come on! I was woozy from low blood sugar. I must've fallen off the bridge. I was out there with my sign for a while, you know.

And people don't toss food nor coin at the 'end is nigh' weirdos like yours truly."

Dr. Linslow shakes his head as he leaves the room. Cassy blows a raspberry at his receding back. Their conversation has me stumbling from bed toward her.

"Hey, look at me." My voice sounds like it used to when Nettie first came to live with me and would keep her eyes glued to the floor. For a moment, Cassy's eyes remind me of my sweet Nettie's—big, round, innocent. A whoosh of air escapes my lungs when our eye contact doesn't warrant a suicide alert. So she really wasn't trying to kill herself. But she did lie when she told me that she'd checked herself in. As if reading my thoughts, Cassy shrugs, then offers a sheepish grin.

"It spooked me, falling in the water. I was so weak and hungry, I couldn't move. It's weird, knowing the world is ending and being so fixated on it that when the concept of death—my death, all alone and not alongside the entire world—was upon me, I'm pretty sure I pissed myself, I was so scared. Sorry I lied. I really do check myself in often to get my shit vacuumed out though, if it means anything."

I sit back on my bed, my hand coiled around the bar with all the tubes that connect to me. "You should come with me." As soon as I can get out of here, that is. Cassy's exchange with the doctor completely sidetracked me from asking about how soon that can be.

"Yeah, sure. Where to?"

I look at her and see so many of my dearly beloved rescues. She looks scared and alone, burying her vulnerability with drugs and her motormouth. I liked her immediately. In a way, I imagine she is what Sandy could have been, had I managed to save her and not break my promise to her. When Cassy's playful smile falls and turns somber, I hold her gaze steady. "We're going home."

Chapter Twenty-Three – Stefan

My phone battery is holding on better than I could've hoped. I'm thankful that my ringtone bothered Phillis enough for her to switch it off. If Detective Landers hadn't been so desperate to get a hold of me, I wouldn't be able to do this right now.

The phone trills against my ear as I jog across the street at an intersection. A few cars creep by through the neighborhood, nobody in any kind of hurry like I'd have expected right outside the big city. I switch over to my maps app and check where I'm headed before listening to more ringing.

Will Mona answer? Did she make it home from the hospital? Is that woman okay? I should've stayed and waited for her to make sure everyone was okay. I'm such a selfish ass for making it all about me. She was so worried about her friend, of course she barely registered my existence when I showed up out of the blue after all this time. She may not have recognized me at all, and that's okay. What matters now is that she's safe, her friend is all right, and that Mona knows I'm sorry for the way I acted but I'm here for her now.

The phone continues to ring. I run across another intersection and turn where the maps app prompts me.

"Stefan?"

I stumble into oncoming traffic and lurch back to a series of angry honks and someone yelling out the car window.

"Mona? Hi, it's Stefan!" I say awkwardly, then pause. "Look, I'm sorry about everything. I'm going to make it up to you. Are you okay? Is your friend all right?"

"I...my friend? I'm okay..." But behind her words I hear another woman's voice say, "Who's that? Your boyfriend? Is he hot?"

Relief floods through me. So they're okay. "Good. I'm glad everyone's all right. I'm sorry about yester—I mean, the other day. I was so happy to see you but then I...it was so selfish and I..." I had all the words planned in my head, but here now, talking with my sweet Mona on the phone, hearing her voice after so long and I can't think straight. I wander down a road unthinking and unsure if I'm going in the right direction.

"What do you mean? Where are you? Stefan?"

"I'm going to make everything right. I'm going to fix this, I promise. And Mona...thank you, for everything. For being there for me after all these years. You mean a lot to me, you know."

My chest clenches as my face heats. I hadn't meant to say all that. A knot forms in my throat as I wait for a response. But the only sound is the maps app beep; it sounds strange, another beep overlapping it. "Listen, I'll see you soon, but I've got to go. I've got to fix something before I see you, okay? Mona?"

I pull back and stare at the black phone screen. Shit, guess my battery wasn't as full as I thought.

• • • •

"I'M HERE TO TURN MYSELF in," I say with frustration and irritation leeching into my voice. I know there's nothing I did but Detective Landers didn't seem to believe that if the look of hatred he gave me was any indication. But the desk cop doesn't so much as blink at my obvious impatience.

"What was your name again?"

I launch into my tirade for the third time and demand to speak with the detective and to know what they've done with Barry.

"This all from the Chicago department, you're saying?"

"Yes!" I practice the soothing breaths that would normally keep my anxiety at bay but they do little to calm my rising frustration. "It's about the missing person's case, for Bridgett? Bridgett Newman? Detective Landers has been trying to reach me but he didn't leave a return phone number. That's why I'm here. Can you put me in contact with him, please? I believe he may have arrested my business partner in error. It's urgent. Please?"

The man harrumphs into his coffee mug and clacks away on a keyboard. I tap my toe and stare at his dull blue eyes. His time flashes in my mind but I look away and shake the thought from my head.

"Bridgett Newman, you said?"

"Yes." The word escapes through clenched teeth. Maybe the Chicago police care more about it than the Dallas police, but one would assume there'd be some kind of urgency. I flick my gaze back at the desk cop and his greasy blond eyebrows, but his puzzled look gives me pause. My familiar companions fear and anxiety take over.

"What? What is it?"

The man holds up a long, slender finger. "Gonna make a call."

I'm left to stare dumbly at his empty chair. Is he grabbing a crew to come arrest me? Had Barry known something I didn't and now I'm somehow involved? When the man finally returns, I'm practically vibrating in my shoes. I become intensely aware of my filthy clothes that I've been in for far too long and my matted hair and the likelihood that the stink of that house coats my skin and assaults the senses of everyone around me.

"Case is closed."

A lump forms in my throat. Is she dead and her body was found and that's why? Was Barry arrested and I'm next? My eyes flick to the glass behind the man and the busy hive of officers coming and going, but none seem to be headed for me with cuffs at the ready.

I stare at the desk cop expecting more information from him, but he clicks on the mouse in a slow and aimless fashion as if I'd been dismissed. "What does that mean?" My voice squeaks. I clear my throat and try to stand tall despite the quivering of my spine.

"She's alive and well. Can't tell you where, so that's that. Case is closed."

I stand there processing what he'd said. "When?"

He finally looks at me. He blinks in surprise as if he'd expected someone else, someone cleaner, older, wiser. "A while. Who'd you say you were looking for? Chicago didn't have any Landers. Detectives Olma and Yelnats were on the case. No Landers. Sorry, kid."

I collapse on the curb outside. The sun has gifted the air with an unbreathable haze. My shirt clings to my back and the stink on me bakes into my nostrils. Why wasn't Barry answering? I called him and Uncle David before calling Mona. I thought he'd been arrested but if not, then maybe they were mad that I ran off. But after so much time, surely they'd be worried by now. They didn't answer and never bothered to call me once after I ran off. And now my phone is dead. What do I do? I promised Mona I'd see her soon but I didn't accomplish anything. Are Barry and Uncle David back at the hotel? If Bridgett is no longer missing, who is this Landers guy and what's he want with me? Should I stay away from everyone if Landers is a threat? Has he already gotten to Barry and Uncle David and that's the real reason he's been in a hurry to find me?

"There you are! Hey, kid! Are you Tod?" The desk cop staggers out the front door of the station. I peer through the afternoon haze right as a drop of sweat drips into my eye. "I thought you looked familiar. There's an APB out on you, kid. 'Fraid you need to come with me."

I follow him inside and try to make sense of what he's telling me. "Uncle David?"

"Yes, a David Williams has requested the APB. I have his number here. You should let him know where you are."

The cop has returned to looking bored and clacking at his computer. I feel embarrassed at the thought that my stink will cling to the man's desk phone. I instinctively look at the phone in my hand but then feel foolish remembering it's a landline.

Uncle David put out the APB but not Barry? The number dialed in and waiting for me is their home phone. Not either of their cell numbers? So, they returned home instead of waiting at the hotel for me. A sense of betrayal slices my heart but I stop the negative thoughts and try to reason with the emotions that stir. No, they were worried and probably assumed I found my own way home, back to Michigan City, Indiana. They're back home while I'm stuck here in Dallas, Texas, a thousand miles away.

They're worried about me, but they're back home. Maybe Uncle David put out the APB because Barry is sulking and mad at me for leaving. That sounds like Barry. I should've called. But they're safe, Detective Landers doesn't have them in some crazy interrogation somewhere. Maybe I'd heard the name wrong and it wasn't Landers. I should probably make a stop at the Chicago police department before heading home to face Barry.

What about Mona? Will she wait for me to return? Should I stop and see her first, explain everything and tell her I'm done with the death psychic crap? Would Mona even want to see me after how I acted? My battery died before I could get much chance to apologize to her, see how she felt about it all. Can I even expect to come back into her life after so much time has passed? She might have someone. That's right, Nettie, her daughter. If she has a daughter...

I shake my head to clear the dread that forms. One thing at a time. The phone grows heavy in my hand. I'll see them soon. There's too much to be said over the phone anyway. I drop it back on the receiver and leave the desk cop to his game of solitaire. He doesn't even look up as I go.

Chapter Twenty-Four – Desdamona

"Miss Desda?" A soft voice startles me from my thoughts. I nearly drop my phone onto the table. Brice cowers in the doorway, staring at me with wide eyes that remind me of a deer about to flee. I gesture to the chair beside me and watch as he tiptoes into the kitchen.

"Hey, baby, how you doing?" He bobs his head in a stiff nod at my question, then stares at his chest. I reach for his chin and tip his head up until his gaze lands on mine. "What is it?"

"Mel okay?" His voice is a whisper.

"Yeah, I checked on her a little while ago. She's good. She wants to come back. I wanted to talk to you and Nettie about it first. We can help her, but I don't want to put you two at any risk of losing your new friend. I can't promise she won't try that again."

Brice's shoulders slump. "Yeah, I know. I...kinda wish she died. I'm such a shit person." Anger heats his normally gentle voice.

"No, baby, no. You wish she died because you don't like watching people suffer. Her suffering would have been over, she wouldn't have to figure out how to be normal again, like you and me, yeah?"

His eyes whip up and pin me. "How do you know stuff like that? Like you can read deeper into people. You're so wise. I want to be like that. You're strong, caring. Nettie adores you. You think...you think if I try to be like you, she'll adore me too?"

I smirk at him and he hangs his head, but an embarrassed smile accompanies the blush that steals across his cheeks. Yessica was right, love certainly is in the air. I can't stop the chuckle that rises. "Nettie already adores you, baby."

Brice's look is one of apprehensive joy. He fidgets under my stare. My smile fades. Mel is okay. Cassy is now here, among the other recent newcomers awaiting onboarding with my psych and drug team. But Rhiannon is still out there. Candy and Lila. And now Stefan.

What did he mean, he'll make it up to me, that he'll fix this? Fix what?

We've only messaged back and forth here and there, dancing around each other's stuck words and never crossing that line of deeper conversation. So many times I've typed out a message, admitting to all my sins in search of undeserved forgiveness. He's the only person who had ever accepted me as I was. He never begged me to stop, to change, he took me as I was. And I used him and cast him aside. Worse yet, I never told him the truth about what I did to his mother. What I nearly did to him, long before he came back into my life.

And now, after another bout of many years, he's trying to get back in again. Every time he gets close to me, I hurt him. What horrible things will I do to him next time? Do I hunt him down the way I desperately want to? Or do I let him go, once and for all?

"Hey, why wasn't I invited to the party? Yo, the name's Cassy. You the one who likes to hide in his room, the cutey I've heard Nettie's crushing on, ain't ya?"

Brice jumps in his chair startled at Cassy's loud and sudden appearance. He sits frozen with eyes so wide they're about to pop out of his head. I hide my smirk and wait for her words to register. I have to bite back a laugh as a deep red pools over his cheeks.

Cassy plops in the chair across from him on my other side. My fears begin to melt away at her presence and I've yet to find out what it is about her.

"Can't sleep, dear?" I laugh.

"Nope. Some rude bitch took away all my pills," she says with a broad smile. Brice looks at her as if she'd slapped me.

"You'll get used to her," I reassure him with a pat on his shoulder. "Now, why don't you try and get some sleep. Let Nettie know if you're having trouble."

Cassy lets out a childish and taunting, "Ooooooh." I've never seen Brice scamper faster back upstairs. She lets out a hoot and slaps her knee.

"Well, now that I spooked him off, what's the sitch?" At my blank stare, she prods right where it hurts. "Yeah, gimme the deets. You've been sulky since that hot number called you on our way here. So, boyfriend? Husband? Secret lover?" She waggles her eyebrows, then leans in conspiratorially.

"*Former* lover, if you must know. We haven't spoken much in years. I don't know what he was talking about, making it up to me. Nettie says there was someone here that looked excited to see me when Mel was being taken in the ambulance. But I never imagined it was Stefan. If he's here, I don't know what he's planning or what he's trying to make up for, exactly. I was the one who hurt him. Many times. And I've got an arsonist who has it out for me that I need to worry about. I can't just hop in the car again and go hunt Stefan down. Jacob and Adam have already been here for too many nights straight and..."

I stare at Cassy long and hard until she cocks her head at me. "What?"

"I don't do this."

"Do what?" She sits back with look I could only call pride. Or maybe she's smug?

"Talk. About me. Out loud. To other people. This is my business. You're not exactly a close friend or family. Even if you were, I deal with my own things myself."

"What could it hurt? Rely on somebody for once. Like you said, I'm not a friend—yet. Just some weirdo you picked up at a hospital. So, rope me in on some shenanigans. I've got nothing better to do but stand on a corner preaching about the end of the world."

• • • •

I DON'T UNDERSTAND why I'm telling her all this. The sun will be up soon and I'm on my sixth cup of coffee. But I don't feel any caffeine. I have a growing suspicion that Nettie bought a big bag of decaf and poured the grounds into my normal brew's bag. That girl. Cassy just stares and nods as I spill everything about my past and how I came to do what I do. And now, I'm catching her up on all the details on the latest things some random middle-aged white guy has tried to burn and destroy.

Yessica will be here soon. I wonder if she got a new car or how she's getting here. She's a little like me in a way, too stubborn to ask for help when she needs it. I hope she found a ride and doesn't walk through the night to get here on time. Maybe Cassy will have the same effect on her that she has on me. Even now the words are vomiting out of my mouth as if a dam has burst and Cassy just keeps on nodding along, unperturbed by my rambling that's lasted through the night.

"That explains the wonderful ashy graffiti on your porch." Cassy nods as if appreciating high art. I'd scrubbed at the charred word but managed to only give a smudgy outline to those three harsh letters.

"What about it? So you do know something!" Nettie appears in the doorway. Without a glance at the clock, I know she's over an hour early for starting breakfast. She pins me with a look of hurt and distrust. My heart sinks.

"Good morn' to ya, sweet thang! Your mama here was telling me about the arsonist who has it out for you guys. But don't you worry any, that's what I'm here for. I'm the best PI this side of the Mississippi. I'll catch the SOB before he can even think of striking another match, ya feel me?"

Nettie and I both blink at Cassy. She smiles with all her teeth showing. Neither of us are quite sure what to make of her. My heart hammers that maybe Cassy can help bridge the gap that has been growing between Nettie and me. I cast a weary glance at her but she refuses to meet my gaze. With a pout, she turns to making pancakes by clanging together every pot and pan as loudly as she can.

The first rays of the sun begin to streak through the house. Dust particles dance in the golden light. The yellow hue reminds me of Sandy's favorite eyeshadow. Cassy yawns in a deep suck of air that sounds as if someone had dropkicked a donkey. Her chair creaks as she kicks back to balance on two legs. A black ring in my coffee mug draws my eye.

Footsteps of everyone above us brings dirt and insulation to drift from the ceiling. A flake of chipped paint floats down, then perches delicately on the surface of my coffee. Like a soft cherry blossom, it swirls before sinking to the bottom of the black liquid. A knock jerks my attention away from my drink.

Shit. I forgot to unlock the door for Yessica. But when I pull open the thick front door, I stumble back in surprise when I find she's not alone. Her face is twisted in disgust.

"Look who I found lurking around!" She all but screams this like a victorious battle cry before shoving a dark figure forward. The man is clad in a filthy blue hoodie and dark jeans. He stumbles and collapses at my feet. Yessica stomps in to kneel in front of him as she kicks the door behind her. I wince as it slams closed.

The man's hand smacks the old hardwood floor as he tries to reach for his hood but Yessica slaps at him. I stare at the deep color and smooth skin. My voice lodges in my throat.

"What the hell did I ever do to you, huh? I saved up everything I had for that car! I loved that car! Now I have to ride the filthy bus and I fucking hate the bus, *puta madre*!" Yessica's voice cracks on a sob but this only enrages her further. Cassy jumps forward and grabs her arm right as she swings down at the bent over man. I stagger back a step and only then notice Yessica's foot is clamped on the man's other arm. Nettie rushes in with a cast iron pan in her grasp.

I fall to my knees before him. My fingers gingerly reach through golden-tinted air to touch him. His cheeks feel icy on my fingertips. My chest squeezes as tears prick my eyes. A lump forms in my throat. I swallow around it until I can squeeze one word out. "Stefan?"

Cassy pulls Yessica away from him. With his arm freed, he clamors upright and throws off his hoodie. Those glorious golden eyes blink back at me. His fiery brown hair is matted beneath the hoodie and a sudden stink burns my nose. But my lip is trembling and my hand is tingling where it rests on his.

"Hi, Mona."

Chapter Twenty-Five – Stefan

"Hi, Mona." My voice trembles as I stand. My brows furrow in confusion when she shrinks in front of me as I lengthen to my full height. Have I grown since we were kids, happily lazing away the night hours on *Sweetheart*'s deck? Mona seems startled too as her head keeps falling back with every inch that I rise. My thoughts flit to wondering whether I get my height from my father, like how I must've gotten the red in my hair, freckles, and a hint of pale white skin from him, but I quell the curiosity.

"H-hi," she stammers. Her full lips are gnawed between her bright white teeth. Her hand raises toward me but then falls to her side again. My cheek tingles where her fingertips had grazed me. I step forward, then stop myself. I want so badly to wrap my arms around her, but there's a girl over her shoulder holding a skillet looking ready to kill me, and there's the angry woman beside her who threw me inside and is currently pinning me with warring looks of hatred and confusion.

"Ladies, this is Stefan. He's a...really good friend of mine."

"Hi." I nod my head at them. The skillet girl narrows her eyes at me. The angry woman blinks a few times as she processes Mona's words. There's another woman I hadn't noticed before. She stands in the doorway to what I assume is the kitchen. She puts a hand on skillet girl's shoulder, who lowers the skillet and watches as the woman strides forward.

Vibrant pink curls flop with her every step. She stares deep into my eyes. *3:14 a.m.* flashes in my mind. But right when her time fills my thoughts, she cocks her head as if she can hear it too. Her eyes bore into mine and I suddenly feel exposed.

"Hiya, Stefan. Name's Crazy Cassy. But you can call me Crazy. Welcome, handsome. Desda here's told me all about you. She's just nuts about you. So go on." Cassy steps back and pushes Mona toward me, startling us both as she stumbles and bumps into my chest. My arms instinctively surround her. She stares up at me and I can't for the life of me remember when I'd gotten so tall and how her lips could be so far away from mine.

"Jeez, Stefany boy, you reek." Cassy waves a hand under her nose. Mona blinks rapidly and pulls from my awkward embrace.

"Sorry, it was the crack house I've been staying in last couple days—uh, long story."

• • • •

I STARE AT THE PURPLE PVC primer staining my fingers. The new plumbing for the upstairs bathroom shines bright white with flashes of purple amid the old stained wood surrounding it. I mentally tally all the new wood I'll need to pick up at the hardware store. All the while, I can feel her eyes on me.

The ladder shakes as I shift from foot to foot. I glance over my shoulder and meet her dark eyes. She scowls but refuses to look away. My hand massages the base of my neck as Mona—Desda, as she's called now—appears beside me, cold drink in her hand. I take the proffered glass and down the contents while pretending not to notice the silent exchange between her and her daughter. Not for the first time, I wonder about Nettie.

Her dark skin. Her height that almost matches Desda's. How old is she? Desda must have adopted her. How did they meet? Had Desda been with someone, unable to conceive, and they adopted Nettie and now Desda raises her alone? Or is that Adam guy from the van her husband?

I can't help but glance toward the door, waiting for him to trudge through and shake up the happiness that has tentatively built with every passing hour. The angry woman has a thick Mexican accent and chats into a phone while working at a makeshift desk in the dining room next to me. She and the skillet girl—Nettie—have been eyeing me as I've worked on fixing the plumbing that I noticed was leaking.

I pick stray lint off the borrowed shirt I was given after being all but thrown into a bath. The shirt is far too tight and stretches and pops if I breathe too deeply. A lock of my hair hits my face and I swat at it irritably. Nettie strides to stand at the foot of the ladder. She eyes me silently, then stretches out her hand. A hair elastic dangles from her slender fingertips. I take the olive branch and offer a weak smile.

When had my hair gotten so long that I need one of these? After the third attempt to tame my locks into the damn thing, giggling has me freezing in place. All around me are women laughing at my struggle. My face ignites until even my ears and chest are burning. This only makes them laugh harder. The ladder tips as I fight with my hair and their laughter collectively lodges in their throats.

"Here, let me." Desda's gentle touch stills the ladder, and my fight with my hair ends in defeat. Her delicate fingers stir unwarranted sensations as my scalp tingles from her touch. With a few quick twists, my hair is successfully tied back. I straighten from the awkward bend and pat at my head. I must look ridiculous in this teeny t-shirt and this ponytail. But when I glance around the room, I notice Desda and Nettie are blushing as they stare at me. The woman working in the dining room wiggles her eyebrows at me.

"Damn, you are looking fine, Mr. Stefan." Cassy whistles and the noise is so shrill that my ears ring. I bow my head in awkward thanks even though I know I look absolutely foolish. She much be trying to ease my obvious discomfort. "So, what are you gonna fix up next, hottie handyman?"

I twitch as all eyes are back on me. When I'd descended the stairs after scrubbing the crack house stink off of me and then squeezed into this little boy's shirt, a fat drop of water plopped right on the top of my head. The old hardwood floor beneath my feet was soft and weak from years of water damage. The desire to fix that Grandpa had instilled in me begged to address the leak before the water from my bath could dry.

I take in the house around me. The peeling paint, the exposed wires where grand chandeliers used to glitter. The floors that've worn to raw wood that's deeply grooved and chipped all over. The bathroom upstairs looked all original, with a rusty clawfoot tub and tiny pink pedestal sink. As I'd walked up to the house, I noticed broken windows in places and the roof had missing shingles.

A strange feeling of peace washes over me. I think of Grandpa's house and all its warmth. The glossy floors and scent of flowers wafting in from the gardens through the open windows. This old broken down Victorian house gives me that same feeling. *Home.* This is how I can repay her for years of our friendship, how I can make it up to her when I'd abandoned her in her time of need.

"Where shall I start?"

• • • •

MY BONES ARE TIRED. It has been years since I've fallen into bed after exhausting every ounce of energy tackling big house projects. It feels like I've done a few rounds of Grandpa's spring cleaning. My lips lift in the corners as I inhale the scent of Mona's sheets. For so many years I've slept fitfully in hotels around the world, drenched in sweat at the thought of all the people I'll read the next day. The ache that's already starting in my lower back and upper arms is a welcome one. For a moment, it feels as if Grandpa will pop his head in my bedroom door and ask if I'd like to join him for a midnight snack.

For the first time in so long, I'm excited for tomorrow. For the projects I'll tackle, the wood I'll tear out, and the trees I'll plant. For the painting, and the hammering, and the sanding. And for time with Mona. I'll get to see her in her world, see her in daylight without counting down the dwindling minutes. And I won't have to face millions, just a small handful of women and the group of people who also stay here that Mona calls "rescues". Tomorrow with Mona. And the day after, and the day after that.

I begin to drift into a peaceful slumber at that thought when a waking dream teases me. I'd swear I could hear the creak of the bedroom door. I wait for Grandpa's words. Warmth floods my heart at the memory-like dream. But a shift in Mona's bed jerks me fully awake. I freeze and listen, waiting for any indication that I'd really dreamt it.

Then a cool finger reaches through the darkness to stroke my cheek. My breath freezes and my pulse spikes. The bed shifts again.

"Hey," her soft voice whispers.

"Hi," I croak.

"Cassy's a bed hog. Do you mind?"

"Uh-uh."

The silence swallows up the roaring in my ears until I begin to fear I've gone deaf to everything but that sound. But then she sidles up next to me, her warmth igniting the small space between us. And the ache of losing her across time begins to recede. Had I ever told her how much those summer nights meant to me? My anxiety rears its ugly head and whispers doubt in my ear. What if she'd left notes trying to reconnect to all her old clients? What if I'm not really anything all that special to her yet I keep popping up when I need something from her?

I kill the awful thoughts before the excitement her nearness brings can fade. I roll toward her and my hand brushes against her. Was it the softness of her hand I'd grazed? Or the delicate skin of her thigh? Heat spreads through me.

"I-I'm happy you're here. Thanks for all your hard work today. I bet you're really tired since you got here just after dawn and we worked you to the bone. I won't keep you up."

Her words are stiff, as if she were speaking to a paid helping hand and nothing more. Foolishness replaces the warmth that had grown within me. Of course. Any relationship we'd had in the past was paid for. I'd thought I made it clear I wasn't paying for anything more than her freedom and company for a few hours a week, but maybe she thought she owed me. Maybe everything was one-sided and I've only just now realized it.

"Mona?"

"Desda. Please. It's Desdamona, but Desda. That name...was for a different life."

"Oh...sorry, right. Desda." It feels awkward to utter after so many years worshipping her name with my tongue.

"What is it?"

"I missed you. A lot."

Silence greets my admission. Panic grips my throat. I swallow. A noise reaches my ears. Is...is she crying?

"Mo—Desda?"

"I'm sorry. I'm so sorry, Stefan."

My hands search for her. I wrap around her and pull her close to me. "What for?"

Her body is racked with sobs. When she'd disappeared, I remember thinking she'd run off with that guy from her neighborhood whose name I can no longer remember. But as the years have passed, I realized she must've gotten out. She must've escaped from working the streets and made a better life for herself. And after seeing the home and business she's built, the sense of betrayal when she left without goodbye began to lift.

"I stole twenty thousand dollars from you." She hiccups a sob.

Her words freeze me in place. She...what? "When?"

"Y-you don't know?" Her cries fade. I can feel her staring at me. My brow furrows as I search back through my memories.

"I remember my bank questioned our withdrawals, but that's about it."

"So you never looked at how much I was taking from you? Never?"

"Never. I trusted you." And I didn't care. I'd just lost Grandpa. His money may have been in my account, but it wasn't really ever mine. I saw the commas and all the zeroes and it meant nothing to me. The money he left behind wasn't him. The house he left with all his clothes and smells stuck inside wasn't him. Even *Sweetheart* was pale comfort. Mona was all I wanted. She was then and is now.

"You shouldn't have. I siphoned twenty grand from you. I took advantage of you."

"Why?" My question isn't out of accusation, I'm merely curious. Had she asked for the money, I'd have gladly handed it all to her, every last nickel.

"Do you remember Sandy?"

I listen to the horror of what happened to that strange girl I remember. I think I still have the book she'd given me sitting somewhere near my hammock on *Sweetheart*. The last words she ever said to me make my blood turn to ice.

"And after I saw her lying there, gone, I ran. I ran and never looked back. I don't even know what happened to Mama. Her house isn't there anymore. B-but if it means anything, I used the money to start my business. I couldn't save her, but I save as many victims of sex trafficking as I can now, in her honor."

"Mona—shit, sorry, I mean, Desda. I gave her her time of death." Desda grows quiet as she waits for me to explain. "I'd forgotten about it until just now. When I read her she said, 'Yeah, I can do that.' I never figured out what she was talking about. I should've realized what she was planning to do. I could've stopped her. I'm so sor—"

"Don't. Don't blame yourself. I'm the one who could've stopped her but ignored it."

"Ignored what? How could you have known?"

Desda inhales deeply. My heart skips as she nuzzles against my chest. "You know how you can tell the time someone is gonna die? Well...I can do something too. I know if someone is gonna kill themselves and how they're gonna do it. If someone plans to, I'll hear *by car,* or *by bridge* in my mind. That's what my travel business is about, saving people from taking their lives and sending them on life-changing trips to help them embrace life again. And the proceeds go to helping my rescues who've worked the streets."

I process everything she's said. My mind reels from all this insight into the woman I thought I knew. She has a special ability like me. She's like me. So she knew Sandra was about to jump in front of that car.

"And don't say I couldn't've known when she was going to do it. I know it wasn't something I was taking seriously every time I heard those words in my mind whenever she'd look at me. I know I couldn't possibly have realized it was real in time to save her. But I carry her death with me all the same. So don't say it isn't my fault. I don't blame myself for not figuring it out soon enough. I...I blame myself for not buying her freedom sooner. I blame myself for not robbing you sooner."

Desda tries to pull away from me. I pull her tighter to me. Through the darkness, I search for her. My nose taps the bridge of hers. I lean my forehead against hers and nuzzle into the contact. "I'm sorry," I whisper.

"Don't." Her voice is tight as tears threaten to spill. I can hear her struggle against the emotions that make her body tremble. This is the first time I've held her in a bed. This is the first time I've held her without watching the clock and dreading her departure. And this is the first time she's opened up to me. Why did I wait so long to find her?

"I'm glad the money helped you build your dreams. And if you want more, for anything, I'll gladly give it. I'm just happy to see you again. T-to be near you again. Whatever way you think you've wronged me, don't. I forgive y—"

My words are cut off as the most glorious thing happens. Desda presses her lips to mine. Her tears fall on my cheeks and trail along my neck. My hands find their way into her full, wild hair. Her kiss is far too delicate for the raging emotions within me. It has been years since I've felt her touch. Years since I've felt this yearning. She was my first, and my last.

For a moment, I'm back in the park, on that bench where I'd held her close. I'm back in our past when the future looked so bright and the world was still at my fingertips. I can almost feel the sway of my hammock beneath us as Lake Michigan's waves envelop *Sweetheart* in its own tender embrace.

When she pulls back and lays her head against my chest, I wonder about the thoughts swirling in her head. What would it have been like had I been born with the ability to read thoughts instead of death times? Would it have changed anything? Would I have been here, in her arms just like this, far sooner?

Her breath is soft against my burning flesh. Her bed beneath me feels more welcoming than any other I have ever lain in. The house speaks to us in that creaking way that only century-old houses can.

The exhaustion creeps up on me. I settle into her warmth and allow myself to drift off. Strange words chase me into a deep and dreamless sleep.

"I'm sorry I killed your mother."

Chapter Twenty-Six – Desdamona

The sun glistens against his back. I cower in the shadows of the living room and watch as he works on pruning my fruit trees in the front yard. The neighbor woman has suddenly decided the rose bushes dividing our yards also need pruning. I smirk as she does more staring than pruning. I can practically see her mouth watering.

Stefan's long toned limbs stretch for a higher branch and his biceps bulge as he squeezes the pruning tool until the offending branch plops to the ground. A tingle dances up my spine as I watch him. A week has passed since Yessica threw him at my feet. I've barely spoken to him since that night. The night that I kissed him before he could say those words.

I don't deserve his forgiveness. I don't deserve all this effort he's put into fixing up my house. The main level looks bright and clean with its new coat of pale gray flat paint. The bathroom upstairs no longer rains on unsuspecting victims walking below. There's a pile of new hardwood that was delivered by the pallet that is sitting in my front yard, waiting to be laid out in every room. The cost of the wood alone has my panic rising.

I already owe him the twenty grand I'd stolen years ago. With interest, that number has obviously grown. And now all this work he's putting in. I can't not pay him back. It's obvious I'm avoiding him yet he works on, unperturbed. The moment he enters the house, I sneak into a bathroom or empty bedroom and hide. And while he's out, I find myself right back here, cowering in the shadows, staring, yearning.

"Desda? Hello? Are you all right?" Adam lays a hand on my shoulder. The contact and his words have me jumping and biting back a startled squeal.

"What? Yes, just...thinking."

Adam follows my gaze out the front window. His eyes narrow as Stefan hauls tree limbs into a new wheelbarrow. "Want me to make him leave? He's clearly making you uncomfortable. He expecting a fat paycheck for all this?"

Adam practically spits the words. I stare at the ground. "No. He's always been like this, a giver. He's not making me uncomfortable. It's...nothing. Never mind. Have you seen Cassy?"

Adam turns his skeptical look on me. I glance away and find my gaze landing back on Stefan, who waves at the neighbor. She lays a hand on her chest as she waves back, her cheeks blazing.

"Are you sure you don't want me calling the police? It's all over that they're looking for him. Haven't you heard about all the looting and nonsense because of him? I heard there's some girl missing that's got to do with him, too. I don't trust him, Desda."

Adam takes a step toward me, his hand outstretched as if to grab me but I move out of his reach. "He's been there for me for many years. This," I wave a hand around at the house, "is because of him. I owe him this life I live. I don't know all the details of what happened, but we're a safe place for people who need us. And right now, Stefan needs me."

I stomp from the room, unsure why Adam's skepticism has me so rattled.

· · · ·

"DESDA!" STEFAN'S VOICE echoes through the house and shoots straight through me. My heart dances at the deep sound of his commanding voice. I've never heard him speak with such gumption. But there's an urgency that has me running for him. When I find him standing in the doorway, I notice two shadows behind him.

"Hey, girl!" Lila steps around him with her hand raised in greeting. Her face is horribly swollen and her lip is split and openly bleeding down her shirt.

Candy peeks around Stefan and bobs her head at me. "Offer still stand?"

"My God, girls! Yes, of course. Come in, come in! Adam! Get the first aid kit!"

Stefan fidgets in the hallway outside the kitchen. I watch as Jacob expertly stitches Lila's forehead before moving on to her lip. Adam sits at the far end of the table, casting worried glances at the girls and an occasional scowl at Stefan. Nettie busies herself making something that smells sweet.

The girls' pimp found out about our little operation. It was only a matter of time. He attacked them, burned all their things, and was about to mutilate their faces to prevent them ever working the streets again when they'd managed to escape. By the looks of them, they put up a hell of a fight.

Since Cassy arrived, every room has been full here. All six bedrooms are doubled up with the exception of my bedroom where Stefan is staying. I try to sleep on the floor in Cassy's room but that woman never sleeps. Where am I going to squeeze two more? Maybe with Stefan's help I could create a temporary bedroom in the living room.

"We're full up," Jacob's gravelly voice announces in his usual abrupt and direct way. I sigh as their looks of hope fade into apprehension and fear. My eyes flit to Stefan and I catch his gaze. If he weren't here, they could have my room. My heart sinks at the thought of losing him again. But they have to come first.

"We can't stay here," Candy says softly. My pulse begins to pound. Her words...there's something they haven't told us.

"It's nothing all that bad, really." Lila puts her hands up. Her bandages crinkle as she forces a smile. "It's just...when we said he found out...he found out about everything. Including..."

"This house," Candy finishes for her.

Everyone freezes. They said their pimp had set fire to their things. Could it be him? Now that he's lost these two, will he be coming to exact his revenge? Had Yessica's car and the fire graffiti of "die" on the porch been precursors to the grand finale of his vindication?

Lila jumps to her feet. "We told him there were tons of big guys with guns and loads of hidden cameras. He's a pussy, his ass won't dare show up here. Honest!"

"But still, we can't stay here. We should be going anyway. We just..."

Lila sits back down and finishes Candy's words for her. "We hoped you could help. I know we don't deserve it after betraying you like this. But we had nowhere else to go. We're really sorry."

I open my mouth to reassure them but Stefan steps into the room. All eyes turn to him. "They can stay with me. I mean, um...at my grandpa's old place. It's up in Michigan City, back home where we're—I'm from. It's been untouched for years but I can fix up whatever needs fixing."

"You've done enough. Really, I can't ask for more, Stefan." *Please, I already owe you far too much. An entire house for my girls is far beyond anything I deserve.*

But pride aside, their lives are at risk. Everyone here may be at risk. They may not think this guy is a threat, but if he's already set fire to my porch, a fire that could've burned down my entire house had it not been put out in time, who knows what he's capable of.

"Your pimp, what's his name again? Is he white, middle-aged?" Adam leans forward, cutting Stefan's offer out of the conversation.

"I think his name is Miguel but he always made everyone call him Big Daddy. No, he's not white. I think he's from Latin America, actually. Yeah, I'd say he's middle-aged thereabouts or so. Why?" Lila cocks her head to the side, then winces at the movement.

A collective breath leaves us while the girls and Stefan watch in confusion. So it couldn't be their pimp, after all. Unless...he hired someone to do his dirty work. Just as hope had befallen us, more worries niggle their way back in. Everyone's eyes widen and I imagine the same thoughts are racing through all our heads. If he wasn't the one behind it, who could it be? How many more pimps out there know about this place?

Nettie glances at me, then quickly looks away. She still hasn't spoken to me since the accident. My chest throbs but I turn to the issue at hand. I rub a hand over my face and swallow back the protests that rise.

"Okay. Go with Stefan. That's the safest bet. We'll all have to continue to be on high alert. Whether its Miguel or another pimp, he's gotten bolder."

"High alert?" Stefan and Lila question in unison.

"It's nothing for any of you to worry about. We've got it handled. Stefan, are you sure about this?"

His eyes soften as they meet mine. This situation is killing me. The thought of sending him away has my heart aching. Is this how it ends for us? He runs a safe house for my rescues over a thousand miles away and we continue life apart all over again? A nasty thought rises. If he leaves, I can wash my hands of him and my guilt. He'll never have to know the truth.

"Yeah, I have a few things I need to do back home anyway. It's time I settled a few things." His smile is so sincere that I want to hit him.

• • • •

THE NEXT DAY I STAND in the airport parking lot, watching as the plane leaves. I'd avoided him the rest of the night. When he wasn't looking, I slipped a note in his bag. By this time tomorrow, he'll likely have found it and he'll finally know the truth. He'll probably never speak to me again. Sickness settles in my gut knowing I did it again.

I've taken advantage of him. He'll offer a safe place for the rescues who need to get far away even though I'll have hurt and abandoned him again. But it was time he knew the truth. And alongside the note, I put a check for all the money I owe him. Now that the money is gone and out of my reach, I can start focusing on putting more aside to fix Nettie's teeth and the rest of the house.

It's time I start taking care of all the things I've been neglecting while I've focused so much effort on saving up the money to repay him and distracted myself from the guilt of what I've done to him and to his mother. The plane ascends toward the clouds and with each moment that further separates us, I begin to let go of all the guilt. Once I've earned his hatred, I can finally be free from my own backpack full of guilt and shame.

But right as the connection to him severs by my own hand, a new thread wraps around my throat in its place. I can feel the pull. Someone nearby is planning suicide. Without a second glance at the plane, I hop in the rental car I'd picked up to use while I search for a replacement van. The thread squeezes tighter with every turn. I'm puzzled as each passing mile brings me closer and closer to home. Panic sets in as I near my block. But the thread jerks suddenly and I'm passing my house with a breath of relief.

A man in a gray hoodie casts a look at my car, then continues jogging down the sidewalk. I creep next to him when I feel the thread pulling taut. It's him. As his eyes connect with mine, *by fire* fills my mind. But the moment I stop to get out and get to know him, he takes off down an alley. I veer around to go after him, adrenalin pounding through me, but he's nowhere to be found.

I slam on the brakes and focus on my breaths. I can find him. The thread is strong. He'll be a welcome distraction from the pain in my chest.

Chapter Twenty-Seven – Stefan

Candy hand-tills the ground where Grandpa's garden once stood proud. She swipes at the sweat pooling on her forehead. Lila laughs as she struggles to jump on a shovel but her tiny frame does little to drive the spade into the hard earth. I showed them the garden tools in the shed and the old stash of seeds. It's late summer, far too late for any real growth of a vegetable garden, but the task will give them a better sense that this place is their home now. Or for as long as they need it.

We've been here a few days. I've yet to bring myself to visit Barry and Uncle David. And I've fought the urge to go to *Sweetheart*. There are so many emotions painfully swirling within me that I can hardly bring myself to smile as Lila looks up and waves.

I wave back from the kitchen window and look down at the meat I've prepped for dinner. The house is like an eerie time capsule to my past. I can feel Grandpa everywhere in this house. I haven't stepped foot inside once since the day I ran away. But somebody has been coming by, keeping up on everything. All the packages I thought were being sent and stored here by someone Barry hired are nowhere to be found. He must have thrown it all away.

But the thought doesn't give me the angst it normally would have. I let go of the ties I'd clung to from all those that I've read. I still have their names and times all documented, some in notebooks and many in digital format somewhere on the cloud. But one glance at the clock and the names of all those who have death predicted at that exact moment fill my mind, and it confirms that I'll remember all of them for years to come. Their faces may fade and the short time we shared together as we exchanged a few sentences may be forgotten in time, but I'll always remember their names.

Without my trinkets piling up in every corner as I'd expected to find when we first arrived here, the house needed minimal repairs to be returned to working order. The thermostat was left at a comfortable temp so no pipes froze over the many winters it sat abandoned. The toilets were coated and tinted with winterizing solution from whoever Barry paid to come here. He never said a word about it. In a way, it feels almost as if Grandpa's ghost has been keeping the place, and that he and his house have been here, trapped in time, awaiting my return.

The house is smaller than I remember. I have to bow my head slightly through the doorways. My bedroom looks hardly large enough for me to have existed inside at the same time as a bed and a teenage attitude. Grandpa's room and the guest room that was once my mother's are still rooms I find myself unable to go in. Candy and Lila were given free reign of choosing where they wanted to sleep, but both decided to stay in Grandpa's room.

Unable to sleep in my old bed and unwilling to disturb the strange illusion of a time disruption, I sleep on the sofa. The bow its tiny frame forced my back into is almost reminiscent of my hammock on *Sweetheart*. Almost. I stretch my stiff back after sliding the roast into the oven. Movement in the kitchen window catches my eye.

Lila flings dirt at Candy, who laughs and throws something in turn. By Lila's reaction of screaming and dancing, I'd imagine it must've been a bug. Candy's hands are on her knees as she doubles over in laughter. My heart warms at that sight. I don't know these women well, but after listening to their story and their connection with Desda on the trip here, I know laughter and happiness like this is a stranger to them.

I hold up my phone to catch a video to send to Desda right as Lila flings more dirt at Candy. She rubs at her face and scowls back with dirt caked over one eye. Lila runs to her side to assist her and her face is etched in apology beneath her fading bruises. To my surprise and embarrassment, Lila grabs Candy's face and kisses her.

Soon, I'm awkwardly standing slack-jawed in the kitchen recording two women as their kiss turns deeper. I turn away and delete the video. Desda wouldn't have responded if I'd sent it to her anyway.

Ever since we left, she's been ignoring me. She'll be on the phone with one of the girls but at my request to talk to her, something will come up. She's been avoiding me since she kissed me. Just like she would do years ago. I'd felt rejected and used before. Now I feel sad and angry with myself. Candy and Lila have shared so much of their lives that it was a slap in the face for me to realize what intimacy must be like after surviving what they have. Maybe that's how it is with Desda.

Once I finish what I need to here, I'll set things straight with her. I love being near her. I desire her more than anything. But if intimacy is something that's hard for her after the life she's lived, she needs to know that I'll stay by her side, that I'm not interested in doing anything that reminds her of her past. I should stop putting off what I need to do so I can get back to her sooner.

"Dinner's in the oven. It'll take a couple hours. I've got a few things I need to do so..." My words fail as I stare at Candy's hands. She clutches green vines and yanks them from the garden before tossing them onto a pile of pulled vegetation.

"What? Oh no, were those not weeds? I don't know a thing about plants. I'm sorry! Can I just replant them?"

I stare at the potatoes dangling off the wilting vine. I thought nothing from the garden survived. But there, a potato from Grandpa's garden. A potato plant that he and I had put in this very soil many years ago. After all this time, its overgrown and replanted itself.

"No, no, it's fine," I mumble as I rub the dirt off a small spud. Tears prick my eyes. I shove it into my pants pocket and turn to the girls, ignoring their confusion. "Listen, I've got errands to run but I'll be back before the roast is done."

• • • •

IT'S ALL STILL SO BROWN. Just as with Grandpa's house, Uncle David and Barry's is so much smaller than I remember. I feel like a giant on their small, tight porch. There's a stack of newspapers at my feet that I gather while I wait for someone to answer the door. The mail and newspapers make me second-guess that anyone's inside, and I start to wonder if they'd gone off to look for me after I didn't call.

Unease settles in my stomach. I fumble the newspapers to one arm and dig out my phone, finally calling the number I'd avoided for far too long. But the phone blares in my ears an unfamiliar tone I haven't heard in years. Barry's phone is disconnected? What the hell is going on? Irritated and knowing it's useless, I bang hard on their door.

I pound the frail wood with all the anger at myself for running away and my cowardice for never calling. All this time I thought I'd never make the same mistake again as I did with Grandpa and yet I've buried my head in the sand all the harder. But as I lay defeated against the grain, the door suddenly gives way and I find myself bent into a warm familiar chest.

"There you are, baby." Uncle David's voice is soft and comforting. I cry into his embrace as the newspapers plop around our feet. "Come, come."

I'm dragged to the sofa and patted on the back and all the twisted emotions keep pouring out. A hot steamy mug is pressed into my hands and all over again, I'm transported in time. But as I sniffle and take a sip, bitter burned coffee assaults my senses where I'd expected sweet and creamy cocoa. I hide my distaste and set the mug on the coffee table.

The house is as kept as Grandpa's, captured in amber resin and showing no signs that nearly a decade has passed. My eyes dart around the room and its doorways, searching for a scowl. But as Uncle David collapses with a disturbing amount of weakness, my thoughts turn from awaiting Barry's barrage.

Uncle David regards me with sad, drooping eyes. His skin has turned from glossy brown with a pinkish hue to sallow. His cheeks, once round and jiggly as his belly, now hang against his jawline. He runs a hand through his hair that looks disheveled and far from its usual coiffed array. I watch in confusion and horror as his hand falls to his armrest with a strange weightlessness that reminds me of a whisp of ash descending from a once raging fire.

"Where's Barry?"

"I...I don't know, kiddo. He left not long after you." Uncle David says this as if he's on the verge of drifting to sleep.

"Did you two have a fight? Is it because of me? I'm sorry about everything, I should've called. I should've—"

He raises a frail hand and I stop, wait. "No. I'm sorry, Stefan. No easy way to say it but we used you. I'm the one who's sorry, my boy. Jeb would be so angry to know what we've done."

At the mention of my grandfather's name, Uncle David's eyes drift to stare at the wall. He reminds me of the many who've come to see me with terrible illnesses, hoping somehow their time of death could save them, or perhaps free them. Like Bridgett Newman. I wait for him to explain but when he continues staring, I prompt him with, "What do you mean?" to elaborate, all the while my unease grows.

"I'm sick. Have been for some time. Back when Jeb was still around, we found it. My mama, she had it bad. And she fought so hard to win. Yup, win she did." Uncle David nods as if at a church sermon. He sips from a glass of water that's so smudged, it looks like it's been reused for weeks. "My mother did chemo. It killed her."

"I didn't know your mom died of cancer."

"She didn't, she died of old age. But the chemo killed the woman I remember, the carefree hippie who loved life itself. The chemo kicked the cancer. But every cold, every time she slept wrong, it was the cancer coming back. She wasn't afraid of it, but the treatment.

She said food tasted like sand. And everything smelled like burned chemicals. The softest fabrics were like needles in her skin. I could've tried the treatment, but I knew it would change me. I'm tired and things ache more than they used to, but I'm still me. When this thing wins, I'll still be me."

I sit and process what he said. His mother had cancer, survived. He has cancer, has known since Gramps was still around, and he refused treatment. Sorrow clutches my throat as I look at him. He's withered away from the jolly man I remember. Would he still be here had he tried chemo? Would he be even weaker than he is now?

"Barry...he couldn't accept my choice. That's...where you came in." He settles into his chair and reclines the leg support as if settling into a good bedtime story. "With your talent and the dollar signs that sprouted in his eyes when he found out, he had it all figured out. Those papers may say he stole from you, embezzled from your company, then ran with the money, but he did it for me."

He goes silent after this as if that should satisfy me. Embezzlement, ran off, used me, cancer... I dig my palms into my eyes and try to scrub out the sands of time that have lodged there so that I can see clearly. His words don't make any damn sense. Only a couple weeks have passed since I ran from the middle of a tour. Yet staring at the man before me and it feels he was left behind in this place to absorb all the years that the house didn't. Has whatever truth he's trying to tell me, this story I can't make sense of, has it caused him to transform into this shell of the vibrant man who's been by my side all my life?

"I don't...I don't understand what you're talking about. Barry ran off with all the nickels we'd collected? That's why he isn't here?"

A disturbing sound comes from him that has panic rising in my throat. But then I realize he's laughing. It's a strange croaking sound, but he's laughing. "No, no, baby. The millions. The nickels were just show. Those tickets cost thousands."

I knew. Of course I knew he wasn't keeping his promise to never charge more than a nickel. But I kept right on burying my head deeper. I sigh. "But...you said he did it for you. That's what you said, right? Then why'd he run off?"

Uncle David deflates into himself, his once large body sinks into the chair and his eyes flutter closed. "He wanted to be my hero. Not the world's villain."

I open my mouth to question him more, to squeeze more out of him despite that he looks one question away from passing out, when the front door trembles with a knock. He waves a hand toward it with his eyes still closed. I stare at it, brain fogged up with everything he'd said, and wait for it to open. When nothing happens and another knocking round begins, I trudge to the door and throw it open, expecting to find Barry and for this to be some cruel punishment for my disappearance.

But a small delivery woman stands on the porch holding out a bag of something that smells salty and deep fried. She pushes the bag into my hand, then bounces back down the porch steps without a word. I close the door and stare between the bag and Uncle David. He wiggles his fingers in the air, gesturing for the food.

I watch as he comes alive, devouring fries, burgers, chicken tenders, nachos—all his favorites. Then as suddenly as I'd had to grow accustomed to this sluggish version of him, it's as if the garbage food filled up all the empty places and he was almost himself again.

He sits back and lays both hands on his belly, triumphant and satisfied. When he meets my curious gaze, his face falls. "I know this is a lot. I'm sorry to tell you like this. I feel a little better now that I've eaten but it won't last. It's almost the end for me. That's what all this was really about. Barry couldn't accept that I wouldn't do chemo so he became obsessed with alternative medicine. But traveling the world in search of witch doctors and voodoo specialists and underground treatment facilities doesn't come cheap. And well, your talent made it all possible.

"But I still couldn't do it. The weird things they wanted me to eat, the harsh diets they expected me to cling to the rest of my life to somehow starve the cancer. I've lived a long and happy life, simple and exactly how I wanted it to go. But he couldn't let it be. I tried for him. For you. I felt awful how much we put you through for nothing. I know 'sorry' won't make up for it. When I hear from Barry again, I'll make sure the money goes back to you, don't you worry."

I stare at the crumpled junk food wrappers and scowl. "I don't want that money. I said I'd only do it for a nickel and no more, that money doesn't belong to me. I still have more than enough from Gramps. Why didn't you guys just tell me?"

My words twist with emotion. Uncle David lowers his gaze and offers a weak shrug. Anger and betrayal slice through me. But I feel awful for feeling that way when I stare at him and see what the cancer and guilt has done to him. But Barry? He's off somewhere with his millions and he's left Uncle David to die alone, bearing the brunt of the consequences.

"Don't worry, he made sure you were listed only as an employee so when the IRS comes looking for their dues, they can't come after you for any of it."

I leap to my feet and pace the room. "Stop talking about money! Where the hell is Barry? Why the fuck has he left you here alone like this? How can he just disappear on everyone?" I stop in my tracks. Just like me. Running away, abandoning people when they need me most. This is what it's like to be on the other side. I hate this feeling. Never again will I abandon those I care about.

"He didn't, kiddo. He didn't. He'll come back, I know he will. He's off licking his wounds, probably hunting down some miracle worker or gifted shaman who can heal me. A last-ditch effort. He's about ready to accept it. He'll come back when he does."

He tries to talk pleasantly about his day like he hasn't grabbed my world and heaved it all off kilter, but I can't think straight or sit still. I hold up a hand and cut him off. "I'm sorry, I've got to go. I need to think."

• • • •

I HAVEN'T CHANGED AT all. I'm cowering in *Sweetheart*'s embrace. The dusty hammock envelops me like a favorite pair of jeans. I ran from Uncle David when he's at his lowest. I ran away from them weeks ago, leaving them behind to face my rabid followers alone. I turned my back on those followers, who had all looked to me for guidance and a second chance. And I've run to *Sweetheart* instead of returning to my responsibilities when I'd promised Desda I'd look after Candy and Lila.

Sobs rack my body. *Sweetheart* sways gently in the soft waves. I've missed the calming rocking motion of her dance. I've missed the isolation of knowing I could untether her and together we could disappear from the rest of the world, far out into the middle of Lake Michigan where the shores and the people on them are nowhere in sight.

What is it about this houseboat that calls to me the moment everything falls apart? I'd loved coming on board and going on fishing day trips when I was a kid, and I loved the idea of sailing the world on her, but it was never a source of comfort until after that fight with Grandpa. Until...after everything changed forever.

I sit up and look around me. This hammock is where I'd nap in the late afternoons when the fish stopped biting. The deck where we'd fileted our catch of the day only to burn them on the tiny grill. I swipe away my tears and wander up the steps I have avoided for too long. On the upper level, the cabin door screeches as I shove it open. Dust tickles my sinuses. The boxes of collected trinkets stare back at me, wondering why I'd abandoned them there. And behind all the boxes, I know it's still there. Grandpa's own hammock, swaying emp-ty right above mine. Deep in that untouched and buried corner, his ghost is lingering. Just like it is in his bedroom, and his garden, his kitchen.

An odd sensation shifts in my chest. When before I'd stood with bent knees on her rocking deck and looked at the water with a sense of completion, a feeling of *home,* now being here feels like I'd wan-dered into an old abandoned museum. There's the lone pink curtain I'd bought among the others to hide my stash away from Mona on her visits. On the deck below, just beyond the dirty windowpanes, lies the potting containers where I'd kept some of Grandpa's plants alive. I wander back down the steps and look around me with new eyes. The sepia hue fades from my gaze with every step.

A figure stands tall next to the grill and my heart stutters. His back is turned to me, his face gazing out on the water. His graying hair billows despite there being no breeze. The man's warm brown skin and bent posture tickle something in my memory.

"Hello?" I call cautiously. The man jumps and whirls around.

"Oh, hi. Didn't see ya there, Stefan. Didn't know you're back. I'll be off then."

"Mr. Howard! Hi!" I call too loudly and stride forward with a hand raised, only to realize the awkwardness of it. He takes my hand anyway and gives it a lone shake. I'd forgotten I'd asked Barry to find someone to watch *Sweetheart* during our tours. Mr. Howard has been our dock neighbor as long as I can remember. The last time I saw him, he was chasing me down and begging me to come back to shore, to bring back Grandpa's ashes. My face falls at the memory.

"Listen, uh, thank you for watching *Sweetheart* all this time. You've kept up on her well."

"Barry paid me, no thanks needed. I did a job. She's a beaut, so it was a pleasure. You really oughta run her more. Boat like her, she needs to roam. Ain't a dock princess, that's for sure."

We stare out at the water and watch as the sun sets. I fidget with my fingers, feeling confronted with how little I've taken responsibility. Here this virtual stranger is, and he knows more about the boat I'd claimed to love so much. I don't even know how to drive this thing. The dock fees and maintenance costs, all of it Barry took care of right after Gramps passed. It comes right out of that bank account so I've never had to lift a single finger in caring for her.

"You still have your same sailboat?" I ask to fill the silence.

"Nope, not for some years. Had to sell it. Hard to keep since I retired." Mr. Howard doesn't take his eyes off the darkening horizon. Puzzled by his words, I step toward the railing and peer behind us. Sure enough, the shiny sailboat that's always been docked there is now gone. An empty gap now sits in its place. It's been gone years and I never noticed?

"Oh, if it's too hard to maintain *Sweetheart*, you don't have to—"

Mr. Howard holds up a hand with a glance over his shoulder. I rejoin him to watch the last rays of the sun streak purple and orange through the inky black sky. He sighs in what could only be described as bliss. "This water here is my haven. Your *Sweetheart*'s the only excuse I got to come out regularly. That sailboat cost me an arm and a leg and I needed the money. If she was paid off, I'da kept her. But the payments got to be too much. It may be selfish, but I'd like to ask if I can still keep after yours for you."

Boats caught out in the darkness come hauling in. The waves rock *Sweetheart* and we both hold the railing. I rub my palm along the knurled metal pole and the rope dangling from it. The rough texture against my skin takes me back to my childhood when I'd clung to this very rope, petrified we'd capsize with every tiny swell of the water. I savor the taste of the lake air one last time.

I run into my cabin and grab the treasure box I've kept with me for so many years. The book Sandra had given me years ago catches my eye right where I'd left it. I grab it to take back to Desda, then turn back to my treasure box. I stroke the box and think of the contents but don't let myself peek inside. Mama's golden hair and her scarf. Pricey trinkets from readings when I was a kid.

The box makes a *ploop* sound. We both watch as it disappears into the dark water. Mr. Howard quirks a brow but says nothing.

"Mr. Howard, I'd like to give *Sweetheart* to you."

He had to be mid to late thirties, youthful forties maybe. I couldn't see much of his face or his hair with his hood up. He was bent forward while running so I can't estimate his height very well. Not quite six feet. White. Since he was jogging nearby, he probably lives somewhere in this neighborhood. But I've lapped every street for hours every day, and every day has bled into the next searching for him. But that thread tying me to him has gone silent. I can feel it still there, like an afterthought, but the desperate pull to save him has quieted.

He's going to attempt suicide by fire, but not yet. He must be putting his plan on hold for some reason. That gives me time to find him if I can just remember what he looked like. I rub a hand over my face and throw back the last of my coffee. I glance at the pot and see one cup remains. Nettie would be furious if I had any more. I refresh my search and sigh. There are too many men on Facebook fitting the vague description I have of him.

"We're here!" Adam calls from the entryway. Three sets of feet shuffle in as Mel returns. I can already hear Nettie fussing over her and my heart swells with pride. Jacob's gravelly voice asks where I'm hiding.

"In here," I call.

Adam strides in first, his face lit up in a broad smile. I nod and return to my laptop. "Whatcha searchin' for?" Adam leans on the table far too close for my comfort. I lean back as far as the chair will allow.

"Just a guy...it's nothing." I slap the laptop closed and help get Mel settled back in. I've bunked her with Cassy so that somebody can always keep an eye on her. Since Cassy never sleeps, I figure Mel won't feel alone and won't try in the middle of the night a second time. Nettie acts like I'm not there and Mel looks at us both quizzically but says nothing. I sneak off to my room and stare at the empty side of my bed where Stefan had lain a few nights ago.

My heart aches. My phone indicator light flashes with that unopened voicemail from him. I can't bring myself to listen. He'd texted pleasantries and called a few times but this is the first voicemail. He must've found my note. I'm afraid to hear the betrayal and hatred in his voice. He forgave me so quickly when I confessed to stealing from him, but this is something beyond forgiveness.

But when I find myself cuddling the pillow that still smells like him, I know there's a thread still attached despite that I've tried to let him go. I stare at the icon and hover my thumb over it. I need to hear it. I need him to tell me he never wants to see me again. And I'll listen to it over and over again until that thread finally snaps.

I press the icon and listen to the voicemail prompts with my heart pounding and my stomach churning. Sweat breaks out on my brow as the voicemail begins. "Desda, hi. I really need to talk—"

"Mama?" Nettie pops her head in my doorway. I squeal and throw my phone. She looks at me with deep concern but a twinkle of laughter in her eyes.

"Nothing, I'm fine. You scared me is all. Is Mel...?"

"Fine, she's good. Gonna get a nap in before dinner. If Cassy shuts up long enough, that is."

I chuckle. Nettie continues to stare at me with her head stuck in the doorway and her body hiding in the hallway. I pat the bedspread, asking her to sit next to me.

When she sits down but too far for me to wrap my arm around her, I sigh and begin. "I know you're mad at me. I'm sorry about the accident. I was too tired and shouldn't have risked driving that late."

"That's what you think this is about? Because of the wreck?" Nettie jumps to her feet and stares down at me, her hands on her hips. "What were you doing just now when Mel got here?"

"I was on Facebook," I say cautiously, but I know I've been caught.

"Yeah, watching cat videos like the rest of us, huh? Bullshit." My eyes widen as her voice rises. "You were looking for more people to save, weren't you! There's no more room here, have you noticed? We're not just full, we're doubled in every room! But it's just not good enough for you, is it? You won't stop until you've saved the whole goddamn world, right?"

"Woah, Nettie, don't talk to me like that—"

"Or what? You're not my mother anymore. My mama cared about me. She wanted to be there for me. But who are you? You're some stranger obsessed with other strangers. And I have to cook and clean for all of the people you bring back here. But where are you? Out searching for every last person trying to save everyone. God forbid anyone gets a papercut or you'll grab 'em and give 'em a room! Look out, everyone! It's our lord and savior Desdamona!"

Nettie waves her hands over her head in exaggeration. I'm left stricken at her outburst. "I'm trying so fucking hard, don't you get that? Yes, I am trying to save people from hurting themselves or from being forced to do what you and I had to. Don't you wish I'd found you and saved you sooner? What if I'd found Brice before it was too late? He could've been reunited with his parents, but I was too late!"

"Shut up!" Nettie's command is whisper-yelled. I jump up to tell her she cannot shush me but she slaps a hand over my mouth. I slap her hand away but she puts her hands together as if to beg. "What if he hears you? You can't go saying shit like that. He's only just now accepting that loss. Don't get him all twisted again. You have got to get over yourself! You can't save everyone and you sure as hell can't blame yourself for everyone's problems. You think I blame you for that nasty old man's dick I had in my mouth just before you got me off the streets?"

"Nettie!" I stumble back as if she'd slapped me. "Yes! Of course I'm to blame. I knew the street I found you on was a hot spot. I should've marched over there the second I learned about it instead of—"

"Instead nothing! There is no excuse because you're not to blame! You're not the one forcing people like us to work the street. You're not your mother!"

The door flies open making us both jump. "Hey, will you two shut the hell up? I just got sweety Mel to sleep and then you had to go have your pissing contest. What the hell's up with y'all? Raging teenage hormones? What!" Cassy yells as if to be heard over us despite that we're both staring wide-eyed at her.

"Nothing. We're fine." Nettie makes like she's running to her room just like the last time she confronted me, but Cassy blocks her path and slams the door shut behind her.

"Nope, not buying it. Out with it. Gimme the deets. Don't give me that 'it's not my business' crap because the way you two were screaming, the whole neighborhood can hear ya. Now what's this about?"

"She's trying to save the entire world and I'm sick of it. She's killing herself and where will that leave all of us *rescues* once she's dead? How does her collecting us like trophies save anybody?" Nettie crosses her arms over her chest and falls to my bed with a pout.

"Well, hate to break it to ya, kid, but the world's gonna end. I ain't bullshittin' neither. Them's the breaks. Now, you. What's your beef?" Cassy nods at me. I can't help but feel like mother hen has come to stop the quarreling between her chicks.

"No, she's right. I haven't been here for her. I've been running myself ragged and it's catching up to me, I know. Nettie," I sit down beside her and feel hopeful when she doesn't jerk away from my hand on her shoulder. "There's something I need to tell you. It's about my best friend growing up. She worked the streets alongside me and was the only reason I got through it. Come, sit, Cassy. Let me tell you both about Sandy."

• • • •

"MAMA, THAT WASN'T YOUR fault then, neither."

"Yeah, I agree with her. Sounds like she did it to herself." Cassy and Nettie nod in unison.

"I know, I know. But her face still haunts me all the same. If I can save someone from the life we led or stop someone from ending it all, it feels like she's forgiven me, little by little. Every person who gets a happy ending from what I do, I believe it makes her smile. Wherever she is."

"She isn't out there, watching you. If she's out anywhere, it's enjoying the afterlife and not haunting you. She wanted out so she got out, her own way. Not your way, not anybody else's way but her own. She left you behind to face it alone, and that's on her. You gotta let that shit go and move forward. I've seen some shit in my time and let me tell you, ain't no forgetting, only moving forward. Let her go so Nettie can have her mama."

Tears well until I can no longer see Cassy perched on the armrest of the chair beside my bed that holds all of the clothes I haven't had time to put away. Moving forward, letting go, carrying it with me but carrying on, it's everything I told Brice on the porch not long ago. I preach and preach about how to carry your guilt and shame with you, but I've been trying to carry everyone else's pain too. It's not mine to bear. I hate the thought of Nettie or Brice or Cassy carrying my pain.

"I'm sorry. I'm so sorry, Nettie."

"Mama!" Nettie sobs into my shoulder. I squeeze her tight against me. Her small frame is no longer small. She's firm in the arms from the work she does for me. She's gotten taller and her chest is softer, larger. My little girl is far from little anymore. How long has it been since I've held her? The thought makes me sob harder.

Cassy wraps her arms around us both and pats our backs. "There, there." The ridiculousness of this woman has both Nettie and me chuckling through our cries.

Sandy's face fills my mind. She smiles sweetly, her overly pink cheeks flush darker. But then her smile falls and her eyes widen. I freeze in Nettie's arms. Sandy mouths to me behind my closed eyes.

Go!

A crash rattles through the house. A second later, I can hear the yells from the men downstairs and further crashing. Cassy bolts out the door first with me close behind her. Nettie is on my heels but I point at Brice's door as we run past.

"Shit! Fuck! Get the fire extinguisher, Jacob!" Adam is panting out commands.

"What's going on?" I scream at the sight before me. Three piles of something dance with flames in my living room. The flames spread across the red rug and lick the legs of the coffee table. The vinyl of the sofa blackens under the spreading blaze.

Jacob runs in with the extinguisher right as Cassy jumps in to join Adam in stomping the violent flames. In seconds, my living room is caked in white foam and the smoke is a white cloud gripping my throat. I stand frozen with the soppy cream clinging to my ankles. I watch as if from another planet as Nettie leads everyone outside. The night air is gentle and warm as the sirens emerge from some-where far off.

Nettie holds Brice, who shakes uncontrollably. Firemen and po-lice and EMTs swarm my front yard. There's someone speaking to me but I can't figure out what they're saying. Cassy and Adam take over for me as I watch from somewhere else.

"Three bricks wrapped in fuel-soaked cloth. No notes, no threats of any kind. Any idea who could've done this?" a man clad in a thick yellow outfit asks Cassy.

Yessica had already left for the day. Had she been here, she might never return after another fire attack. But she wasn't here. She definitely isn't the one this person is after. Movement in the corner of my yard near the street catches my eyes. The crowd is gathering and blocking my view. I wander over, listless and unthinking.

The pallets of my new flooring Stefan had ordered is smoldering. The firemen work to soak the beautiful rustic hickory that has now become charcoal and melted plastic. The tarp that was covering the wood clutches onto the remaining pieces with ferocity. Tears prick my eyes.

A sudden spark of electric heat sears through the haze of my shock. The thread from before snaps to attention. I whip my head toward the crowd. My eyes lock on a pale blue pair.

By fire.

The coffee tastes perfect. The turkey sandwich, chicken noodle soup, and blueberry pie are incredible. I look around The Corner Café and am deeply pleased to notice nothing has changed. The old man who was always here every time I'd ever come is still sitting as if he never left. Brenda still waits the tables and no one else appears to be aware of this place.

The windows have a sheen to them. The air is muggy and somehow just right. My hair swallows the moisture in the air and my tame curls become frizzy. I stare at the hair elastic Nettie had given me and smile as I tie my hair back. Maybe Desda can give me a haircut when I get back.

Candy and Lila had devoured my pot roast and were already in bed by the time I made it back home. For the first time in so many years, I slept without yearning for *Sweetheart*'s hammock embrace. Brenda tops up my coffee and offers a wink. There's a comfort in knowing I can return here and find everything exactly the same—Grandpa's house, Uncle David's, The Corner Café, and maybe I'll even still get to see *Sweetheart* on my visits.

I turn to sprinkle water on Bob, only to find he looks different. The leaves are deeper green, the shine unnatural. I watch as the water stagnates on the soil's surface. The plant is a fake plastic one.

"Sorry, sugar. Bob died some time ago. I brought that silk one in so another one never had to die." Brenda sets a piece of sweet potato pie in front of me. "Your pie fiend buddy gonna be joinin' you?"

The last time I was here—no, just about every time I come—Barry finds me. For a moment, I find myself watching the door expecting him to waltz in like nothing had happened. I shake my head in answer and stare into my coffee cup. Brenda hovers beside the table.

"Listen, you can tell when someone is going to die, right?" she whispers softly.

I blink up at her in surprise. In a way, I'd had a delusion that just about everything in this town was frozen away from the rest of the world and that the goings-on outside this place existed in a different plane of time and space. To hear her voice my talent, something I've never spoken to her about, startles me. But of course she knows. My face has been plastered all over. I nod with brows furrowed.

Brenda slides into the opposite side of my booth. "Will you read me, please?" She places a nickel and a picture in front of me. The photo is old and worn, as if she's carried it everywhere with her. In it she poses with two little girls, one a couple years older than the other. They both look like spitting images of her with rosy cheeks and toothy grins.

"Um, yeah, okay. Your time of death is..."

Her hands are shaking. She sets the coffee pot onto the table and hides her hands in her lap. Her lower lip quivers. What will she do once she knows? Will she quit this job and try for a college degree to better her life for the sake of her children? When I do return here sometime in the future, will Brenda's disappearance from here set off a chain reaction that'll break this spell that holds this town captive in time?

"It's...9:54 p.m."

She nods, then beams ear to ear. "Thank you, sugar. Now how 'bout some ice cream?"

• • • •

UNCLE DAVID SWIPES a hand over his mouth. He sets down the plastic fork and sighs in contentment. His meal of tacos enough to feed three reinvigorates him again. I find myself glancing in the shadows in search of Barry. But every day I visit, I leave feeling equally relieved and disappointed. Every day I cook and clean for the girls, then wander over to check in on Uncle David. But it's time I head back to Desda. Which means another painful goodbye. At least I get to say it this time.

"So I got rid of *Sweetheart*."

Uncle David chokes on his soda. "Y-you did what now?" He sputters while starting at me, startled.

"I'm moving to Dallas to be with Desda. With a girl I've been in love with for many years. I gave *Sweetheart* to Mr. Howard. I know he'll take good care of her. And I don't want to hear about it. It was time to let her go."

He nods but thankfully says nothing. Was it the right decision? Was it presumptuous to let go of my happy place before making sure Desda even wants me around? Probably. But my ties here are to ghosts, and it's time I let them move on.

"He saved up everything for that boat. He'll be happy it's in the hands of his good friend."

"I didn't know he and Mr. Howard were close."

He nods and stares at the wall. "'Bout as close as two old men can be when neither of 'em got much to say."

"Can I ask you something?" When he waves a hand for me to go ahead, I continue. "Why did Gramps keep working so hard until the day he died if he had all that money saved up?"

Uncle David seems to mull something over as his eyes bore into the brown paneling. "He had to stay busy. He hated being idle. Wasn't always that way. He wanted a life of leisure and simplicity when he was with your grandma. After her accident, he started back to working for your mother and then you. But after your mama passed too, he couldn't bear it. He had to keep his hands working or his mind would wander. At least he's with his family now."

He smiles at the sky at this and the shadows beneath his eyes coupled with the sunken sag to his cheeks has goosebumps rising on my arms. I rub away the chill.

"What'd Jeb tell you about your mama's passing?"

"She got sick when I was too little to remember. Why?"

His brows furrow but at my quizzical look, he flashes a forced smile. My thoughts run wild at his sudden question.

"It's nothing, never mind. Hey, hand me the keyring on the kitchen counter, will you?"

I run to retrieve as he'd asked with curiosity burning at every step. The keyring is a comically huge ring like out of a cartoon and chock-full of many keys.

But when I reach out to hand him the massive ring, he shakes his head. "That's for the storage for your...collection."

I look down at the possibly hundreds of keys. "Which one?"

"All of them."

• • • •

I ENLIST CANDY AND Lila to help me scour the storage units for anything interesting and worth keeping. I pick the first unit and work through the keys one after another until Lila points out the tiny numbers on them. But searching for the right number etched on the small keys is no more time-saving than trying each one in the lock. After the twentieth attempt, the padlock falls to the ground.

Once we have four units open and are halfway through tearing them apart, a shadowy figure comes hauling toward us from the other end of the lot. "Hey, get out of there, thieves!"

The storage manager stares at us, perplexed. "Sorry about the mix-up." His red face turns impossibly more scarlet. "No one ever opens these. About once a month or so, a box truck shows up, another unit is rented and the truck unloaded. I hand off a new key and that's that. No one has ever opened one after it's locked, and the people unloading are always different."

The girls have disappeared into different units in different buildings. I pick through the keys and notice no numbers missing.

"Yup, just about full up and they're all yours, so it seems. Whatcha collecting anyhow?"

"They were gifts." I shrug and he smiles with confusion etched in his features but he doesn't press for more information.

A feather boa snakes around Candy. A fur coat drapes on Lila's shoulders. Their fingers glitter with numerous rings and necklaces of all kinds twinkle from their necks. They look rich and ridiculous. We laugh as dust billows from their scavenged goods and a sneezing fit seizes us.

I stare at the boxes upon boxes spilling out of several open units. The keyring feels like twenty pounds in my hand and the thin metal digs a deep groove into my palm. I jangle the mass of metal and look at the girls.

"Well, get everything you want?"

"I don't know, do we look fabulous enough?" They laugh as they wander back to my rental car.

"Excuse me, sir!" I call after the storage manager as he pretends to be busy with a small empty unit nearby. He wipes a hand over his dry forehead as I approach. "I don't need any of this anymore."

His brows raise to his hairline. "W-what do you mean?"

"How about you sell everything and keep whatever you make? I'll keep paying for the units until you sell 'em clean, how about it?"

The storage manager waves as I drive away. Behind him, my years and years of trinkets spill out onto the ground. I think of the WWI and WWII items I've been given, the Hummel figurines, the jewelry the girls didn't want. But there's also the buttons and broken toys, the sparkly hairbrushes and the paper clips.

I feel thousands of pounds lighter.

Candy and Lila giggle up the steps to Grandpa's house. They kiss and stumble into the front door with distracted goodbye waves back at me. I smile as I make my way to Uncle David's place before heading for the airport. Only a couple hours and I'll get to see Desda again. I should've known she wouldn't answer my calls or texts. The conversation we need to have isn't something that can be done in any other way but in person.

Maybe I'll take her to a nice private dinner tonight. I whistle as I bound up the porch steps, then bang on the door. I let myself in as I have been doing after announcing my presence. But his favorite chair in the living room is empty.

"Uncle David? You in the bathroom?" I wander in and plop on the sofa. After a few minutes, I call out for him again. No answer. A feeling of unease settles in and I find myself running from room to room and jumping at every shadow. But I don't find him passed out on the floor in a puddle of his own fluids as I was expecting.

I huff in relief as I lean on the counter. Maybe he's out for a walk or was feeling up for eating out. I bet he's sitting at The Corner Café right now, inhaling his sixth piece of pie. My hand slips on a paper on the counter. What's this?

Stefan

Hey, baby. I'm so sorry to leave you like this. And I'm sorry about everything. Barry came back for me. Please don't look for us. We love you dearly. Enjoy your new life in Dallas. We're proud of the man you've become and we know Jeb would be too.

Uncle David

I'm in a daze on the plane ride back to Dallas. Barry came back and Uncle David left with him. Why couldn't either of them say goodbye? I think of Uncle David's sickly pallor and frail, sunken body. Will I ever see him again? Part of me doesn't want to see Barry ever again, but Uncle David...

Tears begin to well but I sniff them back as the plane ascends. Lake Michigan glitters beneath us. My heart sags as I look down at the water and can practically see *Sweetheart* bobbing there, beckoning to me. I try to chase the melancholy away and decide to distract myself with music. My earbuds coil around everything in my bag and it takes ten minutes until I can pull them halfway free.

My plane ticket ensnares the remaining wires but as I unwrap the final coil, I notice strange markings that give me pause. This isn't my ticket, it's a check. A check from Desda for over twenty grand!

"What the hell?" The old lady in the seat beside me scowls at my language. I bow my head in apology.

Behind the check is a folded piece of paper. My throat squeezes. Not another letter. Uncle David just abandoned me with a letter. My hands shake as I unfold the handwritten note.

Chapter Thirty – Desdamona

*S*tefan's fingers trail along my neck. Shivers course through my feverish body.

"Kiss me. Kiss me, please, Stefan."

But as I continue to beg, he only smiles down at me as if waiting for something.

"Open for me." His voice is husky. I try to oblige but instead of spreading for him, my chest cracks open. What?

"Wider," he whispers against my ear. My ribs spill out around me until my chest is spread apart like a book. His smile is wide and toothy. His eyes darken to almost black. Goosebumps rise as he bends over me. I arch into his touch.

"There." Stefan holds my pounding heart in his dripping fists. I watch in horror as he bites into it like an apple. It makes a sickening sound that has my stomach churning. "This is for killing my mother."

"Yo! Will you wake up already!" I'm slapped across the face.

"Ah! What the hell?" I lurch up in bed, only to come face-to-face with Cassy.

"You were moaning for your boyfriend. But then it got real weird toward the end. Wanna talk about it?"

I rub the sand from my eyes and the soreness from my cheek. An ache settles at the back of my neck. "What time is it?"

Cassy glances at her wristwatch. "Five. Top of the morning to ya, sleepyhead."

"Five? You woke me up from a dream at *five*?"

"Yeah, yeah. Death dreams, right? I get 'em too. Heard you hollerin', thought I could be of service." Cassy slips into bed beside me. I stare at her with wide eyes. How could she know? "So, tell me about it."

"No, I told you before, I don't do that. What's mine to know is mine to deal with. Alone."

But she just pats the bed in front of her as if offering to cuddle me. I scoff at the invitation and rise from the warmth of my bed. No point going back to sleep now.

"Come on, let it out. You'll feel better." Cassy sidles up behind me to rub my shoulders.

"Fuck, that feels good."

"Yeah, I can make it feel even better." She whispers in my ear, her hot breath tickling my neck. "It'll feel so good if you lay it all out on me."

I can't help but laugh at her. "You're a weirdo, you know that?"

"And proud of it! So, tell me who dies in your dreams?"

I whip around to face her. In the dim light from my side table, her wild hair looks like dancing flames around her head. "What do you know about it?" My eyes narrow at her unnervingly easy smile.

"That's just how it is with people like us. Near-death experiences do that to you. I've met a few and we're all alike. Death dreams and a newfound ability that scares the piss outta normies."

My chest heaves. I sputter out a cough to cover it up but too late. Cassy is over me in an instant, that annoying and knowing smile hovering above my eyes. I fall back onto my bed and stare at the shadowed ceiling. "Near-death experiences, huh? But I didn't almost die from that car wreck, barely had so much as an achy muscle the next day."

She just stares at me, knowing. Dammit. I wasn't planning to tell her anything more. What is it about this woman?

"I was maybe five years old or so. Stefan not quite two. He was my neighbor when I was really little, before...before Mama started training me. In those days, life was easy and simple. Stefan and I played together nearly every day while everybody was out working. Looking back, I realize now how shitty it was that I was left in charge of a one-year-old but..."

I stare off into the painful memories I've shunned for so many years. My filthy secret coats my insides like tar. I never even told Sandy this. Cassy stares back at me but my throat tightens, and the words turn to ash on my tongue. Somehow, putting the truth out into the air makes it all real and not a bad dream. But I've already told Stefan in my letter. The truth is already out there. It's time I purged it like the demon it is. The demon I am.

"In my dreams, I watch as the world ends. Y'know, what's coming and all the shit I'm always preaching. I hate sleeping like you, too. 'Cause when I do sleep, I watch as babies are crushed, and puppies are on fire. Eyes popping from skulls and seriously the worst shit nobody is ever meant to see. That's why the pills. Pop 'em to stay awake as long as I can. And when I can't take it anymore, I take a few too many to hopefully sleep deep enough where those nasty dreams can't find me. But they always find me."

She says all this and then she smiles that same smile. Is any of her dream real? I've always shrugged mine off as guilt, but she views them like omens of something to come. The world, if it is ending, will my guilt finally rest?

I drape an arm over my eyes. "I remember Stefan's dad. He was a nasty man. Sometimes I look at Stefan's brown-red hair and golden eyes and it makes me think of his father. He was mean. So mean that neither Stefan nor his mom could hardly make a sound before he'd come after them, swinging. I was never allowed to play over there because of it but every time I went to pick Stefan up for a play date, his dad would be chasing one of them or hitting them if he caught them.

"I went to pick him up one day. But when I knocked, it was like somebody was knocking back. I kept knocking and the sound kept mocking me. Being a kid, I was getting ticked and thinking Stefan was inside playing a trick on me. But when I opened the door...and what I saw... Ira—that's his mom's name—she took one look at the horror on my face, and she grabbed Stefan and we ran. She was bloody, Stefan was unconscious, but we ran. I don't know why we didn't just go to my place, why we didn't get help. I followed her, running and running.

"It was so damn cold. The wind was vicious that day. He came after us, but we lost him in the woods. And we kept running. When we stopped to rest, Stefan still hadn't woken up. I remember looking at him and wondering what kind of spoiled brat could sleep through all that. Of course, I didn't see the gash on the side of his head. Ira was trying to hide his face from me. While we sat there catching our breath, she kept falling asleep. I'd hear a noise behind us and try to wake her."

Cassy lays her head against my chest. Her fading pink curls tickle my cheek. She intertwines her fingers with mine. Her hand is darkened from the sun, but a white band encircles her ring finger.

"Then she looked at me and said, 'Take him. Go that way until you see a little yellow house. That's his granddaddy. You take him there. I'll just rest a little longer and I'll be right behind you, okay?' I was so angry at her. I was hardly much bigger than Stefan myself and yet she was making me carry this sleeping boy through the woods alone.

"Well, anyway. I ran the way she pointed, but it was getting dark, and I was so tired. I could see the house through the trees, but it felt so far off. I thought I deserved a nap. So I dropped Stefan out of anger and annoyance that he was still sleeping and that Ira made me carry him all this way. But then I fell on top of him. I woke up in the hospital next. There were so many people there. Police wanting to know what happened and where Ira was, doctors and nurses staring at me like I was an alien. It was my body heat that kept Stefan alive long enough that they were able to revive him pretty easily. But they said I was frozen solid, they thought I was dead."

Tears choke my words, but I force through to the end. It's almost over. I'm close to purging the darkness from within. I inhale deeply to steady myself. "Stefan's grandfather asked where Ira was. I was so angry about all of it that I kept my mouth shut. I could've saved her, but I was too selfish and nasty. By the time the search dogs had found her, she had been dead so long that the birds had gotten to her. Stefan must've stayed living with his grandpa after that. His dad completely disappeared and was never seen again. Any time I'd ask to play with Stefan, my mama would tell me to mind my own and get to work.

"If...if I'd left Stefan with his mama and run to his grandpa's house, she'd still be alive. I could've run there and back if I didn't try carrying him the rest of the way. We wouldn't have nearly died, and she would still be here. Stefan and Ira probably would've lived with his grandpa and their lives would've been so much happier. But I ruined everything. And I killed her."

"You know what I think?" Cassy says after a while. Her voice is soft and soothing, so unlike her bubbly and charismatic self that I feel for a moment that a mask has slipped out of place. "I think Ira knew it was her time. I think she wanted you and Stefan gone so you wouldn't have to see it. Yeah, it was shitty that she got you involved and put all that on you when you were so little yourself. But I think she knew there was nothing that could be done except get Stefan as far away as possible. And I think your Nettie is right. You blame yourself for far too much. But who am I to judge? I think I can save the world, too. So I won't stop you from carrying that weight, but you should know that I don't think any of that's on you."

"I told Stefan the truth. In a letter when he left. I don't think I'll ever see him again."

The sun has begun to stretch from sleep. Yellow fingers of light seep through the cracks of my blinds. I close my eyes and imagine, just for a moment, that it's Stefan's head against my chest and his warm hand wrapped in mine.

"I love you." The words whisper from my lips at the phantom in my grasp.

Cassy chuckles in her ridiculous way. "Love you, too, sweet cheeks."

Chapter Thirty-One – Stefan

The black Victorian house is cast in shadows with touches of gold from the rising sun. My eyes are puffy, and my cheeks feel sunken. There are boards over the front room's windows that catch my stare. What did I miss?

It's my fault your mama's dead. I'm so sorry, Stefan. I should've told you sooner. I kept lying to myself that you must've remembered me, that you knew. But you were too young and that was my selfishness wanting to keep you. It's time you learned the truth.

I don't remember any of it. I don't remember my father at all. Not even a twinge of memory for my mother. Desda and I were childhood friends and I blanked it all out? I was almost two years old, and I died. Desda died. My mother died. As I stare at Desda's house and feel the cool air snake through my clothes, part of me wishes I were nothing more than a ghost watching over her. Had I stayed dead that day, I could be with my mama. I'd be with Gramps, too. And I'd get to meet Grandma. And that means I'd be there to greet Uncle David.

But I stand here on the street after a restless night in a hotel. So many truths coming to light had my head pounding. I wasn't ready to face Desda after everything, not until I had a moment to process. Once I had sprawled out on the thin mattress in that cheap room, I knew the truth. I was running away again. I was hiding and avoiding facing reality. I'd given *Sweetheart* away because I thought I had over-come wanting to dig my head in the sand, yet I ran away again.

All these years, my Mona has carried this burden. All this time she must've been looking out for me because of my mother placing that burden on her. I read her letter and never once blamed her for what happened. I couldn't help but wonder if any of what we had was real. Or was she with me out of pity, out of guilt and shame?

As I stumble over the stairs to the front door, my thoughts roam. She asked me to hate her. Her letter was a goodbye. She never wanted to see me again. She couldn't face me now that I know the truth.

I lay my head against the hardwood of the front door. As I press my palm into its rough wood, the door falls open. I scramble onto the floor in the entryway. My breath locks in my lungs as I listen for any sound that I'd woken anyone. But the house remains silent. Who the hell left the door cracked open?

Creaking upstairs has me freezing in place as I rise to my feet. I strain to listen. Do I announce my presence and risk waking everyone up? Should I wait down here until a reasonable hour? Should I try calling Desda and see if she'll answer this time?

"S-stop. Don't!" Someone's muffled cries have my heart leaping in my throat. Is someone having a bad dream? I tiptoe to the stairs, squinting into the darkness. Someone is crying. But it isn't soft and feminine, it's deep and masculine. With all the people Desda saves and brings back here, I've seen a couple men come and go. But the muffled cries don't sound like they're from a bad dream.

A door squeaks open somewhere farther into the darkness. I freeze halfway up the stairs as the step pops beneath my feet. There's silence through the house for several moments. Have they gone back to sleep? Had the emotions running rampant through me and my exhaustion caught up with me and I'd imagined it all? If anybody finds me standing on these stairs in the middle of the dark early morning...

"Brice? Where are you?" a soft feminine voice calls in the dark. A shadow looms at the top of the stairs.

"No, don't!" someone above me whispers.

"There you are." There's a dark and sinister voice beside the other one. A shuffling and blurring is coming from the landing above me, but I can't tell what the hell is going on. And then a woman screams.

"Get off me!"

It's Nettie! I run up the remaining steps right as someone flips on a light. I blink through the blinding bulb's assault and can't make sense of the crowd ahead of me. There's a young blond, white boy cowering on the floor in the hallway. I think his name is Brice. Cassy stands at the light switch with a hand on her hip but her face pales as she makes sense of the scene before I can. Our eyes fall on the couple in the center of the hallway.

A strange smell hits my nose. My mind flashes to *Sweetheart's* deck and summers spent drifting on the lake while Barry douses too much lighter fluid onto the grill. My nose scrunches from the offending stench. Nettie thrashes as the fluid is squeezed over her head.

"Get away from my baby!" Desda screams and launches at the man clutching Nettie in his grasp.

A filthy, wrinkled jacket catches my eye. "Don't move! Or I'll light her up right now!"

That voice, I know I've heard it somewhere. "Hey! Let go of her!" I yell to get the man's attention. Just like I'd planned, all eyes land on me. Their times fly into my head, Nettie's is 6:12 a.m. but I focus on his. *6:09 a.m.*

"Detective Landers?" His eyes widen, then narrow at me. Wait, no, there isn't a Detective Landers. 6:09 a.m.... "Neil Newman!"

Neil blinks as I point at him and the memories come rushing forward. How did I not recognize him before when I was in the hospital? "You're Bridgett's husband. What the hell are you doing with Nettie?"

"Stay back! All of you, or I'll do it!" Neil's eyes are wide and bloodshot. He looks like he hasn't slept since I last saw him. He holds a lighter in his grasp and poises his thumb to strike it to light. Nettie stares at the metal square in terror. Brice sobs at my feet.

"Wait, Bridgett? Bridgett Newman? That's what this is about?" Desda steps forward but stops when Neil waves the lighter.

"Yes, that's what this is about!" Neil spits the words. "You took her from me! We had the rest of our lives together and then you got into her head. You stole her from me! Where is she? Tell me where she is, or I'll take someone important away from you! This is your daughter, right? She's really pretty. Sure would be a shame."

Neil squeezes Nettie against his chest until she squeaks from the crushing pressure. I hover on the top step trying to process what the hell he's talking about. After they came to have their times read, I never heard from them again. What does Desda have to do with this? My eyes land on her face but she can't look away from Nettie. She's frozen in terror, a haunting look is carved into her beautiful features.

"Hey, name's Crazy Cassy, how are ya? Been better, huh? Put that lighter down and we can chat about—"

Neil strikes the lighter and holds the flame closer to silence Cassy. But instead of fear, I see anger cross her face.

"Look here, asshole. You need to move on. It sure as shit ain't easy but it's not impossible. Your wife left. It sucks, I know. My husband left me, too. He was the love of my life and I did everything for him. Y'know he was so terrified we'd accidently have a kid that I got a hysterectomy so there'd be no chance? Yeah, well, he's remarried now and has five kids. I'm not trying to light one of 'em on fire, no! 'Cause I moved on. We can help you move on, too!"

"I just want my Bridgey back!" His face crumples. "Please, please give her to me."

"Neil, listen, honey..." Desda steps slowly toward him. He clutches the lighter but makes no other move. "Bridgett is safe. She's happy. I know it hurts right now, but please, we can help you, too. We can help you move—"

"She's the love of my life! I can't move on from that! Don't you know anything about love like that?"

Desda's eyes land on mine. So many emotions flash in her gaze. My heart twists. "Yes, yes I do. I know the pain you're feeling, trust me, I do. But I can't give you Bridgett. She came to me asking to be set free. She loved you, too, Neil. She said it was because she loved you that she needed to let you go. She left so that you could let her go."

"That's bullshit! I just want to talk to her. I need her!"

"You have to let her go." Cassy puts a hand out toward the lighter. She steps cautiously toward him. My shoulders sag in relief as he begins to hand it over.

"I'll never let her go!" The lighter flicks to life and falls through the air. Neil's eyes squeeze shut, and a smile pulls his lips as Nettie begins to scream.

There's a rush as we all run forward but someone shoves me aside. Flames erupt in a violent burst that singes some of my hair. I leap out of the way as two figures fall over one another down the stairs. Small flames lick the banister and stair nose.

"Brice!" Nettie screams beside me and runs after the ball of fire.

I grab the extinguisher on the wall upstairs as Desda and Cassy run down after Nettie. The small flames on the stairs flicker out from the wind of everyone rushing by. Desda is frantically smacking Nettie's legs as fire eats its way up her pajama pants. I aim the extinguisher at Nettie and shoot. Cassy runs in from the kitchen with another extinguisher and sets to blasting the writhing figures on the floor.

When the fire is mostly out, we stand around the two charred bodies at our feet. Neil is no more. But Brice's upper half is still intact. He smiles warily and reaches out for Nettie.

"No, no, why, Brice!" Nettie sobs as she sinks to her blistered knees.

I toss my phone at Cassy and direct her to call an ambulance. Desda hovers behind Nettie with her hand on her throat. I lay a hand on Desda's shoulder. She turns to me and buries her face in my chest.

"I'm sorry I've been such a coward, Nettie," Brice croaks.

"Shh, shh, no more words. Please, baby." Nettie lays a gentle hand on his face. He winces. She leans over him and presses her lips to his. When she rises, a broad smile paints his soot-coated face.

"I love you. I'll always...watch over...you."

"Please don't leave me." Nettie sobs. Desda burrows against me as her body is racked with her cries. My tears drip into her long hair.

"I have to...go." Brice chokes and launches into a croaking coughing fit. His eyes briefly catch mine. *6:13 a.m.* It's almost time. "Please, Nettie, let me go. I wanna see my mommy and daddy again."

His words slice through us all. Cassy told me his story. About being kidnapped as a little boy and holding on long enough to be reunited with his parents, only to learn years later that he was too late. Nettie grabs his blackened hand, but the skin crumbles in her grasp. He reaches up with his surviving hand.

Nettie's keening cry and Brice's distant gaze as he reaches toward someone who isn't there has something within me snapping. I drag Desda toward the ground and hold her close as I join Nettie in screaming toward the sky.

Six Months Later

"I can't believe I'm doing this." The needle hovers over my arm. Stefan's hand is wrapped in mine. His wrist glistens. Cassy laughs over his shoulder and snaps an obscene number of pictures.

"Ready?" the tattoo artist asks, a smirk twisting her full lips. I nod and feel a cold sweat coat my brow as the machine begins buzzing. I watch as if floating above myself as the letters are etched into the skin on my inner wrist.

"Yay! Now we're all Deviants!" Cassy does a happy dance on the way to the new van. The glossy mural painted on its side still warms my heart. *Safe Haven: Join the fight to end sex trafficking. Only YOU can make a difference.* Nettie poses with me beside our first brick and mortar nonprofit location in the vibrant painted scheme.

Stefan's hand swings with mine. The spring air is warm and inviting. I feel well-rested for the first time in years. When we pull up to the house, Nettie waves from the porch, a fresh pie in her grasp. Her leg wounds have mostly healed, and she proudly wears shorts to show off her scars like a badge of honor. *"He died saving me, now I want everyone to know his story. This way, people will ask about my scars, and I can tell the world about Brice."*

"Wait, let's get a pic of all our wrists before we go in. The sunlight is perfect out here!" Cassy holds out her pink tattoo and Stefan holds out his black version. My blue letters burn with the memory of that terrible needle.

"I still can't understand how we settled on this name. Why couldn't we go with 'Angels' like I wanted? Deviants? You make it seem like we're pervs."

"Dancing with death is kinda pervy if you ask me. Besides, it's cool as hell! Angels? That's reprehensible." Cassy makes a face, sticking her tongue out and acting as though she'd eaten something sour.

"That's a five-dollar word." I laugh. "Calling ourselves angels is reprehensible and I suppose calling ourselves deviants is laudable, is it?"

"Looks who's talking about five-dollar words! Now shut up and get in here for the picture." The camera snaps right as something falls at our feet. Stefan sucks in a breath.

"Look! It's a big peach." He scoops up the large fruit and rubs a gentle thumb over its soft flesh.

Cassy leans in for a better look. "Yummy, bring it in, we'll have it with Nettie's pie!"

"Nope, by then it'll be too late. The universe dropped this at our feet and it's telling us to stop what we're doing and eat." Stefan's smile is so damn sweet and innocent.

Stefan rips the juicy peach into haphazard thirds. We suck at the fruit's flesh with orange syrupy liquid dripping down our chins. Laughter bubbles out of me and the love of my life and my best friend join in.

"Hey!" Nettie yells from the porch. "Give me some of that. I've been watching for that to fall all week!"

She runs over and nibbles on some of Cassie's share. Nettie laps at the syrup that dribbles from the corner of her lips. Her eyes light up in laughter. I glance at Stefan and see that he's watching her, a smile on his orange-stained mouth and tears welling in his eyes. Cassy gives me a knowing wink.

I grab Stefan and pull his mouth to mine. He blinks in surprise but soon melts into my kiss. My heart swells with love for him, for my daughter, and for my best friend. My family. Stefan deepens the kiss, dipping me low and invading my senses with the sweet taste of the peach on his tongue.

The house is loud with laughter as I look around the table at my family. Jacob and Adam will be by soon with their report of the nonprofit's building schedule. Mel will stop by to help us set up for tonight's meeting before she's off to work with Yessica at Last Chance Travel Agency's first real location. Another old Victorian house like this one, but in much better condition.

But just when I'd thought my fight was finally getting easier, when I'd finally had enough on my team to really put a dent in the disgusting sex trafficking industry and enough employees to make my travel agency profitable, Cassy had other plans. The flyer she'd hung around town shines an offensively neon orange on every corner and telephone pole.

"Near-death experience leave you feeling abnormal? Do you dream of death every night? Your family think you're weird and off your rocker? Join us the last Saturday of the month at 8 p.m.!"

Cassy's curly handwriting makes the poster look like a child's ad for a lemonade stand. I didn't expect anyone to respond or show up. But Nettie baked enough for dozens of people, and Stefan has been working hard all month to finish my new hardwood floors and repair the windows. My eyes close in bliss as I walk through my house and not a single surface protests or screams at me. Even the stairs are all repaired and silent. Halfway to my bedroom for an afternoon nap and the new doorbell rings.

"It's a little early for anybody to be showing up." Stefan's head pokes out of the kitchen doorway. "Don't worry, I'll take care of it. You go nap."

My heart warms. I slowly continue up the steps, relishing in the silence and sturdiness under my feet.

"Desda, it's for you!" Stefan calls from the front door. Dammit. So much for napping.

Her long dark hair billows in the wind. Behind her, my freshly planted gardens blow their floral fragrance around her. A pair of vibrant green eyes regard me with suspicion. She has her mother's dark hair but nothing else. Her skin is a medium brown and her lips pulled into a tight frown. I stand corrected, she has her mother's stubbornness.

I have to bite back laughter when the little girl perched on her mother's hip narrows her eyes at me. "Hi, Rhiannon. Who's this?"

"Sylvana, say hi."

"No." Her eyes stay narrowed. So this is what kept Rhiannon working. She's had a daughter. Maybe there are other children, too. My pulse begins to pound in that way it would when I was close to saving someone from plummeting off a bridge. I breathe in the scent of her and of the flowers from my garden to calm the adrenalin that rises.

"I've seen your van around. So you're a nonprofit now, huh?"

"Yup, Safe Haven."

We move to the porch swing and Rhiannon rocks beside me. Sylvana climbs on the new rocking chair Stefan made for me. Daffodils and tulips stretch from the ground around the base of my fruit trees. Stefan's potato plant from his grandpa's garden looks like an out-of-place weed but the small shoots disrupting the layout of the flower garden warm my heart. Creeping red thyme coats the ground where only a few months ago there was nothing but dead grass and dirt. The fiery flowers make my front yard look as if it were on fire. In a way, the tiny blooms remind me of what I'd nearly lost to the flame.

I look over at Rhiannon, whose head is tipped back, and her lips are turned up at the corners. She sighs in contentment. My neighbor's dead lawn catches my gaze, and I can't help but smile at the thought of the futility of maintaining grass in Texas. Ice clinks in our glasses as midday mimosas bubble.

Stefan is inside somewhere, likely tinkering with something that he'll decide to repair before it can break. Nettie is putting more cookies and pies into the oven while Cassy sets up chairs in the dining room where Yessica used to feign working while browsing Facebook.

"I'm still working the streets, if you were wondering," Rhiannon says to the porch ceiling. I tip my head back and look at the pristine robin's egg blue paint that now coats the wood. The floorboards beneath my feet are glossy with new blue paint, the burned-in graffiti long since removed. A black Victorian with a touch of blue. A subtle flash of color made this place finally start to feel like home.

"And I still look for you when I drive at night."

Rhiannon chuckles. "Still trying to save everyone?"

"What can I say? It's what I do." I shrug as she beams at me.

"Well, I'm still happy doing what I do. I like..." she glances at her daughter before leaning toward me to whisper, "S-E-X. And the good money is a nice perk. I put an offer on a house. White picket fence and everything. And I applied to the school of my dreams. I think I'm gonna get in, too." She sips her mimosa, exhaling with an exaggerated *ahh*. "I know most people look down at the way I live my life. But I'm happy that I worked to achieve my dreams, my own way. I came here to tell you. I won't be doing this for much longer. Oh, and your 'Safe Haven' nonprofit van came driving through my area one day and they gave me this."

Rhiannon hands me one of our covert business cards. It looks like any other lawn service card, cleverly disguising that the real contact info is for anyone needing help. Because of these cards and expanding to multiple locations, the nonprofit organization is being credited for ending sex trafficking for the local area. But Rhiannon has always been that reminder that it's still not enough.

"Ah! See, that face. Don't do that. Don't think of me as the one that got away. You've got to let go."

"No, no, you're right. I have. It's hard sometimes with cases like you. But I've come across a few, actually. It's helping, you being here. You both looking happy and healthy. Well, she doesn't seem to like me much, though."

Rhiannon throws her head back and laughs. "She's so much like me, isn't she? But that complexion, she gets that from her daddy. She's beautiful, isn't she."

I wave them off as they drive away. I can't help but worry what she'll tell Sylvana about her work and if she'll grow up believing it's okay. *You can't save everyone.* I huff out a breath. Rhiannon is getting out soon, soon enough her daughter probably has no idea about any of it. I really do need to stop worrying about everyone so much.

"How's the world's mama?" Cassy cocks a hip against the table in the entryway.

I realign the stack of brochures that I've laid out beside Nettie's plethora of baked goodies. "The what now?"

"You dope. You'd try to mother the whole world if we let ya. You're still thinking about Rhiannon, aren't ya?"

I lower my head as a blush creeps across my cheeks. I'm clapped on the back as Cassy opens the door for the first to arrive. People begin streaming in one after another until all the seats are filled and people have to gather in a small crowd in the back of the dining room. As we being the meeting, more people continue filling the hallway.

"How many here have had a near-death experience or know someone who has?" Stefan calls. The majority of the crowd has hands raised. I stand in shock as I look around. Stefan has sweat beading on his forehead and his hands are shaking. But he stands in front of everyone with a façade of calm and control. I slip my hand in his. He surprises me by leaning over and kissing the top of my head.

"That's what I thought. You're all here because you haven't felt the same since. People who haven't experienced what you have, do they tell you to just get over it and move on?"

Heads bob in answer. Cassy walks up to the podium. In the background, I can see Nettie as she clears the entry table of all the empty pans. The house soon fills with the smell of more baking cookies.

"People ask God to spare a child. When innocents die, they say, 'If God were real, He wouldn't let bad things like this happen.'" Cassy shakes her fist to the sky. My brow furrows at her speech. Where is she going with this? As if reading my thoughts, she turns and winks over her shoulder.

"So He saves the child. When does His almighty protection of children end? On the twelfth hour on the eve of their eighteenth birthday? And they ask, why did the child's mother have to die? So all children and mothers get protected. But then the father dies, and mother can't protect the children from attackers. Why take the father? So now all parents and children are protected. But some fathers and mothers attack others. Why did God let these bad things happen? Maybe they were hungry or sick. So, say God ends hunger and illness. Now the exact amount of food is always available, no one ever dies an untimely death or gets sick. No one has to fight or be afraid. And...then what? No one would try to be good or work or build for the future or improve or create medicine or find ways to feed the hungry. Nobody would have to do anything, so what would be the point of any life at all? Educate to do what? Not to work or improve yourself or the world. Work to do what, provide food that's already plentiful or medicine that isn't needed?

"I'm sure you're wondering what this has to do with near-death experiences. Well, I died and came back, and now I know when the world is going to end. My friends behind me, one can tell the time you'll die and the other knows if you're gonna kill yourself. I bet you all have abilities like that too, don't you? Well, I believe we have touched the other side, and now we're tasked with saving the world, in our own ways. What I said earlier, that's what the normies say. It's God's fault, God should save the world. But we know that's not how this works. We've seen the other side. We have the power. Will you join us Deviants in using yours?"

The crowd hoots and hollers. Some throw fists in the air. Stefan's hand slips from mine as he steps forward. Cassy quirks a brow and steps back.

"I was once known around the world as Tod, the Death Psychic. I can tell when someone is going to die. And for many years, I used my ability for selfish reasons. I saw a waitress slaving over tables with little hope for a much better future. And I thought, if she would embrace life and had a second chance, what would she do differently? I thought she'd go to college, get some flashy degree, make big bucks, and put her kids through college. Instead, she took extra time to read to them a little more each night and really listen to their woes. I saw a homeless man and thought, if he knew when he was gonna die, surely he'd get sober and get work and rekindle old relationships and build anew. But he didn't.

"I laughed at people who mocked God when He wouldn't hand them life on a silver platter. And then I tried handing life to people on a silver platter and expected them to understand it for what it was. I thought my answer was *the* answer and all anybody ever needed was a second chance. It isn't my job to fix the world. *Humanity* has to do it together. If somebody can finally quit their job and travel the world all because I give them a time, then I'll gladly help. But it's what we Deviants can do together that'll make the world just a little bit brighter."

I shake off my feeling of awe at their words and step forward to add a little of my own. Stefan's arm wraps around my shoulders. I nuzzle his shoulder, then face the crowd. "I thought it was my responsibility to end sex trafficking and suicide. I worked day and night until I nearly took my daughter's mother away from her by obsessing over saving others. I don't have to—no, I can't possibly—save everyone. What 'perfect' means to a model is the ideal weight and looks. To a surgeon, it's flawless surgery with a perfect cure and survival rate. To a mother, it's a child's smile. To be saved is just as personal. Saving oneself can be as broad as starting a new career and truly living like you'll be dead in the next minute. It can also be as small as a reminder to take an extra few minutes to tuck your kids in at night. Being saved from oneself can also take the form of realizing that some external mystery magic doesn't hold the answer. Our grand delusions to save the world and its people may have been just that—the delusions of a socially awkward anthropophobe," Stefan bows his head at my gesture toward him, "or the delusions of a victim of the streets with survivor's guilt," I bow my head, then look at Cassy, "or the delusions of a housewife whose world as she knew it had ended. Is the world coming to an end? Maybe. Can little ol' me, or him, or her, or you stop it? Maybe, maybe not. But we Deviants can work to make things a little more comfortable for whenever the sky does rain down on us. What do you say? Will you join us?"

The crowd erupts. Tears are shed. Clapping goes on for far too long. We look at each other unsure if our words were really all that powerful to have such a reaction.

"I can tell if someone is going to have a heart attack within the week!"

"I know who someone was in a past life and how they died."

People in the crowd set aside their pies and cookies and stand one by one, confessing to their near-death experiences and how their lives have been impacted. They talk about how Cassy's poster went viral and we discover that only a small handful of people are local. Many others have flown in to tell their story.

"I'm so happy. I've felt so alone. None of my family understands why I collect obituaries. I know just by looking at their photos if their deaths were by murder and were misruled. I want to join the Deviants so I can help save the world!"

"I want to help save the world!"

The crowd chants and Cassy whoops. The toothy grin that splits her face and has tears welling in her eyes has my heart skipping. It feels like the first genuine smile of hers that I've seen.

Chapter Thirty-Three – Stefan

I startle awake at 11:14 p.m. and the tears are immediate. Desda leaps forward in bed and consoles me. Uncle David's face flashes in my mind and he smiles, waves, then fades away. Desda gasps and grips my arm. She can feel what is coming. Her ability is screaming that she do something to stop him.

"It's okay. I know. You won't get to him in time. Let him." When 12:41 a.m. came, I was all cried out but knew Barry had joined him. A few days later when I heard Cassy calling for me, I knew.

"Stefany! Letter!"

I collapse onto the new sofa with Desda beside me. The tears rise before I can even break the envelope's seal.

Stefan,

If you're reading this, I have passed on. We both knew this was coming. And knowing Barry, you should assume he's joined me on the other side by now as well. I've said it many times, but I am sorry about everything. Part of me wishes I had done any one of the treatments Barry wanted so that maybe what we put you through could've been worth it. But I know that's just my guilt talking. I don't have much to pass on to you, but our house is yours, if you want it. I'll have my lawyer get this to you once I'm gone. I'm sure the IRS will take everything they can find, so the house may not end up being something I can even pass on to you.

I'm sorry again. Cancer isn't something that you can understand until a bored white man in a lab coat throws it at you. I'm such a coward that I could never tell you what happened with Bridgett. I know they thought you had something to do with it, but it was me. I saw her, that signature headscarf, and the loved one, I think it was her husband, obsessing over her. I saw myself in her. And I told her to run away. I told her about this group I'd heard about that helps people get a second chance. I didn't think she'd go through with it, but I was happy when she did. But I was too much of a coward to tell you. And I was too much of a coward to run away myself.

I hope you're happier where you're at now. I'm glad you found someone. Just do me a favor, if her time comes before you, if she ever, God forbid, gets slapped with a cancer diagnosis, learn to accept her choice, whatever it may be. And learn to let her go. It will kill you, but please, as my dying wish, if that ever happens, let her go. The way I hope you can let me go.

I love you, my dearest nephew. I'll say hi to Jeb for you. We'll be waiting. But give us time to catch all the fish first, okay? Don't worry, we'll have them all fileted before you and your pansy nose can get here.

Uncle David

Desda reads the letter and her face pales. She runs to the new at-home office setup in the lower-level bedroom and rummages through some paperwork. She returns to the living room and hands me the travel itinerary she planned for Bridgett Newman.

"It happened so fast. She came in the middle of the night, demanding to be freed from her life and I whipped up this one-way travel plan to Bora Bora for her. She paid in cash, left to wait for her flight at the airport, and I didn't think anything else of it. I forgot her name. It's all my fault. They blamed you and it's all—"

"Nobody but Neil blamed me." I fill her in on how Neil had paraded around as a detective and harassed me about Bridgett's disappearance. He must've somehow found out that she went to Desda for help to escape and set his sights on her for his revenge.

I kiss away her fears. She melts in my arms. Her fingers trail up my chest as I talk endlessly about memories of Gramps, Uncle David, and Barry.

• • • •

"OF COURSE I'M SURE. I'm a Top Fan on your page. And I've been like, your number one fan from the beginning." Cassy smiles in that way where I can't tell if she's serious.

"I don't even know what to say. Hasn't everybody sorta forgot about me by now?"

"Well, they've stopped rioting, if that's what you mean. But there are a few social media pages out there with fans dedicated to finding you. See? Here's one where somebody hunted down some cop you talked to here in Texas." Cassy holds up her phone and I see that lazy desk cop smiling back at me. "Says here the cop tried begging you to call your family who put out an APB on you, but he says you ran out."

Sweat stings my armpits. They were able to find out that much, it's only a matter of time before I'm found here at Desda's house. And now that she no longer does business out of her house, this place is starting to feel like our home, our happy place. My new *Sweetheart*. I have to do this. I can't have anyone showing up here and destroying the peace we've begun to rebuild.

"Okay, I'll do it. But not here. If they know I'm in Texas, I can't have any connections to this house, or they'll find me here."

"Yeah, no shit. Your fans are fucking nuts, man. No, I was thinking we'd do this outside of the travel agency's new shop. That or one of the nonprofit's locations. Hell, we could do a little of both if you wanted."

My followers developed an unhealthy attachment once I'd read their time. I wasn't the only one fighting for a connection. But in a way, I think they thought of me as some kind of messiah, a savior here to guide them through this hellish life. When I ran away, they nearly set the world on fire searching for me. Maybe some of them still are but I can't bring myself to watch the news anymore.

So I'll say goodbye to them like Cassy suggests. But I can redirect them to help fight for the Deviant's cause. "Cassy, remind me again, what is the Deviant's cause?"

She smirks, then flashes that same damned smile. "To save the world, duh." Right, how could I forget?

She points the camera at me as the warm sun beats against my back. The brick wall behind me looms in familiarity. It's odd to think how the side of a brick building set forth so much in motion. When before, the graffiti covering the brick from my past was riddled with bullet holes, this graffiti was performed by a hired local artist and promises a brighter future.

An artist's rendition of Desda's business logo for her new non-profit organization covers the entire side of the building of the first of many locations sprouting up all around the city and soon, the state. Cassy fiddles with the camera as I appreciate the graffiti design. Hope for others like Desda and Nettie rises. While my attempts to save the world were futile and ended in more chaos, Desda was working around the clock I was enslaved to and she saved so many, one at a time. She's made the real difference.

"Hello, um, everyone." I raise a hand, then lower it and feel utterly ridiculous. Sweat stings my skin. "It's been a while."

Cassy's eyes widen. Her mouth hangs open and for a moment I think the end of the world has arrived and a portal to the underworld must've opened in the wall behind me.

"What? Was it that bad? You weren't live, right? Let's just go again."

"That was...oh Great One, that was amazing!" She giggles.

"Shut up! You scared me. Seriously though, was it okay?"

My thoughts became jumbled as I spoke. I lost the direction I'd intended and the notecards in my grasp had slipped away to flutter in the wind. My mouth kept right on moving even though my brain had shut down. I still have no idea what I said.

"You were great. It was perfect. All your followers are sure to help. Here, let's check." Cassy scrolls through something on her phone while I shift from foot to foot and try to calm my frantic breaths. "Holy shit! It already has like a hundred thousand viewers watching right now! And fuck me, look at this. They're donating like crazy!"

The nonprofit's donation counter on her website is whirling as the numbers climb. Desdamona's nonprofit and travel agency social media profiles begin gaining my followers in droves. Maybe they'll help spread the word and maybe their donation can help save other sex trafficking victims. But...

"How is any of this going to save the world?" I ask aloud later that night over dinner. Desda's hand covers mine.

"I don't know." Cassy shrugs. I stare at her. "Okay, look. I know when the world is going to end. And in my dreams, well, it sure as shit ain't pretty." At Desda's glare, Cassy bows in apology at Nettie for her language. Nettie rolls her eyes and laughs at her mother's overprotectiveness.

"That said, I got this theory. You see, Dezzy here can tell if someone is about to off themselves, right? But she jumps in and stops it. And you, you can tell when someone's gonna die. Now tell me, what was Nettie's time before Neil went psycho?"

My eyes widen at her insight. I hadn't told anyone about that. I look between all three of them as they stare back expectantly. "Um, well...it changed...if that's what you're asking." Nettie's time was 6:12 a.m., shortly after Neil's. She was meant to die with him. But now, her time is 3:14 a.m.

Cassy nods. "Mm-hmm, mm-hmm. That's what I thought. So, it can be changed. And tell me, too, did a lot of people who came to our first Deviant meeting all have the same time of death?"

"Yes...3:14 a.m." I swallow the lump in my throat and stare at my plate.

"Suicide can be prevented. None of this death stuff us all are privy to seems to be set in stone. So, I think we can change the end."

"Wait, what's that have to do with all those people having the same time of death?"

Cassy gives me a look that tells me I'm bring obtuse. "That's the time of the apocalypse, apparently. I've always known the date. Now we know the time, too."

"The world is going to end at 3:14 a.m.?" Nettie cocks her head to the side. I can't tell if she believes any of this or if she is humoring Cassy, but she shows no fear nor mocking doubt.

"Poetic, no? It's like some big cosmic joke." At our blank looks, Cassy rolls her eyes. "You know, three point one four, pi? Everything's coming full circle. Ugh, y'all are too much."

"So, you want us to stop the apocalypse?" Desda chuckles. Her eyes are glossy, and her skin has a healthy glow. These past few months have seemed to wash away the pain she's carried for as long as I've known her. Nettie laughs with her mother and her new front teeth flash. It took far too much pushing but I'm glad Desda finally accepted that I wasn't taking the money back.

Cassy's face falls and turns serious. Our laughter dies at the shock of Cassy's haunted look. "No. I don't think we can stop it. I don't know, can't you feel it? The Earth, she's tired. All she wants is to sleep. No, I think the end is inevitable. I don't know for sure. But I do think we can make it peaceful."

"You want to make the apocalypse *peaceful*? What does that even mean?" I can't help but scoff at the notion.

"Yes, peaceful." Cassy wrinkles her nose at my mocking. "Like in that Ray Bradbury story, what was it, "The Last Night of the World", I think?"

"Ray who?" we collectively ask.

"Oh, you uncultured swine." She lays a hand over her heart. "He's only the single greatest writer of all time. Jeez, anyway, in his story, the world just ends, peacefully. He says in the story that it's like 'the closing of a book'. See? Peaceful. Every night I dream about the horrible things that are coming. I think we Deviants with our abilities, we can stop it from being so gruesome. And if it's meant to happen, then it still will. But it'll be like someone simply turned out the light. The end."

Desda and I exchange glances. After Cassy lost everything—her career, her husband, her future—it makes sense that she'd want the world to end. But both Desda and I think maybe Cassy's own situation may be tainting her prediction about the coming apocalypse. I believe it is coming, and her ability is as legitimate as mine or Desda's, but I don't think it's impossible to thwart it, not with so many eager to join our cause.

Silence befalls us as we eat our dinner and chew over Cassy's words. The world is tired and wants to sleep. Sleep doesn't sound so bad. Cassy's theory doesn't sound as scary as I'd always thought the end of the world would be. She knows when it's going to happen and it's soon enough that she wants to put a stop to whatever it is she dreams about yet far enough away that she believes we can make a difference. That means there's still time for us all.

Desda and I can continue exploring our relationship, at our own pace. And Nettie can finish growing up and maybe even make it through college and building a life for herself. Maybe Desda and I will have children or adopt more. And we'll work to end sex trafficking and save people from suicide. Maybe I'll read a few people their times, for old time's sake. Or I could use my ability to help Desda thwart those attempting suicide. And we'll work on growing the Deviants to help Cassy's hope for the end come to pass, whether the end happens tomorrow, or in ten years, or fifty. Most of all, we can show Cassy that there's a reason to fight for tomorrow, that we can fight together as a family to put a stop to anything that comes our way.

Who could ask for a more peaceful ending than that?

"Read it again, Mommy!" If Brenda had a nickel for every time she heard that one. Brenda laughs and reads the bedtime story over and over until two snores rise from the tangle of blankets. Looks like she'll be sharing her bed with both her daughters again tonight. She glances at her wristwatch, 9:20 p.m.

He hasn't been in to see her for a while. Brenda wonders if Stefan is eating well. If he's finally catching up on the sleep that he needs. She thought after his long absence that she would never see that sweet boy again. But then he came striding back into her life with all the air of a full-grown man swirling around him.

Ira would've been so proud of the man he's become. Brenda's mind wanders to her childhood and the great years she spent growing up beside Ira. She missed those simpler times. But as she watches her girls slumber, wrapped up around each other—how they'd hate it if either of them woke up and found out—and she can't help but think these are the happiest years of her life. Her heart aches at the sense of betrayal for her dear friend.

Ira gave her the best years she'd had until she had her daughters. At first it was out of loyalty to her that she made sure to slip Stefan extra food whenever he came in. She knew the moment he first walked in as a young teen that he was her boy. He had her eyes. Over the years of his frequent visits before he was dragged off for that death psychic nonsense, Stefan became something of the son she never had.

9:53 p.m. She stares at the minute hand as it ticks around. Her heart begins to pound. She feels foolish every time but can't make herself look away until the minute is over. When 9:54 comes and goes and her brain hasn't imploded or her heart crumpled, she breathes a sigh of relief.

Careful not to wake her sleeping angels, she peels herself from the blankets and tiptoes to the living room. The various jars tucked in the corners need to be dusted. But she sets to work watering what her girls lovingly call the jungle room. Bob has grown and expanded so much over the years that she's had to divide him into many planters. His vast vines and waxy leaves seem to dance as she waters each of his numerous containers.

Her mantle and her coffee table and all her shelving have disappeared beneath his reach. Brenda smiles as she refills her watering can and offers more water to Stefan's pet plant. Her eyes wander to one of the many jars in the room. The plethora of nickels flash in the pale light. He always tipped her with tons of nickels. For some odd reason, she could never bring herself to cash them with her other tips.

Maybe one day she'll lug all these in and put them in a savings account for the girls' college tuition bills. But for now, the nickels and Bob give her company as she sits in her favorite rocking chair and feels like a mother wondering after her grown son.

"Ira, you did good. Stefan is everything you hoped he'd be." Brenda smiles as she stares out into the darkness beyond her living room window. Beneath tufts of late-season new-fallen snow, yellow cups illuminate her gardens. "Look, Ira. Daffodils, your favorite."

Acknowledgements

I have so many to thank for this novel. Your inspiration and assistance was immeasurable.

To my editors, Anita and Christie, for not only squeezing me in last minute but getting the manuscript back to me in parts to help me reach my ARC deadline.

To my book cover designer, Sarah Kil. Thank you for the many rounds trying to find the right cover and for schooling me on magical realism.

To Alexia Howell, my sensitivity reader. Your notes helped me to better represent black characters and you gave me the confidence to move forward with this book.

To my husband, Spencer, for the never ending encouragement.

To my sister, Kirstie, for wrangling my hellion of a son so that I can get some writing done once in a while.

Thanks for reading!

If you enjoyed *A Nickel and A Trinket*, be sure to leave a review[1]!
Reviews are very important and help authors and readers alike!
Want to connect?
www.Twitter.com/MaxWatsonBooks[2]
www.Facebook.com/MaxWatsonBooks[3]
www.Goodreads.com/MaxWatsonBooks
Want free stuff?
Check out my website www.MaxWatsonBooks.com[4] where you can sign up for my newsletter to get free books, get notified about new book releases, enter giveaways, and more!

---

1. https://www.amazon.com/review/create-review?&asin=B09327F91Z

2. http://www.Twitter.com/MaxWatsonBooks

3. http://www.Facebook.com/MaxWatsonBooks

4. http://www.MaxWatsonBooks.com

Don't miss out!

Visit the website below and you can sign up to receive emails whenever Max Watson publishes a new book. There's no charge and no obligation.

https://books2read.com/r/B-A-WAOJ-VOJPB

BOOKS 2 READ

Connecting independent readers to independent writers.

About the Author

Max Watson braves the sweltering heat of Dallas, Texas along with her husband Spencer, their son Jack, and their three kitty overlords. From roofing, to flipping houses and businesses, to building race cars, to ladder-climbing in corporate America, Max Watson loves to jump from one challenge to the next. In her career working for the man, she frequently found herself enthralled by the human psyche and was always daydreaming twisted tales. Running away screaming from corporate America, she decided to tackle the itch just under the skin and begin her writing career.